THE RULES FOR DISAPPEARING

THE RULES FOR DISAPPEARING

ASHLEY ELSTON

HYPERION
Los Angeles • New York

Printed in the United States of America
First Hyperion paperback edition, 2014
10 9 8 7 6 5 4 3 2 1
V475-2873-0-14046

Designed by Marci Senders
Library of Congress Control Number for Hardcover Edition: 2012035122
ISBN 978-1-4231-6926-0

Visit www.hyperionteens.com

For Dean, my best friend and true love

Chapter 1

"WHAT do you want your name to be this time? We have about thirty minutes."

I stare at the muted television. The only light in the room comes from the flashing images on the small screen, one of those old Meg Ryan movies that's on all the time. A movie I've seen so often that sound isn't necessary.

All the other times they asked me this question, I'd stressed out searching for the perfect name. I used each available moment going back and forth, trying to decide.

Not this time.

"Meg," I answer.

"Meg. Do you want just Meg or maybe Megan with Meg for short?"

"I don't care."

"What about her?" A hand points down to the lump of girl next to me. My arm curls around her sleeping form, and I fight the temptation to pull her in close.

It's very late, somewhere around three in the morning, and I hate to wake her for this. She was pissed when I made this decision for her last time. I picked the wrong girl's name from that show she likes. Luckily for her, it had been our shortest identity.

I shake her gently.

"Hey," I whisper. It's been hammered into us not to use our real names. Ever. With the suits watching, I can't call her anything. "What name do you want? I don't want to pick for you again."

She tosses around, trying to wake up. Slowly, her eyes open. "What'd you choose?" Her voice is hoarse.

"I went with 'Meg.'"

Lines race across her crumpled forehead. It's almost like I can hear the wheels in her brain turning over possibilities. Each time she's had to make this decision, she's chosen a TV character she likes. Can't think if there's one left she hasn't used.

"I don't care," she answers in a ragged huff.

Just like that she shuts off. Her eyes close and her knees curl in closer to her chest. My throat constricts. I hate seeing her like this. "What about Mary? You'd be a cute Mary."

She's quiet a moment more and then gives me a small nod.

If she doesn't like it, I'm sure we'll be changing them again soon. At this rate we will go through a dozen names. "We'll be the M&M girls. How's that?"

A ghost of a smile crosses her face, and she drifts back to sleep. I watch her for a few seconds. She's talking less and less with each move, and I'm scared she'll stop altogether. She doesn't act like an eleven-year-old anymore. Most days she needs help bathing and doing her hair, like she's five or six. And it's not like Mom's up to the task.

The woman taps her pen against a clipboard in an annoying *rat-tat-tat*. She told me her name at some point, but I'd stopped trying to remember them all months ago. I assume my earlier position.

"Mary. She'll be Mary." I'm exhausted. Drained.

"Do you have a preference for middle names?"

"No."

"All right, Meg." Just like that, we are Meg and Mary. We will not be called anything else until the next move. "The only thing left is your appearance. From your file pictures, I see that you have—until this point—gotten away without any major alterations. Sorry to tell you—that's not the case this time." The woman squats lower.

"I brought a few things. We can start with you, and let Mary sleep a little longer." She shifts around the bed until she's blocking the TV. Her feet are planted squarely on the floor, and both hands ball into fists at her waist.

"We'll have to cut your hair and change the color. I also brought contacts for you to change your eyes from blue to brown. Hopefully, that will be enough." She talks slow and draws every syllable out like she's trying to get through to an old person or a small child.

Ignoring her, I stare ahead as if I can still make out the images on the TV behind her. The old me would have revolted. My hair and eyes are my most striking features, and I know it. Up until this point, I've only lost my name. After this I will be unrecognizable.

I count to sixty in my head before I start moving. Inch by inch, I slide from the bed, careful not to wake "Mary" up. Her new name doesn't fit, but that will change in a few days. The bathroom is small and smells like mildew. There's only one light over the sink. It's a single bare bulb that gives off a really hard light compared to the muted images from the bedroom. I force my shoulders back and step in front of the sink.

No matter what changes the suits make, that girl in the mirror bolted with this last move. Gone. Pieces splintered away with each new identity, but the last big chunk shattered the second the suits yanked us from our beds in the middle of the night and threw us into that windowless van. No tears after this loss. Not after everything else that's gone.

My long blond hair is thick and streaked with natural highlights that can only come from hours in the sun. It's straight and falls well below my bra strap. It's beautiful hair.

"Cut it off." My voice is firm.

The woman comes up behind me and gathers my hair into a ponytail. Once it's secured, she pulls it down, loosening it a small amount. She withdraws a large pair of scissors from her bag and takes a deep breath, as if she too understands what a travesty this is, and begins to cut. It takes a few moments and several attempts, but finally the entire ponytail is gone.

She holds the hair, still bound together, in her hand and offers it to me.

I can't look at it. "Just throw it away."

The woman takes the scissors and cuts smaller pieces here and there. I watch as a short pixie-like style begins to appear. She puts the scissors down and reaches back into the bag. Pulling out an over-the-counter package of hair dye, she studies the directions on the back. In my other life I would never have stooped so low.

I glance at the box and read the color as "Espresso on the Double." The woman works the color through my hair, and I relax my clenched hands from the edge of the porcelain bowl.

Rinsed, I get the first glance at my new look. The woman takes out a pair of colored contacts and hands them to me.

She demonstrates, using her own contacts, how to put them in and how to care for them when I take them out. After several tries I finally get the lens in the right spot. I examine my reflection for a few moments more. The changes transform my face. My eyes are larger. The angles are stronger. My face looks too thin. The woman is right—no one from my former life would ever recognize me. I am truly gone.

Chapter 2

RULES FOR DISAPPEARING
BY WITNESS PROTECTION PRISONER #18A7R04M:

Live on the fringe of society. You don't want to be in a nice neighborhood because those people are all in your business and want to know everything about you. And you don't want to be in a bad one, well . . . because it's bad. If you go to all this trouble to hide from bad guys, it'd suck to get shot just because you live in a crappy area.

MY dad never calls anyone by their real name. Men he worked with, people from our neighborhood, and every guy who ever took me out on a date had some stupid nickname. The worst ones were Bud, Sport, or Champ. It's awful when your date picks you up and your dad thumps his back a few times and calls him some really dumb name. I always thought it was rude, like he can't be bothered to remember anyone's real name. My sister and I have nicknames, too. My sister's is pretty cute—Teeny Tiny. She was, like, four pounds when she was born. It doesn't matter that she's taller than most girls her age now; she'll always be Teeny Tiny to Dad.

Mine, on the other hand, is not very original. It's Sissy. Yes, Sissy. Dad started calling me that when Teeny was born since I was obviously a big sister. I always hated that nickname, was mortified when Dad would call me that in front of my friends, but now it's different. With each placement came new names, but the nicknames stayed the same. We all use them between the four of us in private now. The suits would freak out, but so what? That stupid nickname has become really important: it's the only thing anchoring me to my past.

I turn and watch Teeny. She showed no more interest in her haircut and color than I had. In fact, her eyes never once moved to the mirror. At least Teeny's new style isn't as severe as mine. The woman left her with a short bob that falls a few inches below her ears. We favor each other in many ways, with the blond hair and the naturally bronzed skin, but I'm the only one who has blue eyes. Teeny's are a soft brown, and thankfully she won't have to suffer the contacts.

"Do you think they did this to Mom's hair, too?" Teeny's voice is hollow.

We haven't seen our parents since we were brought to this "safe house." The suits usually meet with them for a while after we leave a placement—I guess trying to figure out what keeps going wrong—but this is the longest we've gone without seeing them.

"Probably. I'm sure we'll all match with the dark hair just like we did with the blond." My dad has the same natural blond hair as Teeny and me, but Mom matched hers to ours through a box. I suppose she didn't want to be the only one in the family who wasn't blond. This dark color would actually be more like her normal shade, but that's a guess since I've only seen her natural color in old pictures.

I flop back on the bed and run my hands over my eyes. I'm exhausted. Every time I fall asleep I'm plagued with nightmares and wake up to Teeny's screams mixed in with mine. Not sure who starts first, but it's seriously freaking me out.

The woman comes back and hands me a sheet of paper. I hate

what's next. We'll be drilled on our new backgrounds and names.

"Okay, Meg, Mary, your exact full names are Megan Rose Jones and Mary Claire Jones. Your ages will remain the same, with you, Meg, at seventeen and Mary at eleven. But your birthdays are different. Meg, yours is November fourth, and, Mary, yours is April third."

Teeny traces the floral pattern on the bedspread. She's not hearing a single word.

"Your parents are Emily and Bill Jones. You've moved here from Arkansas. Your dad, Bill, will be working at an auto parts manufacturing plant." The woman pauses a moment before continuing. "Your mom, Emily, will not be employed in this placement."

It's not good if they aren't making her work. I wonder if they know how bad the drinking is, or if there's another reason. The same "reason" that caused the bad dye job and contacts.

The woman details the remaining facts of my new life. I'm surprised that even though I don't like and would have never chosen "Rose" as my middle name, I really don't care. And this is the first time Dad's job won't be behind some desk. He's probably pissed he's going to be working in a factory, but he'll fake enthusiasm for our benefit. I hate to think what Mom will do all day at home alone.

As I read all the pertinent details, I find I'm missing a big one. "You said we moved here from Arkansas, but you never said where here is."

"Natchitoches, Louisiana."

Louisiana. All you ever hear about Louisiana is hurricanes and oil spills. Perfect.

"Well, today is Friday, January eighth. You'll have the rest of the weekend to get this information memorized, and then we'll move you into new housing on Sunday. Both of you will start school on Monday morning."

We lived in houses for our first two moves, but since we were burning through new identities so fast, apartments made more sense. Wonder what type of "new housing" we'll get this time. I pore over the details of my new past.

Great. Another boring life summed up in three neatly typed paragraphs.

The suit shuffles her folders around. I put my paper down and ask, "What's different this time?"

She stops but doesn't look up at me. "Nothing. Why would you ask that?"

"Oh, I don't know." I can't hide the sharp tone. "I mean, we've been in a rush to leave a placement before, but dragging us out of bed in the middle of the night seems a bit extreme. Then the hair, the contacts. Surely we didn't do makeovers because we were bored here."

Teeny buries her head next to me. The suit gives her a glance but then fixes on me.

"I'm not at liberty to say."

Great, standard bullshit. She gathers her briefcase and heads to the door, pausing before she leaves the room. "Just be careful," she says without looking back.

Our parents make an appearance later in the afternoon. *Rough* is the only way to describe them. They're dyed and styled but not in a good way. They've turned into the "before" picture. I honestly would not have recognized them on the street.

Teeny and I slouch on the bed in the room that has been home for almost thirty-six hours. Mom comes in and sits down beside us while Dad leans against the wall, arms folded across his chest.

"How are my girls holding up?" Mom slurs. I've never seen her like this with the suits around. "Both of you look really cute with your new looks." It's a bad lie, but what else can she really say?

"How much longer before we get out of this rat hole?" I ask.

"It shouldn't be much longer. We're not far from where we'll be living." Mom strokes through Teeny's short bob. She's a touchy-feely drunk. No telling how she talked someone into getting her some booze here.

Mom looks down at Teeny. "You picked Mary? What show is that from?"

Teeny shakes her head. "It's not fun being famous people anymore."

Mom gives us both a weak smile and swivels toward Dad, almost falling off the bed. He grabs her by the shoulders, holding her up but slightly away from him, like he can't stand to be near her.

"Girls, I know these moves are getting harder, but it really is for the best. None of these changes are permanent," Dad says.

I roll my eyes in the exaggerated way I know he hates. "Whatever."

I'm so sick of this. Witness Protection sucks, and I'm done playing along. Dad's the only thing stopping Mom's drunk ass from falling off the bed. Teeny's off in never-never land, and I look like some terminally ill kid with a bad wig. This family has fallen apart.

"I've had it with your attitude. It won't make things any different."

I stopped tiptoeing around him three moves ago. "Well, then, I guess it won't make things any different if you tell me—what did you do? Because whatever it is—we're all paying for your mistake."

Dad looks like he's about to explode. Maybe I've finally pissed him off enough for him to spill it. What he did. Why we're here. But the words seem stuck in his throat. He finally blows out, "It's late and we're leaving early in the morning. Go to bed."

"Go to bed? Is that really all you can say to me?"

Mom's head lolls around, and Teeny scrunches into a smaller ball, if that's even possible.

Dad's face gets blotchy as his white-knuckled grip digs into Mom's shoulders. He mutters something I can't make out and then hauls ass from the room, dragging Mom with him. I fall back on the bed in utter disgust.

I learned on the third move to always have a bag ready. It's full of underwear, a toothbrush and toothpaste, pj's, and a change of clothes. The stuff the suits give us is hideous. My makeup bag stays in there too, because luxury items are never provided for us. I've tried to explain that makeup is a necessity, not a luxury item, but no success there. It sucks earning money to buy the same stuff over and over. The bag was almost history on the last move. Luckily, it'd been beside me, next to the bed, so I'd grabbed it on my way out.

The time in between placements drags on. No one makes sure you have something to do, so by the fifth move I'd added a few paperbacks and my iPod. I started throwing in similar stuff for Teeny to help keep her busy. The bag has gotten ridiculously big and heavy, but I loathe parting with anything in it. Right now Teeny's working on one of those Sudoku books she loves so much.

We're in the van again; the kind that has no windows. The front seats are blocked by darkly tinted glass. It's like riding around in a box. The suits will let us out to use the bathroom and get our bearings only after we are a good distance from where we started. It must be a new suit driving us, because he obviously doesn't know the rules. The local radio station is on, and it only takes two commercials to figure out the safe house is in Shreveport. Although that means nothing to me, I'm feeling pretty smug to have that info.

Once I hear the town's name from the local station, I put in my earbuds and crank the music on my iPod. Perfect time to write in my journal.

I started it the same time as the go-bag. It's full of personal things, but also some short stories, poems, and just random stuff that floats through my head. The suits would be pissed if they knew I wrote about what we've been through, so I have to hide it. I don't use our names or the cities we lived in, but I write about what this ordeal has been like. It's the only place I can be honest.

We travel for almost an hour before we come to a stop. I figure we're getting out for a bathroom break, so I'm really surprised when we unload in the middle of a driveway that's sandwiched between two rows of cottages tucked back off the main street. They're made of old brick, and French doors with tall wood shutters span the front. It's charming until you get close—the chipped paint and rusted handles remind me that we're not in the best part of town.

This must be it, our new, albeit temporary, home. At least it's not one of those gross apartment complexes.

I grab my bag, putting Teeny's book back inside, and we follow the suit to one of the middle houses. The same woman who cut my hair opens the door to #12.

"Hello, Jones family, welcome home." Her bright cheery smile is overdone, and I can't help but groan out loud. "Since this is a college town, no apartments were available on such short notice. These are old Creole cottages, and I thought it'd be more of a homey feel anyway."

Dad nods at her and says, "Agent Parker, nice to see you again."

"You too, Mr. Jones." She points to a small building at the end of the long driveway and says, "You'll find washers and dryers in there."

It's totally depressing on the inside. White walls. Brown carpet. It's sparsely furnished with secondhand furniture that doesn't match. The material is worn through in some places, showing the outline of the springs, and you can see remnants of stains. Yuck.

"This is a two-bedroom." She looks at me quickly with a small frown and says, "Sorry, Meg, but you and Mary will have to share a room."

"That's fine." Truthfully, it's better this way.

"Let me show you around." Her arms spread wide likes she's one of those game show hosts and the curtain's just been pulled back.

There's no reason for a tour. The den, kitchen, and small eating area are basically the same room. There is a short hallway with three doors, which I assume are two bedrooms and the bathroom.

I don't wait for the suit to show me the way—I just start opening doors. The first one has two twin beds with matching comforters in pale pink. Obviously our room. It also has a small desk and chair and a polka-dotted beanbag chair on the floor.

The next door is the bathroom. It's tiny, with room enough for just a small counter with a sink, toilet, and bath/shower combo. The lingering smell of cleaner stings my nose but makes me feel better about taking a bath later. The last door is my parents' room. A double bed covered with a frayed quilt sits in the center, and a single wingback chair takes up the corner next to a small dresser.

I walk back to my room and open the closet door. I already know what to expect: very generic clothes for us both.

Teeny comes in a few moments later, and I let her choose her bed. She sits on it and picks at the comforter. "I'm glad we're sharing a room."

"Me too." After fleeing our last placement in the middle of the night, I want Teeny right next to me.

"Are you nervous about school?"

She leans down and pulls her book out of my bag. "No."

I lie back on my bed and think about tomorrow. Coming in midyear sucks, but this time I don't care.

So much for senior year.

Teeny and I hole up in our room the rest of the evening. She falls asleep early, but it's harder for me. I toss and turn most of the night until I can't stand being in the bed a minute longer. As the soft morning light filters through the small window, I give up the fight and grab my jacket and journal to escape outside.

It's cold. A fine layer of dewy ice coats the front steps, so I sit on my jacket rather than wear it. No one is out this early, and the only sounds come from the occasional bird searching for its first meal of the day. I rub my hands over my arms, hoping the friction will keep the chill away.

Aside from the first placement, I started every new school believing that we would last. I made friends, joined school clubs, and in the third placement even got a spot on the dance line—anything to make that new school feel like home. But each time, those men in suits showed up. I lost everything over and over. There are countless friends I've made around the country who must think I fell off the face of the earth. Not again. If our track record shows anything, it's that we won't be here more than a month. I can't do it again.

Opening the journal, I find a crisp blank page and write:

1. I will not join any clubs
2. I will not try out for cheerleading or any other sport/team
3. I will not make any friends
4. I will discover the truth no matter what

I underline and star number four until it's almost hard to read. The list is short but powerful, and I make a vow to live by every word.

I tiptoe back into the cottage and get Teeny up for school. Looking at the clothes makes me depressed. The last person who stocked a closet for us at least had a small sense of style. No luck this time. The choices seem pitiful even by Witness Protection standards. I pull out an ugly gray hoodie and it makes me laugh. I wouldn't have been caught dead wearing anything like this just a few short months ago, but now it seems like the best option for today.

I shower, dress, and put on makeup in record time. The stupid brown contacts give me a little trouble, but I finally get them in the right spot. Hair is towel dried. It's so short, there aren't a lot of options, so I leave it sticking up everywhere.

"Sissy, where are we again? I forgot." Teeny's fumbling with her hair, and I step over to help her fix it. The second I take over, she slumps down. She would have never tolerated being babied like this in our old life.

"We're in Louisiana. The city is named Natchitoches."

Reciting the major facts again, I try not to think about how much of her slips away with every move. I quiz her on our new identities, and she answers most of them right.

"I think I should stay home today."

Teeny says this every time she's about to leave wherever it is we're living. She's terrified we're going to be relocated without her. "No, you'll be fine. I'll see you right after school. Mom will be here when we get home. It's all good," I answer. In the second placement, the suits packed everything while Teeny was gone, and she came home to an empty house. She freaked and it took her forever to believe we wouldn't leave without her.

Dad's dressed and waiting for us in the kitchen, but Mom's a no-show.

By the fourth placement, Mom had changed. She lost all desire to keep the apartment clean or pay attention to Teeny. Back home, my parents were very social. We always had people over for some sort of function or another—any excuse to have a party. Mom loved to entertain. And she would drink—beer and margaritas around the pool, wine with dinner, gin and tonic late night—but only when we had people over.

I close my eyes and picture Mom in the kitchen of our old house. She'd dance around, mimicking some move she'd seen somewhere, and sing along to the music using a cooking utensil as a microphone. Even though it was embarrassing, my friends loved hanging out with her and thought she was the coolest mom. She was the life of the party.

Her favorite thing was to throw these ridiculous formal dinners that lasted forever. The only ones I looked forward to included Dad's boss, Mr. Price, and only then if his son, Brandon, came. I can't remember a time in high school when I didn't have a crush on him. I would beg Mom to let me be in charge of the seating, and I always made sure to put him right next to me. Those were the only nights Mom's dinner parties were too short.

I push thoughts of Brandon away. Thinking about him always makes me feel raw inside.

But two placements ago, Mom moved the drinking to a whole new level. She wasn't drinking to be social—she was drinking to get drunk. Dad won't talk about it. He just cleans up her mess or hides her from us. The suits must know her drinking is getting out of control since they didn't find her a job this time.

"I can take you and Teeny to school today. My job doesn't start until tomorrow. After that, you'll have to take the school bus."

"I don't get why I can't have a license. You and Mom get them in your new names."

Not the first time we've had this discussion. Dad lets out a frustrated snort. "I don't know why either. They have a certain way they do things, and one of them is no minors get licenses."

Teeny scans the room. "Where's Mama?"

Dad rinses out his coffeecup, ignoring her.

Then the coffeepot.

Coward.

I move to Teeny. "Sleeping in. She doesn't feel good," I answer, and lead her outside and wait for Dad to show us which car is ours. A funny feeling says it's the old green station wagon with wood paneling down the side.

And sure enough, Dad heads directly to the driver's side. The suits must really hate us—this is the most hideous ride I've ever seen.

With one car and Dad working twelve-hour shifts, it looks like Mom will be stranded here all day.

But then again, she probably won't get out of bed, so it really might not matter.

Chapter 3

RULES FOR DISAPPEARING
BY WITNESS PROTECTION PRISONER #18A7R04M:

Don't make eye contact or strike up conversations with random people. This may make you seem interesting and therefore attract the attention of others. And you don't want that . . . right?

THERE'S nothing really exciting or different about the area, just the same as our last three placements, until you go a couple of blocks toward the historic district.

The town is cute. Really cute. Everything's old but in a cool way. Front Street runs right next to a river, and the road is paved with old cobblestones. Driving over them sends vibrations through the wagon. Little restaurants and bars mixed with souvenir shops line the sidewalk. Most buildings are made of old brick and wood, like our cottage, and have second-story balconies trimmed in scrolled black iron. It must be like walking into someone's home rather than their store.

We cross a narrow bridge, and the shops turn into houses, the rambling kind with big yards, porch swings, and shrubs so thick and full they look like small trees.

We pull up to a school, and I see all the little kids.

"Okay, Teeny, we're here." Dad peeks at her in the rearview

mirror. The worse Teeny gets, the less Dad deals with her. It's like he's not equipped to handle this change.

She's crouched down in the backseat, her backpack clutched to her chest. I paste the biggest, brightest smile on my face. "Teeny, you'll do great. I'll see you after school. No worries."

She smiles, but it's forced. She gets out of the car, and Dad and I watch her walk slowly toward the building. Her head hangs low and her shoulders hunch over.

The air is heavy with all of the things we both want to say to each other, but neither of us speaks. I fiddle with the heater vent and Dad scrapes away something nasty from the windshield.

Once Teeny's out of sight, Dad pulls away from the curb.

At my request, he stops a block away to let me out. He mutters something about being here after school, but I'm out before he finishes.

Going in with The Plan does little to ease the nerves in my stomach. I take my iPod out and put in the earbuds.

It's easy to blend in with the crowd as everyone heads to the front door of the old school. Stealing glances at the kids shows me there's money in this area as well—lots of designer clothes and bags, everyone very put together. And I thought I'd blend in with these hideous clothes.

The halls are crowded and filled with the sounds of lockers banging open and shut. By now I thought I'd heard every accent out there, but these voices are so different—definitely Southern, but something else, too.

I spot the office and inch the door open. The woman behind the counter is frantic, shuffling papers around and barking into the phone. Her expression is exhausted even though it's not even 8 a.m. I take one earbud out. "This is my first day. I need my schedule."

The woman starts flipping through papers again. "Name."

"Meg Jones."

She rustles through another pile. "Have a seat. It's not in this stack."

The only vacant seat sandwiches me between two very different-looking guys with the same problem. They both got the crap beat out of them.

The one on my left has a swollen eye and a cut lip. There's blood covering his varsity jacket, and he's wiggling what may be a loose tooth. The one to my right has the beginnings of a bruise that covers his entire cheek. It's mostly red and swollen, rimmed with purple. Even with half his face discolored, he's cute, in a bad boy sort of way. The sleeve of his camouflage coat is hanging by a thread, and his boots are caked in mud.

The jock looks straight at me. "New girl?"

I blink a few times. "Uh, yeah. First day."

"Cool—don't get many transfers. You'll like it here. One piece of advice—stay away from that son of a bitch sitting on your other side and you'll be just fine."

Camo boy leans forward and says to the jock, "Hey, how about you take your advice and shove it up your ass, you stupid prick."

The jock lunges toward camo boy, and I cover my head with my hands, preparing for impact, when a sharp command stops the boys in midair.

"That's enough! In my office immediately." Both freeze with fists cocked back and swivel around to face the man in the doorway.

I peek through my fingers. The voice belongs to a very tall, heavy-set man dressed in a suit that seems way too nice for someone who works in the public school system.

Camo boy and jock stand up, but it only takes a few seconds before they're both blaming each other again. The man holds up his hand.

"No one breathes another word until I give you permission to do so. Understood?"

The guys quiet down and follow him into an office marked PRINCIPAL. Just before the jock goes inside, he raises one eyebrow and says quietly, "Don't say I didn't warn you."

Welcome to Natchitoches High School.

I take two wrong turns and finally find my homeroom after the final bell rings. The teacher looks up from her podium and gives me a quick glance. "You must be Megan. Go find a seat."

Looking across the room, I see an empty one in the back row. Thank God. Everyone scans me up and down and then dismisses me. The urge to pull my hoodie up over my head is overwhelming. I know what I look like to them—I would have acted the same way if some freak-looking girl showed up at my old school—but it doesn't make the stares hurt any less.

A loud screech fills the room, and I'm on the floor near my desk before I even realize I fell. The announcements start playing over the intercom, and the room fills with laughter.

"It's the intercom speaker. It's busted and sounds horrible when it comes on," the girl in front of me says. She looks sorry for me, which I hate, but at least she's not laughing like the others.

I put my earbuds back in and wait for the bell to change classes.

The morning goes by in a haze. New teachers, new classes. All these schools are starting to run together. This one isn't that big, so I share most classes with a handful of the same people.

I follow the crowd through the double doors into the cafeteria. A few girls I had a class with this morning, including the one from homeroom, signal me to sit with them. My legs itch to walk to their table and drop down in the chair they have pulled out, but before I take the first step, I check myself and remember The Plan. No friends. Grabbing a banana and a bottle of water, I give a half wave in their direction and flee the cafeteria.

Lugging my go-bag, I walk down the hall in search of a quiet place. Deep down there is a twinge of regret for isolating myself like this. I knew it would be hard, but I never believed it would be this hard, and it's only the first day.

The windows down a side hall overlook a small deserted courtyard, a circular area with several stone tables and benches surrounded by overgrown bushes. It's the perfect hiding spot, so I decide to brave the elements. January is colder than I thought it would be in Louisiana. I figured the hoodie would be enough, but the temperature is hovering around the freezing mark.

The benches are too cold to sit on, so I plop down on the mossy ground, pulling the hood over my head and sliding my earbuds into place as I crank the music. I take out my journal and write a while before my thoughts start to wander. One month. One month to figure things out. If I fail, I'll have to start all over in the next placement. The thought of this isolation being permanent makes me almost throw up, but I know I'm stronger than that now. The old me wouldn't have been able to do this. I shove the banana into my bag along with the journal and use the bag as a pillow. Closing my eyes, I let the music wash over me and try not to think.

A dark shadow passes over. I jerk upright.

It's camo boy. His lips are moving, but my music is so loud I can't hear what he's saying. I take the earbuds out, and he repeats himself.

"Not fitting in so well, huh? Must be pretty bad in there if you decided to freeze your ass off rather than sit inside with everybody else." He drops down beside me.

"Are you always so blunt?"

"Yep." He pops open a Coke. "What's your name?"

"Meg."

"I'm Ethan Landry. So, Meg. What's up? Why all alone out here?"

I shrug and lean back against my bag. If I ignore him, maybe he'll go away. I give him a quick once-over, noticing that the caked-on dirt covering his boots is also on his jeans and jacket. Why is he so dirty at school?

"Did you roll around in the mud or what?" I want to clamp my hand over my mouth the second the words leave my lips. So much for ignoring him.

He lets out a loud, sharp laugh. "I guess you could say that. Had to help my dad this morning."

"So your dad fell in the mud and you had to get him out?" Quit asking him questions!

He smiles. There's a dimple on the bruised side that is probably adorable when not discolored. "Something like that. Tractor got stuck and I had to go pull him out."

I lean over and wrap my arms around my knees. "So you live on a farm?" I ask.

"No, but we have a farm right outside of town."

His hands are rough and calloused, like they belong to a man more than a boy. I wonder if they feel as rough as they look.

My eyes move quickly back to his face, hoping my brief trip to the gutter doesn't show.

"Ya know, you're a pretty good singer," he says.

What.

A grin breaks out across his face. "I guess you didn't know you were singing out loud?"

Oh. My. God.

"Uh, no . . . um, I . . ." There are no words. I'm humiliated because I know, really know, what a bad singer I am.

My face is on fire and probably looks like a tomato.

Ethan chuckles, then nudges my foot with his. "I didn't mean to embarrass you, although it's pretty cute the way your cheeks get all pink like that. So what classes do you have this afternoon?" he asks.

He called me cute. Or at least my red-stained cheeks cute. The excitement this brings is replaced immediately with dread. I'm not doing this. Making friends. No matter how nice (or hot) they are.

"Look, I gotta go." I stand up, and he grabs my ankle.

"Don't be mad. Bell won't ring for another ten minutes."

God, he's adorable even with the ugly bruise marking his cheek. And that accent. I want nothing more than to sit back down and spend the next ten minutes flirting with him.

Instead, I shake my leg free.

"You must be pretty desperate to hunt down the new girl, farm boy. If I wanted to hang out with some hick, I'd have stayed in the cafeteria, where it's warm." Brutally harsh, but I've seen that look before. Interest. Interest in me and who I am, and I can't handle that. Not again.

He drops his hand, surprised, and squints at me. I swallow down the guilt. I'm really doing him a favor. I put the earbuds back in and walk inside.

I glance over my shoulder to where Ethan is still sitting, and I already regret walking away from him.

There's no way I'll make it a month.

Chapter 4

RULES FOR DISAPPEARING
BY WITNESS PROTECTION PRISONER #18A7R04M:

Be forgettable. No name-brand clothes or anything remotely cute—and that goes for shoes, too. It's not like anyone in these small towns will appreciate a good pair of Jimmy Choos anyway.

DAD'S waiting where he said he would, with Teeny in the car. Her head pops up just a bit when she sees me, and I try not to run the last block.

Every change between classes, I saw Ethan. Once I literally ran into him trying to go through the same classroom door, and we both dropped all our books. It didn't help that the jock with the cut lip was in that class, too. Ethan didn't try to talk to me again, but he kept eyeing me. It makes me nervous, the way he watches, and a bit tingly, too, which is bad, bad, bad. I'm also pretty sure I blushed like a fool every time he got near me.

Teeny is quiet. I ask about her teacher, her school, and the kids in her class, everything down to what she ate for lunch. Every answer is one word.

Dad takes a different route back home than the one we took this morning.

"Where are we going?" I ask.

He takes a moment to answer. "Thought we would do some sightseeing this afternoon. Get our bearings around town."

This is code for: Mom's hammered and Dad's giving her time to pass out before we get home.

I go along with it because it won't hurt to see what this town has to offer. Plus, I'm in no rush to have a drunken conversation with my mother.

Those never end well.

The streets near the river are narrow and very crowded. We end up driving in circles since most streets are one-way, until we manage to get away from the historic district. The farther we get, the more it changes. Quaint mom-and-pop shops are replaced with Taco Bells and Olive Gardens.

I watch Dad as he drives. He's staring more at the rearview mirror than through the windshield. I glance behind us a few times but don't see anything that looks weird. After he takes several quick turns without putting on the blinker first, I ask, "What are you looking for?"

"What?" He taps the brake and we lunge forward. "What are you talking about?"

"You keep looking in the rearview mirror. Like a lot. Is somebody back there?" I glance behind us again, but see nothing odd.

Dad shakes his head and mumbles under his breath. He's gotten really good at the mumbling.

After about thirty minutes, he pulls up into the parking lot of an ice-cream shop next to an Old Navy.

"How about we stop in here?" Dad throws the wagon in park.

I hop out of the car, go-bag clutched to my chest, and nearly bump into a girl I recognize from school. It's actually a group of girls piling out of an SUV, and most of them were in several of my classes.

As I scoot past them to the sidewalk, they giggle and whisper to each other, and once I catch my reflection in the plate glass window, I know why they're laughing. The cute towel-dried style from this morning didn't last. My hair is glued to my head and has no shape or body at all. In the plain jeans and gray hoodie I could pass for a boy. And not a very cute one.

Dad and Teeny follow me inside the ice-cream store and we pick a booth in the back.

Dad ambles off to the counter to order for us.

Teeny gives me a small smile. "Do those girls go to your school?"

"Yeah. They're in some of my classes," I say, my voice too high and my enthusiasm forced.

"Are they mean to you?" I don't give Teeny nearly enough credit—she picks up on everything.

"It's just the first day. I don't even know them, really." I fidget with the napkin dispenser and ask, "Were the kids in your class nice to you today?"

Teeny leans back against the booth and focuses on the ceiling without answering me.

Dad, balancing three ice-cream cones, slides in next to Teeny a few minutes later. She's more interested in peeling the paper off the cone than licking the ice cream. Dad uses a spoon even though his is in a cone, too. What a nerd.

I take long slow licks and try to think about what to say to Dad.

Number four on my list is to figure out what he did to get us into Witness Protection, and I won't get a better opportunity than this.

"Dad, what are we waiting for?"

Dad peeks over his shoulder and examines the room. "What do you mean?"

I lean in close. "Are we waiting for a trial or something? Why are we here?"

He presses his lips together and they turn white. He whispers, "This is not the place to discuss this."

Before The Plan, I would have backed off, but not now. "There's never a good time. Every time I bring this up you blow me off. Just tell me. The suits won't move us around forever, will they?"

Dad digs in his cone, his head shaking. "There may be a trial at some point," he answers through clenched teeth.

"What's the holdup? Don't we get out of the program after that?"

Dad's head comes up and his expression is odd. Like I'm crazy. "It's not as simple as that." He stands and throws his cone into the trash. He won't look at me. "We're not going back home. We're in this program for the foreseeable future, so please don't make things any more difficult than they already are."

"Dad, something's different this time. I don't know what it is— things just feel wrong."

"Stop talking about it!" Teeny screams, then throws her cone on the floor and runs from the store. I chase her out, dumping my cone on the way. I catch her at the wagon and try to pull her in close, but she's shaking and hitting me with her fists. I don't stop her.

I glance through the window, and Dad's cleaning up the spilled ice cream. God forbid he leaves the mess there to check on his daughter, who is completely. Freaking. Out.

When Dad finally comes out, he picks up Teeny, who's kicking and screaming now, and carries her to the car. She's really loud and draws a crowd pretty quickly, including the cheerleaders, who walked out of Old Navy straight into my family breakdown.

Everyone watches as Dad tries to stuff Teeny into the car. Her legs are so long they're making a helicopter motion in the air. One foot clips Dad on the side of his head, and he lets out a loud yelp. He finally gets her bottom half inside the wagon, but she grabs on to the door. He pries her fingers loose and slams the door shut, leaning against it as Teeny beats on the window. Most people have walked away by now, except the group of cheerleaders, who cluster together and start whispering like crazy.

Teeny's in the car crying, and Dad's breathing hard. I stand in front of the cheerleaders, hoping to block some of their view.

"Show's over. Go find someone else to gawk at." I hate that they saw Teeny like this.

The whispering stops as every eye turns to me. A dark-haired cheerleader steps forward. "Excuse me?" She actually made *excuse me* six syllables.

"You heard me. There's nothing else to see here." I may regret this later, but I can't seem to stop myself.

"You're right," the dark-haired girl says, then looks me up and down. Slowly. "Nothing worth seeing here."

A few ugly remarks float my way as they get into their car, but at least they've stopped talking about Teeny.

Class tomorrow should be loads of fun.

Mom is sprawled on the couch with an empty gin bottle and a box of tissues. There are, like, a million little pieces torn up on the floor.

Dad barely glances at her. "Girls, why don't you go to your room and get started on homework. I'll help Mom clean up this mess."

As if she's going to be any help at all. We head down the hall to our room, where Teeny throws herself across her bed, covering her face. She's ignored me since her meltdown.

Stretching back on my bed, I pull out my homework. I haven't worried about my grades for the last three placements, since my transcript won't follow me to the next school, but I make sure I know just enough to not look like a dumb-ass if I'm called on in class.

I think back to my conversation with Dad. The Plan took a major hit today. I never thought this situation would be permanent. The way Dad talks—we're in this for life. But I'm more determined than ever now. No way in hell I'm moving around and living like this forever.

"I don't have any homework, so can I have my book from the bag?" Teeny's hand is out, but she's still turned away from me. At least she's talking.

"Sure." I hand her the book she was working on yesterday. "Do you want to talk about it?"

"No."

She starts a new puzzle, and the concentration on her face is intense.

"I get scared sometimes, too. We have each other, Teeny. If you need to complain, or yell, or get mad—it's okay. I'm here for you."

She ignores me completely.

Dad knocks on the door some time later and pokes his head in. "I meant to stop by the grocery store while we were out this afternoon. I'm going to that pizza shop on the corner. Is pepperoni good?"

I swing my legs off the side of the bed. "I'll go. It's just a couple of blocks. You stay with Mom." I'm so not up for dealing with her when she's hammered, and I would love nothing more than to get out of this house.

Dad hesitates, runs a hand through his hair, and lets out a deep sigh but doesn't say anything more.

"What?" I ask.

He shakes his head. "Nothing. I guess that's fine."

"I asked you this earlier—what's different? You're acting all weird and I can tell something's wrong. Is it a problem for me to go three blocks to the pizza place?"

Dad says, "No. We just need to be really cautious."

I park my hands on my hips. "Did the suits tell *you* we're supposed to be extra cautious this time? Because they don't tell me crap."

He doesn't say anything.

"Did they tell you we shouldn't leave the house?"

"No. I'm probably being paranoid. Just go straight there and back." Dad hands me ten dollars. The suits give us very little extra money. Whatever I can get for ten bucks will barely feed Teeny and me, much less Mom and him.

I'll have to add a little of my own money to get us enough food. I have some extra cash from my last job, but it won't last long at this rate. I'm going to have to find some work.

It's dark and really cold out when I leave. The wind stings my cheeks, and the contacts are hurting my eyes.

The pizza place is about three corners up, one street away from the cobblestone street that runs next to Cane River. I walk fast and look behind me often: I guess Dad's paranoia is rubbing off on me. By the time I get to the restaurant my hands are frozen and my nose is numb. The warmth and savory smell of pizza pour out of the restaurant when I open the door.

I get to the counter and study the menu written on a huge chalkboard above the cashier's head, wrinkling my nose at some of the choices. Swamp pizza? What is that? I read the ingredients: crab, crawfish, jalapeños, shrimp, and andouille sausage. You have got to be kidding me.

"Can I help you?"

The woman behind the counter is older, maybe in her late fifties, and has a head of solid white hair. I check the prices on the normal stuff. "I'll take a large pepperoni pizza to go."

"Be ready in about ten minutes." She rings me up and then shuffles to the kitchen. There are several people eating, but she seems to be the only person working.

I clear my throat loud enough for her to peek through the small window between the front of the restaurant and the kitchen. "Need something else?" she asks.

"A job, if you have an opening." This place would be perfect since it's in walking distance from the house. Teeny might be able to hang here with me in the afternoons at one of the tables in the corner.

"Ever work in a restaurant before?"

This is the hard part. I have no résumé and certainly no references. I've had odd jobs since our third placement, but that's the extent of my work history, including the time from my old life. I don't think playing hostess at Mom's parties counts for much.

"Yes."

"What's your name?"

"Meg Jones."

The woman stops what she's doing and asks, "You in school?"

"Yes. At Natchitoches."

"Well, you caught me at the right time. The girl helping me quit this afternoon. Any chance you can start tonight?"

I think about Teeny back at home. Mom's a wreck but at least Dad's there. "Yeah. I need to take that pizza home first, and then I can come right back."

"Perfect. And just for that—the pizza's on me. I'll throw in some breadsticks, too," the woman says. "Come back here, and I'll show you around while it's cooking. You can have a T-shirt, too. I always give the first one away, but after that you're gonna have to pay if you want another one."

I walk into the kitchen, and the woman introduces herself as Pearl. She hands me a red T-shirt with the logo of the restaurant on the front. "My son works here during the day, so it'll be you and me in the afternoons and evenings. You work the front register and keep the dining area clean, and I make all the food. We're closed on Sundays. Can you be here after school? We're open till eight."

I think about Teeny again. Dad starts his job at the plant tomorrow, and he'll be working twelve-hour shifts from seven in the morning to seven at night. I'll be lucky if Mom can take care of herself, much less Teeny. And the way Dad is acting, I'd rather she was here with me.

"Pearl, I have a younger sister that kinda depends on me in the afternoons. Is there any way she can hang out here until my dad gets off work at seven?"

Pearl puts her hands on her hips and taps her orthopedic shoe on the floor. "This ain't no day care, girlie."

"She's no trouble at all. Very quiet. She'll sit in a booth in the corner and do her homework, promise."

"Only 'cause you caught me in a bind. First sign of that girl messing things up or getting in the way, and she's out of here."

"Of course. She'll be no problem."

Once my pizza and breadsticks are ready, I hurry back to the house and tell Dad and Teeny about my new job.

Dad stops in mid-motion of putting a slice of pizza on a plate for Teeny. "What about your schoolwork? And how are you getting there? Are you walking back and forth?"

I run to my room so I can make a quick change into the T-shirt Pearl gave me. I don't answer Dad until I'm back in the kitchen. "Teeny can hang out with me after school. You can pick her up on your way home from work, and I'll walk home when my shift ends."

Dad sits down next to Teeny. "I don't think this is a good idea."

"No, Dad, it'll be fine." I point to Mom, who is snoring loudly on the couch. "Teeny and I can't stay here all afternoon with her like this." It's true and he knows it.

"I'll come back to pick you up. I don't like you walking alone," he says.

"Is there something I should know?"

His jaw twitches but he doesn't answer.

"Then I'll walk home when my shift is over. No big deal," I say.

"Straight home," he adds.

"Sissy, can I go with you tonight?" Teeny's sad eyes make me feel like I'm deserting her.

"Tomorrow." I squeeze her in a quick hug and grab a piece of pizza as I head out the door. "The name of the restaurant is Pearl's. The number's on the box if something comes up."

The pizza parlor is packed by the time I make it back. There's a line at the counter and half the tables are full. Pearl waves me over the second I step through the door.

"Meg, you're gonna have to jump right in."

There is a steady stream of customers for almost an hour. I don't know how Pearl would have pulled this off by herself. A few people come in from school. They nod but don't speak to me other than placing their order. Eventually, things settle down enough that I can wander around the dining room picking up trash and refilling napkin dispensers. The door dings and I glance up.

It's him. Ethan. He's concentrating on his phone, his baseball cap shielding part of his face, so he hasn't spotted me yet. I spin and try not to run to the back room, hoping that maybe Pearl can take his order. Great, she's on the phone.

Standing a little taller, I walk to the register. I can do this.

"May I help you?" I hope my voice didn't come out as stiff as I think it did.

His eyes leave the phone and fly to my face. His mouth opens a bit, but no words come out. We both stand there for several seconds before he glances back at his phone. He texts something, then shoves the phone into his pocket. "Large swamp pizza, extra jalapeños."

It amazes me how many people order this pizza. I thought it would look better than it sounds. Not even close.

"To go?" Hope rings in my voice.

He smirks. "Dine in." He throws some money down on the counter.

This may be my shortest employment yet. I toss his money into the drawer and yell his order back to Pearl.

Ethan sits at a table that gives him a direct view of me behind the counter, and, as if on cue, my face flames red. I can't even look at him without blushing. This sucks. I try to stay busy while his pizza cooks, but it's very unnerving knowing he's watching me. Pearl calls out when his order is ready.

I drop his pizza on the table and then do the same with his change. He's made me nervous, and I hate that. When I turn to go, he grabs my wrist, not rough but firm. I'm two seconds from bruising his other cheek when he yells, "Aunt Pearl? Mind if Meg takes a break and helps me with this pizza?"

Aunt Pearl! You have got to be kidding me.

Pearl pokes her head out of the kitchen. "Hey, Ethan. Should have known it was you. Sure, Meg, take a break. Keep my nephew in line," she cackles, and disappears back into the kitchen. I stand there openmouthed.

I shake my arm free. "I don't need a break. I just got here."

"I'm sorry I embarrassed you earlier. Maybe we can start over."

My brain screams to get out of here, but I can't. He still has a smudge of dirt on the side of his chin, and I have to resist the urge to brush it off. The bruise has turned a really deep purple, but it doesn't diminish his striking features. "Meg, sit with me for ten minutes." He sounds put out.

I plop down in the chair before I can talk myself out of it. He's smiling at me, dimple digging into the side of his cheek. I smile back before I can stop myself. I'm so pathetic. I can't make it one day on The Plan.

"Okay, so here I am. You've got ten minutes."

He puts a slice of pizza on a plate and slides it to me, then gets one for himself. "You're gonna have to eat some of this."

Extreme hunger couldn't make me take a bite of that pizza.

He swallows down a huge piece. "Come on, just one bite," he says, his Southern drawl dragging out his words.

"You look even dirtier than you did this morning." I try to make this sound really rude and offensive, but it comes out more like I'm curious. Which I guess I am.

"Yeah. Working on a farm will do that to you." Ethan rubs his hands down his coat sleeves, knocking dirt on the floor. A huge chunk falls on the table, and before I think twice about what I'm doing, I flick it at him, hitting him square in the forehead.

His expression is perfect. Completely amused and surprised at the same time.

"You're gonna get it now," he says as a wicked grin spreads across his face.

I push away from the table, laughing, but I'm in a bind, with Ethan blocking any possible escape.

I try to scoot one way, and he mirrors my move. Not sure what he has in mind once he catches me, so I hold up both hands and say, "Truce. We're even now."

"Even?" His hands go out to his sides like he's confused. "How do you figure we're even?"

"You made fun of my singing. That deserved a little bit of retaliation."

Ethan drops back down in his seat and pulls mine closer to the table with his foot. "For the record, I said you sounded good. Not my fault if you can't take a compliment."

I move my seat a little farther from the table before sitting down, not trusting he won't go for some sort of revenge.

"What do you grow?" For some reason, this whole farm thing fascinates me. I've never known anyone who actually had a farm or grew things. Or looked so cute covered in dirt.

"Mostly cotton, some corn and soybeans."

"So what do you do there, exactly?"

Ethan lifts up his cap and slides it back and forth a few times before fitting it back on his head. "Well, this time of year we mostly fix equipment and get the fields ready. We have cows, too, so you gotta make sure they have plenty of food since it's so cold out."

His face looks chapped from the wind, and the tips of his dark hair curl over the edge of his cap. And that voice, deep and smooth, those words rolling right out . . .

"Why were you fighting with that other guy?"

Ethan's smile drops. "He's an asshole."

I wait for him to explain, but apparently that's all I'm going to get.

"Did you get in trouble? It kinda surprised me that you didn't get suspended." I tear off a small chunk of crust and pop it into my mouth.

"Technically, the fight happened off school grounds," he says, putting "off school grounds" in air quotes. "Principal couldn't touch us. That jackass wanted to keep going once we hit the parking lot. That's why we got called in."

I'm starving, so I give in and pull the plate closer. There probably won't be any leftovers at home, so this may be my only chance to eat. I pick every single thing off the pizza, and Ethan laughs at me as he shovels his fourth piece into his mouth. It's a good thing Teeny and I don't have appetites like that, or we would have starved months ago.

"Now my turn for a question. What's the story on Meg Jones?"

Loaded question if there ever was one. "Not much. Just moved here from Arkansas. My dad got a job here. That's pretty much it."

The guilt eats at me every time I lie. I'm going to need counseling at some point—maybe I should find a Liars Anonymous meeting. *"Hi, I'm Meg from Louisiana. No, that's not right. I'm Suzie from Texas. No, not that either . . ."*

"What part?"

"Um, Lewisville."

Ethan's face lights up. "No friggin' way. Ever see the Fouke Monster?"

What the . . . Fouke Monster? There was no mention of a monster in the neatly typed three paragraphs I was given. I shake my head. Surely *No!* is the right answer here.

He watches me a second. I tuck a few short strands behind my ear and try not to panic.

"So, how'd you end up working here? This is your first day, right?"

"Came in and ordered a pizza. Asked for a job. The last waitress quit, so lucky for me." Ethan's mouth opens, I assume for another question, but I'm saved by the door chimes. I jump up from the table.

A few new customers trickle in to pick up to-go orders. Once they leave, I want nothing more than to run back to that table. I force myself to stay at the counter. Ethan walks over when it's clear I'm not coming back.

Before he can say anything, I put my hand up. "Ethan, thanks for the pizza, but I need to get back to work. I don't want to make Pearl mad or lose my job." It had been too nice—a simple conversation with a cute boy. It wouldn't take long for it to progress to something else. And then what? Ethan would look for me one day at school, and there would be no trace of me left. I lost myself for a few minutes, but it's not too late to pull back.

He slides his hat off and back on again and studies me. Leaning over the counter, he grabs a cardboard pizza box from underneath and yells, "Bye, Aunt Pearl! See ya later."

Pearl sticks her head out of the kitchen. "You going already? Well, bye, hon." She nods toward me. "Meg, you can go on and go, too. You weren't planning on working tonight. I can handle it from here. Be back at four tomorrow."

I grab my hoodie and go-bag from behind the counter and head out the door. It opens and closes behind me, but I don't turn back—just keep walking. A moment later, a truck comes up beside me and the window rolls down.

"Are you walking home?"

I don't answer.

"It's too cold to walk."

No shit. "I'm fine. It's not far." I pick up my pace. A loud noise from the bushes almost brings me to the ground. My heart's in my throat until I see a little squirrel dart from the shrubbery. Dad's paranoia is definitely rubbing off on me.

"Meg, let me take you home."

God, I probably look like an idiot. The fumes from the exhaust fill the air around me. There are still two and a half blocks to go, and I'm freezing. The wind is whipping right through my hoodie, and my teeth are chattering. I jump in his truck and point up the road. "I live in one of the little cottages up there."

We pull in to the driveway and Ethan leans back in his seat. My playful attitude turned considerably frosty, and I'm sure he's trying to figure out why. I jump out of the truck before he can say anything else, and don't look back. I don't hear the truck drive away until I shut the front door.

Chapter 5

RULES FOR DISAPPEARING
BY WITNESS PROTECTION PRISONER #18A7R04M:

Only use public transportation. It's the one true way to look completely uninteresting. That is, unless, you have a hideous wood-paneled station wagon. That'll work, too.

I wake up in a cold sweat. The room is dark, but I can make out Teeny's sleeping form in the twin bed next to me. My T-shirt is wet and my hair is plastered to my face. I can't catch my breath. *It was a dream*, I repeat in my head. It's the same dream that has haunted me for months, where I'm stuck in a room and I'm scared to death. There are people in the room, but I can't hear what they're saying. It's been weeks since I've had this dream, but that doesn't make it any better when it shows up.

My legs get tangled in the sheets and I end up falling out of bed. I grab the journal from my bag and start to write, squinting in the dark.

> Flashing lights. I'm trapped. I'm scared. I can't breathe. It's like I'm drowning.

I'm hoping this will help me make some sense out of the nightmares, but all I can pull out of them are the flashing lights and the feeling of being trapped, which isn't surprising since that's exactly what Witness Protection feels like. As soon as I wake up, the images evaporate.

My throat's on fire. I run to the kitchen for some water and drink a glassful in seconds. It isn't until I fill the glass for the second time that a movement catches my attention.

The glass slips and shatters on the floor. Mom is hunched over the kitchen table. "I didn't mean to scare you." Her words are slurred.

"Mom, what are you doing up?" I glance at the clock on the oven. "It's two in the morning." Tiptoeing around the shards of glass, I get the broom and dustpan from the small closet.

"Can't sleep. Miss my bed at home. Not the same here."

No kidding. "Mom, you need to get to bed."

"I have failed you girls. I can't even remember the names they gave you." She puts her head on the table and sobs.

How many times have we sat in the dark like this? I want to feel sorry for her, but I'm tapped out. I run my hand through her messy hair, trying to untangle a few of the knots. If her face didn't show the damage from all the alcohol, she would be beautiful. The darker hair looks so much better than the fake blond did.

"It's Meg and Mary. I'm Meg. Meg Jones. You are Emily Jones. Dad is Bill Jones. We're in Louisiana." Hearing all the basic facts of our new life seems to calm her down, just as it did for Teeny this morning. "C'mon, Mom."

Mom gets up from the table, and I put an arm around her waist. She's leaning against me, and it's a struggle to get her down the hall.

She points a finger back toward the kitchen as we leave. "We don't even have food here. I never would have had an empty refrigerator."

"I know, Mom. I'll go to the store tomorrow. Keep walking, we're almost there."

We stumble into her room. I'm sure Dad's aware of what's happening, but he doesn't move or say a word. I should've turned the lights on and made him deal with this. Mom snores softly before I even get the covers over her.

Mom made an appearance this morning, eyes red and puffy, but didn't mention our earlier conversation. Dad put an envelope in my room with money for food before he left. I'm sure he didn't trust Mom with it. Let me add *find a way to get to the grocery store before work and do all the shopping* to my to-do list. Then again, there's always pizza.

I step off the bus in front of school. It's humiliating to show up your senior year on a bus. My old friends back home, especially Elle and Laura, would have a field day if they could see me now. As soon as the thought seeps into my brain, I push it back out. Just thinking about them makes my stomach hurt. How can I want to go back home more than anything, and at the same time never want to see my two best friends ever again?

I can't think about them right now.

I join the sea of people wandering through the front doors, and head to my locker. I'm so nervous, and it's totally Ethan's fault. I took extra time with my hair this morning in the hopes that I won't look like a boy by the end of the day. This goes totally against The Plan, I know. There's no reason to look cute for a boy you're desperately trying to ignore. His locker is close to mine, so I peek past the metal door to spy on him. He's easy to spot, leaning against the wall near the bathrooms, talking to a small group of people. I grab my books and sneak into homeroom.

My seat in the back is available, so I slide in. Before I can start my music, the guy in front of me turns around. It's the jock that fought with Ethan. His eye is an array of disgusting colors and almost swollen shut.

"I didn't catch your name yesterday, new girl."

"Meg Jones."

"Well, hey, Meg. I'm Ben Dufrene."

I don't answer, just crank the volume up.

Ben takes the hint and doesn't try to talk to me again.

After sitting through my first two classes, I've decided it takes a lot of effort to be a loner. In the other schools I worked hard to fit in, but a few hours into my second day here and I'm physically exhausted from not making eye contact or initiating conversation.

Third period begins, and my teacher turns the class into a study hall and runs out of the room in tears. Bits of gossip throughout the room suggest that she was having an affair with one of the coaches and he broke it off with her this morning. Classy.

But it's fine by me. One less class I have to worry about. The room is broken up into little groups, everyone enjoying this unexpected hour of freedom, but I sit all alone. Busy doesn't look as pathetic, so I pull out the journal and put in my earbuds. About halfway through the hour, a girl drops down in the desk in front of mine. Her eyes peek to the page I'm writing on, so I close the book.

I recognize her as the cheerleader that was front and center for Teeny's meltdown yesterday. A group of her minions watch and giggle from across the room.

From the expressions on their faces, this probably won't be good. Elle used to do this same crap to Nicole Payne. That girl made Elle look stupid during a mock debate in speech, and Elle never let it go. I'd sit back and watch, just like this cheerleader's friends are doing now, and I can still remember that feeling of nervousness mixed with excitement when I saw Elle move in. I pop the earbuds out and try to prepare for what's coming.

"Okay, so my friends and I have a question."

I don't take the bait. I'm going to make her work for this.

"That girl who was with you yesterday, was that your sister? Is something *wrong* with her?" Her face crinkles into a fake sympathetic expression. "Is she *special*?"

So *not* what I was expecting. I feel like I've been punched in the stomach. This bitch is sitting here making fun of Teeny in front of all these people, when she has no idea what we've been through in the past eight months. But I refuse to give them what they want, which is some sort of scene.

"Hello?" The cheerleader giggles and glances back toward the group behind her. "I guess it runs in the family."

She gets up from the seat in front of me, and I can't resist—I stick my foot out just as she starts to walk away, and she goes flying across the floor. Her skirt comes up and her bare butt (except for the small strip her thong covers) is there for the world to see.

The entire room bursts out laughing, and for a moment I sit there stunned. Then I grab my go-bag and sprint into the hall toward the bathroom. I may have just started WWIII.

The bathroom door slams against the wall, and the noise echoes through the room. A girl jumps and grabs her purse protectively.

"You scared the shit out of me!" She jams something into the wall. The girl's sketchy, dressed in black from head to toe with hot-pink stripes in her hair. She shoves a bunch of crap into her bag and races from the bathroom.

I walk to where she was standing and look at the brick wall. What did she do? I brush my hand against the bricks and feel around, but nothing. Leaning against the wall, I slide to the floor and pull my knees up to my chin.

How could I have lost control like that? It must have been too many thoughts of home and my old life this morning. Elle and Laura were my best friends, but they had a habit of finding their amusement at others' expense. Now I know how bad it sucks to be on the receiving end of that.

The Plan is going to hell—I'm failing miserably at going unnoticed. I have to get back on track. Dad's a dead end. He wasn't much on talking in our old life, so I don't know why I thought he'd open up now. Maybe I can Google something, but what? *How to get out of Witness Protection*? I've been terrified of the Internet ever since what happened the last time I surfed around. Trying that could be like a one-way ticket to the next placement. As much as this one sucks, the next one could be just as bad. Or worse.

I drop my head on my arms. There's always Mom. Maybe I can get her talking while she's drunk. My stomach turns as soon as I think this. It seems wrong, but I'm desperate.

A shrill ring vibrates through the bathroom, and I join the swarm of people in the hall.

Word must have gotten out about what just happened. Before, no one paid me much attention, but now I'm getting all kinds of looks. Most of them not good, but there are a couple of kids who looked pleased. I can't be the only person who's ever wanted to knock that girl on her ass.

It's incredibly hard to act like none of this bothers me. There's no protection when you're a loner. I'm like that one little baby duck you see on those wildlife shows that gets separated from the group as the nasty alligator hovers just below the water's surface. *Chomp, chomp.*

As soon as my next class is over, I make a break for it. After grabbing lunch from the cafeteria, I peek out the window into the courtyard, where I ate yesterday—hoping I can hide there again—but Ethan is there, lying on the stone picnic table. He's got his backpack under his head and his earbuds in. It's almost the same exact pose I was in yesterday, except I was on the ground.

I'm not going out there. I'll have to find some other little hole to crawl in and wait out the lunch hour. It's way too easy hanging out with Ethan, and it's stupid to get too close. And yet I find myself walking outside.

The door makes a loud creaky noise, and Ethan's head pops up. No sane argument in my head could have stopped my legs from walking out here. He smiles when he sees me but doesn't get up.

He plucks his earbuds out and says, "So, I heard you're fitting in nicely, making friends, warming up to the locals."

"Ha-ha." I drop my go-bag on the ground and use it as a cushion, then balance my lunch in my lap. "You're funny. Those girls seriously hate me now—and they started it! I'll need eyes in the back of my head."

Ethan sits up and takes a deep swig of Coke. "That's because you're new. We've all been in school together since kindergarten, so there's nothing left to get worked up about."

"You and Ben don't seem to have that problem."

"That's because Ben is a pain in my ass that won't go away."

"So, why are you out here and not hanging out with your friends? Or do you not have any of those?" I ask between bites of turkey sandwich. I know that's not the case, since he's surrounded by people every time I turn a corner, but it is strange that he hangs out here at lunch by himself.

"I thought you might be back. Wanted to see how you were handling what happened this morning."

I stop chewing and look at him. That is the nicest thing anyone has said to me in a long time, but I can't ruin The Plan over some sweet words. "I'm fine. You don't need to worry about me."

"Good. So, have you had a chance to check things out around town? You got here at the right time—Mardi Gras kicks off soon, and you can usually find a good party on parade nights."

"I thought that was only in New Orleans." My remark may make me seem stupid. I'm supposed to be from Arkansas, which is next to Louisiana, so I should probably know all this.

He shakes his head and doesn't seem thrown off by my question. "No, there are lots of smaller parades all through the state. The best ones are down there, though."

Ethan digs in his bag and pulls out a sheet of paper.

"What's that?" I ask.

He shakes it a few times. "Read it."

I take it but know instantly that this is not going to turn out well. It's a Wikipedia article about the Fouke Monster, which is basically a Big Foot–type creature that is believed to be in, well, Fouke. The article says there was even a movie about it, and a little map shows that Fouke is near Lewisville. The town is crazy about the myth, and people come from all over to try to get a sight of the monster. My mouth gets dry. I'm so screwed.

Ethan takes a swig of Coke. "I don't think you're from Lewisville."

And there it is. The suits explained what to do if someone questions your story, but he's called me out.

"What? Of course I'm from Lewisville." I try hard to look offended. Jumping up, I heave the go-bag to my chest. "I've got to go to the bathroom."

I cringe at my choice of words, but beat it to the door anyway.

At this point, I'm sure he thinks I'm nuts. Multiple personalities or something. He doesn't say anything, just watches me run back into school.

Chapter 6

RULES FOR DISAPPEARING
BY WITNESS PROTECTION PRISONER #18A7R04M:

Do not join clubs, dance line, or any other really fun organized group at school. This leads to making friends and really awkward questions like, "What's wrong with your mom?"

TO say it was a bad day would be like saying the *Titanic* had a little accident. My new archenemy wasted no opportunity to make snide comments about my hair, clothes, and overall existence throughout the day. And then I *had* to come back with something equally ugly. War has officially commenced.

I expected Ethan to show up at Pearl's tonight. Every time that door dinged, my neck hairs stood up. But he never showed, and that was almost worse. The walk home from Pearl's is brutal—three blocks in the freezing cold. I need to buy a pair of gloves or my fingers may very well fall off.

I start to climb the front steps of our cottage, lugging the few groceries I was able to carry from the store near Pearl's.

"Where have you been?"

I almost fall backward. Dad is sitting on the top step in the dark.

I hold up the bags like *duh.*

"I thought you were coming straight here. That was the deal if you're going to walk home." He gets up and grabs a few of the bags from me. "Teeny fell asleep crying in her room. She thought you weren't coming back."

I follow him in the house, dropping my remaining bags on the table, and check the clock. "I'm not that late. Did you try to convince her everything was okay?"

He had brought Chinese home for dinner, and the empty containers are scattered all over the counters. I throw out the trash while Dad puts away the groceries.

"Of course. But she wouldn't talk to me. Sissy, we're not on vacation. You have to be careful. Don't go anywhere unnecessarily."

I twist my face into the worst surprised expression I can manage and say, "What? You mean this crap shack isn't part of the Four Seasons? Shocking."

He doesn't answer, just goes to his room once we're finished putting everything away. God, what an asshole.

I jump in the shower and it isn't until the hot water pours over me that I start to warm up. Dad is freaking me out. In our old life I had plenty of freedom, coming and going pretty much as I wanted. Mom was always off doing whatever moms who don't work do when they get together, and Dad was at work. All the time. When we got into the program, both of my parents took more interest in my whereabouts, but we still tried to act normal about it. That's the suits' motto, in fact—Act Normal. But Dad is not acting normal.

After I shower I head to bed. I barely get the covers over me when Teeny whispers.

"Sissy, is that you?"

"Yeah, it's me. Are you okay?"

She gets up from her bed and jumps into mine. "Can I sleep with you tonight?" She doesn't wait for my answer, just snuggles in under the covers.

I can't say no, even though this is a twin bed and neither one of us will get a decent night's sleep if we're both in it.

She curls up next to me. "I thought something happened to you."

"I know. I'm sorry. I'll call if I'm running late next time. I didn't know you would worry like that."

She's shaking under the covers, and I have the feeling there's something more to it. "What happened around here after Dad brought you home?"

It takes a while before she answers. "Mom and Dad had a bad fight. They went in their room, but I could still hear their voices."

I run my hands through her short hair. "What was the fight about?"

Teeny squirms around. "I don't know. I could only hear the parts they said really loud. Mom said the F-word a lot."

Holy shit. This is kind of a big deal for them. Back home, my parents were the ridiculous type of couple who still seemed to actually like each other. If Dad wasn't at work, he was with Mom. They used to watch movies together on the couch late at night, and Mom rubbed his feet. Totally gross, but she seemed to like it. They fought, but it was always short, and they hardly ever raised their voices. And as crazy as Mom could be, she never said the F-word.

I can tell the fight really bothers Teeny, and I don't want to force it out of her, but I need to know if they said anything about what got us here. "What else?"

"She did yell out once that it was time for Dad to tell the truth.

Then Dad started yelling about how much she drinks, and then she started crying."

Oh. My. God. What's he been lying about? My mind races with accusations. Teeny gets quiet, and I continue to stroke her hair. Finally, her breathing changes. She's asleep. I lie in there thinking.

There are so few bits and pieces to work through that nothing makes sense. My parents have been totally silent about our situation, and it makes me crazy. If Teeny and I have to live through all these moves, it's only fair we know why.

Two days into The Plan and I have more questions than answers.

I allow my mind to drift, and replay scenes from the day. Those cheerleaders are vicious, but I let them get the better of me. And Ethan. Out of everything that happened, he's the one thing I'm the most worried about. I think he's on to me.

Stupid-ass Fouke Monster.

The bus ride home on Friday afternoon is like heaven. Well, as close to heaven as you can get riding a school bus when you're months away from being a legal adult.

It was a tough first week. The entire cheerleading squad is out to get me, and I finally learned the name of my new archenemy. It's Emma. And she and Ben like to hook up. A lot. Against my locker. I'm sure she picked that particular piece of real estate on purpose.

Archenemy and her minions were total bitches all week. Ethan stepped in once or twice and stood up for me, but it seemed to make things worse. There's some crazy thing between Ethan and Emma, and I pray to God he didn't used to date her. I couldn't look at him the same.

I avoided the courtyard (and Ethan) at lunch. He's getting too close for comfort. He hasn't mentioned Lewisville again, or the Fouke Monster, but he's asking about other stuff and trying to trip me up.

The bus rambles on and finally pulls over on the street in front of the row of cottages. There are very few people left once we get to my stop.

I can tell the second the door opens that Mom's bad off. The smell of alcohol assaults me as soon as I step inside. I don't see her until I walk around the side of the couch. She's on the floor, curled into the fetal position, snoring loudly. I check the clock on the oven in the kitchen. Teeny will be here in about ten minutes.

"Mom, get up." I shake her shoulder and she moans. I roll her onto her back, and her breath almost knocks me over.

"Mom, let's get you up."

She makes a halfhearted attempt to move. I pull her into a sitting position.

"Mom, Teeny's gonna be here any minute. Let's get you to your room."

This seems to have some effect. Once she's on her feet, I walk her down the short hallway to the bathroom.

A shower won't hurt. Actually, I'm not sure she's bathed since we've been here. Her hair is greasy and limp. I lean her against the wall and turn on the water.

I start undressing her, trying not to think about how pathetic this is. Mom's super skinny and it's shocking. Once she's naked, I lead her to the tub. I'll be scarred for life after this.

When the water hits her, she opens her eyes and starts sputtering and coughing. She sways into the wall and then back into the curtain. I end up sitting her down to let the water run all over her.

She finally becomes somewhat coherent and helps me wash her hair and body. My mind is reeling. I've never seen her this bad.

Once I get her into her room and she's dressed, I lay her down on the bed and cover her up.

I pick up the clothes on the floor, and something falls out. It's a small piece of paper. Looking back at Mom to make sure she's completely out, I grab it, unfolding it slowly. It's a phone number.

I sprint to the phone in the kitchen, not thinking about what I'm doing, and dial the number.

A man answers on the second ring. "Mrs. Jones?"

Uh-oh. Do I hang up? "No, this is Meg."

It takes a few seconds for him to speak, but he finally says, "Meg, this is Agent Thomas. Is everything all right?"

Great, it's one of the suits.

I don't answer. He asks again, "Do you need something? Is something wrong?"

The last thing I need is for a suit to show up. I'm not sure who I thought was going to be on the other line, or what I was going to get out of this conversation, but I say, "I found your number in my mom's pocket." I let that hang there.

"Yes. How is your mother?"

I think about her thin body and empty eyes. "She's fine."

"Has something happened?" he asks.

"No, I just didn't recognize this number. We don't need anything." I hang up before he can ask me anything else. Why would Mom keep one of the suit's numbers on her? Maybe both my parents keep them—I don't know.

I hear Teeny come in the house.

She spots me and then looks around the room. "Where's Mom?"

"She's taking a nap."

Teeny's not stupid. She watches me for a few seconds and walks into the kitchen. I get her a granola bar and fix a peanut butter sandwich to take with us to Pearl's. Even though I don't have to be there for another twenty minutes, we take off.

"How was school today?" I ask.

Teeny shuffles her feet while we walk, kicking little rocks in every direction. "Fine."

"Did you hang out with anyone today? Have you made any friends?" I haven't been this blunt in my questioning before, but I'm really getting worried about her.

Teeny just shakes her head.

"Are the girls nice to you?" I turn to Teeny, and something catches my attention in the corner of my eye. I whip my head around, but nothing's there. Teeny hasn't looked up from the ground once and seems oblivious to my spastic movements.

We take another few steps before she answers, "One girl is nice."

Okay, something to work with. "What's her name?" I'm trying to concentrate on what she's saying, but I can't shake the feeling that something's going on behind us. My head is swiveling back and forth every few steps. Dad's warnings about walking around alone float through my head.

Teeny answers, "Grace," and I almost forget what we were talking about.

"So, do you eat lunch with Grace or talk to her in the halls? If she's nice, you should be nice back. She could be a new friend for you." I decide to cross over to the opposite side of the street. I still can't tell if anyone is back there, but something just feels wrong. I grab Teeny's hand and pull her along.

She doesn't even look up to see if a car is coming. "I'm tired of making new friends."

Amen, sister.

We walk the next block in silence. I'm Miss Spastic now, checking in front of us, behind us, and the other side of the street.

"Do you think Mom's going to die?" It's the first time she's looked at me since we left the house. We stop walking.

"No." I try to sound reassuring, but I can't. Because I'm not sure I didn't just lie to Teeny.

I grab her hand and we start moving again. For the first time, Teeny realizes we've changed sides. She looks around. "Why are we over here?"

I shrug. "No reason."

We walk the last block to Pearl's. Teeny heads in, but I wait on the sidewalk another minute, scanning the street. Not many people are out right now, and just a few cars go by. It looks normal. No one even glances my way. So why does it feel like someone is watching us?

The nervous feeling I had walking to work stayed with me all night and lingers this morning. I had the nightmare again, too. I crack my eyes as the early morning rays filter into our room, and cringe when I glance at my watch—too early to get up on a Saturday morning. A really bad nightmare leaves me feeling a bit hungover, without all the fun of a night out. Teeny's still sleeping, and I don't hear many other sounds coming from the house. As much as I hate reliving the images, I'm able to hold on to a few details and race to jot them down before they float away.

> I'm stuck in the same room, but this time it's a little different. Books are stacked up around me—huge mounds of them. The pages are full of all the names we've used, written over and over, but they're all crossed out with deep red *X*'s. And every time I open a book it multiplies into three more books. The red *X*'s start running until red ink drips off the pages and covers my hands, arms, and legs. I push all the books away until I get to the bottom of the pile and find Mom's dead body.

I stare at what I've written. It's horrible how real the nightmare felt. Were the books my journal? Am I screwing up by writing all this down?

The first time I dreamed about that room, it scared the shit out of me. But in that first placement, everything scared the shit out of me. I missed my friends—Elle, with her crazy, outrageous plans. Never scared of anything. And Laura. The voice of reason. The calm that kept us all grounded.

And then I would remember none of that was real.

That last night at home, before my life was full of fake names and suits and fear, I discovered my friends weren't the people I thought they were. Some things about that night are so clear, like the smell of Elle's perfume floating into the hall outside her bedroom, followed by the conversation that cut me like a knife. But other parts of that night are hazy . . . and confusing. The party I crashed. How did I get there? The shots I did by the pool. God, it makes me nauseous thinking about it.

I push away the past and tug at the foggy edges of my nightmare, but it's painful, just like everything else, so I let it go.

I stretch around the bed. I'm not sure if it's a good thing that I'm off work or not. There are a lot of hours to fill between now and Monday morning, and I might just be going a little crazy.

After a nice long hot shower, I head to the kitchen and find most of my family awake. Teeny is asleep on the couch. Mom's leaned against the counter, waiting for the coffee to finish brewing. She looks terrible.

"Are you okay?" I say.

Mom stands up straighter. "Yes. Of course." She smooths her hair down and quickly rubs her hands across her face. "What do you have planned for today?"

I shrug. "Don't know. Why?"

She shrugs back. Dad comes in, and he and Mom don't make eye contact. I watch them do this silent dance around the kitchen without actually acknowledging each other.

Mom skulks away, and Dad motions for me to sit with him at the table. I plop down next to him, and we stare at each other for a few awkward moments.

"Do you want to talk about it?" he asks, then sips his coffee.

"If *it* is why we got in this mess, then yes."

He sets his mug down, and brown liquid sloshes over the side. "I heard you last night. You're having nightmares again. It may help to talk about them."

I jump up from the table. "No, I'm fine." I can barely stand to write the dreams down in my journal, so there's no way I'm talking about them with Dad.

"Come on, Teeny. Let's go." I pull her off the couch and out of the house. No way are we hanging around here all day.

With no real destination in mind, we walk at an easy pace. The weather is mild, definitely not as cold as earlier in the week, and it's really nice to be outside. I'm so relieved that the being-followed feeling is missing this morning. A big group of people are hanging out by the river, but it doesn't look like any sort of organized activity, just everyone taking advantage of the weather to get outdoors.

There's a group of kids running around, chasing the ducks that are brave enough to come on land, while their parents scold them from blankets on the ground. Some middle-school-aged kids are playing soccer off to one side, and an older crowd is tossing around a Frisbee.

We walk along the cobblestone street and down the narrow road to the water. There are lots of people milling around, and it's got kind of a street fair feel to it. I buy us both a hot chocolate and a meat pie from a street vendor, and we plop down on a grassy area to people watch. The meat pies are what this little town is known for, although this is the first time we've tried them. Steam rises from the flaky pastry when I unwrap the paper around mine. It's delicious and, of course, the seasoning is on fire. There is never a lack of spices in the food people cook here, even in the cafeteria at school. You have two options—hot and really hot.

The group playing Frisbee seem to be doing it football style. It's pretty rough, with lots of tackling and shoving. Ethan's in the bunch and quickly moving our way.

So much for avoiding him.

He goes up for a high catch and falls to the ground hard, but the Frisbee is still in his hand. A few guys run to him, yelling and cheering—high fives all around.

I can tell the moment he spots us. He breaks away from the group and jogs to where we're sitting.

He falls to the ground next to Teeny, who scoots as close to me as she can without actually getting in my lap. Ethan is sweating and his hair is sticking to his head. He's got little pieces of grass stuck to his face. He looks adorable.

"Who's this?" He nods toward Teeny.

"My sister, Mary," I answer.

"So, what's up?" He throws the Frisbee back to his friends and waves them off.

I shrug. "Not much. Just checking out what's going on."

"Cool. The weather's great today. Y'all want to hang out with us? We're headin' to Gus's in a little while. Best jambalaya in town." That slow Southern drawl is intoxicating. I could sit and listen to him all day.

"What's jambalaya?" Teeny asks.

I don't know what it is either, but if we're from Arkansas we probably should have some sort of clue. I nudge Teeny. "You know what that is." And then I give her the look.

A girl with dark red hair sits down on the other side of Ethan. I recognize her from school as the only one who didn't laugh when I freaked out the first day in homeroom when the intercom came on.

She looks at Ethan and says, "Hey. Everyone's about ready." Then turns to me. "I'm Catherine. We haven't met yet."

I nod and lift my hand in a small wave.

Ethan points at me and Teeny. "This is Meg and her sister Mary. They moved here from Arkansas."

"Nice to meet you. Y'all want to come with us to Gus's?"

I want to go with them. So bad. There's a group waiting off to the side, and it looks like they'd take me in without hesitation, but I can't do it. I'm still raw from the nightmare last night, and faces of all the friends I've left behind parade through my mind.

I glance at Teeny, and I can tell she would go if I wanted to.

"We can't. We've got to get back home, but thanks for asking."

Catherine smiles and says, "Maybe next time." She hops up from the ground and sprints off toward the others.

Ethan is a little slower to leave. "Sure I can't talk you into it?"

God, if he knew the restraint I was using. "No. We really can't."

I watch him head back to his friends.

"Why didn't you want to go?" Teeny asks.

"I did, but it makes things complicated. And I'm tired of things being complicated."

"Me too," Teeny says, and leans into me.

It's not long before Ethan and his friends are piling into Jeeps and trucks and heading away from the river. Ethan looks back once, but it's just a quick glance. We're left watching the small children and middle school kids.

Chapter 7

RULES FOR DISAPPEARING
BY WITNESS PROTECTION PRISONER #18A7R04M:

When the suits tell you not to use the Internet, you should really listen to them.

I hate being the "nobody" at school. Everything in me goes against it. I want to buy products and make this boy haircut cute. Hit the M.A.C. counter and load up on all the goodies I used to have at home. Wear Seven jeans and North Face jackets. I want my little white BMW with the leather seats and manual transmission, which all the guys were impressed I could drive as well as any of them. Every club poster in the hall makes me want to join. I want to be excited about the upcoming Mardi Gras Ball and stress over finding the perfect slinky dress.

Health class is the hardest hour to get through. Ethan's here, and the way he watches me is alarming. I'm afraid he's either one step from calling bullshit on my whole existence, or asking me out on a date. Neither good. I can feel the curiosity and interest coming off of him in waves. Ben's here, too. The hostility between him and Ethan is solid. And then there's Emma, giving me the stink eye every time she passes my desk. I know her type. If I could just keep my mouth shut when she starts crap with me, this would all die down. She'd get bored and move on to someone else. Problem is—I can't seem to ignore her. So let the fun begin.

The class fills up just as the bell rings, and Ben and Emma walk in together. The teacher doesn't even look in their direction. Ben nods and says "Hey" as he walks by, while Emma rolls her eyes and mutters, "Loser."

This is the weirdest class I've ever taken. In the week I've been here, we've only had class in the classroom once. We've been to the library, the gym twice, and outside on the front lawn.

Mr. Knighton steps away from his desk and holds a fishbowl filled with little pieces of crumpled-up paper. Behind him is a similar bowl.

"Okay, class. In this bowl are numbers. Each person will draw one. It'll match with one other person in the class. That will be your partner for the rest of the year." A few groans and whispers fill the room. "People, settle down. After the partners are matched up, one of you will pick from the bowl behind me. That will be your first project, and you'll have three weeks to finish."

Sheer. Freaking. Panic. Last thing I need is to be stuck talking to the same person every single day. One part of me hopes I get teamed up with Ethan, but the other prays I don't.

Holy hell, I could get Emma! I'm dropping out of school if that happens.

Mr. Knighton starts in the front of the room; everyone excitedly starts pulling small pieces of paper out of the bowl. By the time the bowl reaches me, a few people have already hooked up. I pluck out my slip and open it to find the number eight.

Everyone else says their number aloud as soon as it's out of the bowl. I hear my number and turn my head around quickly to see who it is. Ben holds his paper up with the number eight on it.

Oh, no.

He scans the room to see who his partner is, and I nod when his eyes stop on me. Emma looks pissed. My stomach sinks.

"Once you're in pairs, please move the desks so you're near your partner and turn them to face one another."

Ben heads toward the desk behind me and slides in. I turn my desk backward. This is so awkward. I glance around the room and see Ethan and Emma rearranging their desks until they are facing each other. She is really pretty. Long dark hair and startling blue eyes. She and Ethan look amazing together.

"Well, Ethan and Emma, funny how things work out. Should make things easy," Mr. Knighton says, and grabs the second bowl.

Ben grins at me from across the desks. "So, I guess it's me and the new girl."

I give him a small smile and look back to Ethan. He's arguing with Emma. "What did Mr. Knighton mean about them, about it being easier to do their project?"

"That's right, new girl, you don't know. They're twins."

I want to bang my head against the desk. Great. She's his sister. His twin, for God's sake!

"Twins. You've got to be kidding?"

They look so amazing together because they look so much alike. Same dark hair, same blue eyes. How can Ethan have shared a womb with her?

"So you and Emma are together, but you fight with Ethan?" I ask Ben.

"Like her, can't stand him." His smile is huge.

Before I can ask any more questions, Mr. Knighton gets to us with the second fishbowl. Ben looks at me and gestures to the bowl. "You pick."

I pull out a slip of paper that reads, *A Study of the Relationship Between Physical Exercise and Learning Ability.* I show it to Ben, and he shrugs his shoulders like *who cares.*

Mr. Knighton walks to the front of the room after he finishes passing the bowl around. "I will have your packet for your project up here when class is over. For now, I'm handing out questionnaires. Any good partnership requires understanding the person you're working with. Ethan and Emma, this assignment does not apply to you, so I'll ask you to come to the front and help me sort the packets."

This could be a disaster.

Ben takes the form from Mr. Knighton, hands me a blank sheet of paper, and says, "Okay, let's knock this out together. First question: Where were you born?"

"Lewisville, Arkansas." If he asks me about that stupid Fouke Monster, at least I'm prepared.

"Okay, I was born here," he says.

We both scribble our answers, and I start to relax. Maybe this won't be so bad.

"Next question: What is your favorite food? Mine is a big fat juicy steak," Ben says.

I have to think on this. If I answer my favorite, it'll open a ton of questions because I've yet to find it anywhere we've lived so far. So I decide to play it safe. "Pizza."

Ben laughs. "Yeah, pizza would be my second choice." He scans the paper again. "Some of these questions are wack. If you could learn to do anything, what would it be?"

First thoughts: Read minds, become invisible, be invincible. Can't say those, though.

"Um, I'd want to learn how to sail a boat. I love being on the water," I answer instead.

"That's cool. I guess for me, I'd love to learn how to throw the perfect spiral."

My blank look must give away my confusion, because he says, "You know. Football."

Of all things, that's what he picks. Whatever.

"Next question," I say.

"If you could be any superhero, who would it be? Where does Knighton come up with this shit?" Ben thinks for a second or two, and answers, "I'd like to be Tony Stark from Iron Man. Coolest of the superheroes because he's just a regular dude with a kick-ass robot suit. And he's super rich."

Mr. Knighton was right. This questionnaire really helps you know who you will be working with. I wish more than anything that Ethan was filling one of these out and I could just get a little peek at it.

This question stumps me. I know very little about the superhero world, but I remember one that I wouldn't mind being even if just for a day.

"Wonder Woman," I say. With her lasso of truth, I could solve a lot of my problems in just a few hours.

We go through the remaining questions: What chore do you hate doing? Ben: mowing. Me: laundry. What is your favorite body part? Horrible question, if you ask me. Ben: chest (ugh!). Me: Can't say eyes or hair because they look like crap now, so I pick brain. That's the best part I've got working for me right now. And last question: What do you want to be when you grow up? Ben: NFL football player. Me: I want to say free. That's really all I want, to be free, but I say nurse because that sounds normal and that's what's expected.

After class, Ben and I walk up to the desk to get our packet. Ethan starts to hand it to Ben, but Ben motions for it to go to me. "You may as well keep it. I'll just lose it."

Emma walks up to Ben and says, "I can't believe you got stuck with her." She says *her* with enough venom to make my cheeks turn pink. Ben shrugs, then ushers Emma out of the room. Ethan's busy passing out the rest of the packets.

"Why didn't you tell me you were related to her?"

He stops what he's doing and raises his head. He's guarded. "Well, maybe if you didn't run off every time I tried to talk to you, I would have."

He leaves the room, and I feel stuck. I need him to lose interest. Get pissed. Or whatever it takes for him to move on. But I don't like it.

At all.

I stop in the bathroom before my next class. The second I walk through the door, that same girl with the pink-striped hair is there. She's screwing around with the wall again. What the hell is she doing? I try to get closer, but she holds her hand up.

"Back off." She runs from the room, and I stare at the brick wall. Something's not right here, but I can't put my finger on what it is. I bang on the wall a few times, not really expecting anything to happen, and of course—nothing does. And then I figure it out.

That girl is nuts.

I wait for the bus in front of school, praying it will arrive soon, when Ethan's truck pulls up to the curb. The passenger window rolls down, and I step up to the side of the truck.

"Don't tell me you ride the bus."

Embarrassed, I nod.

A man is standing on the other side of the driveway, looking toward the truck. I can see him through Ethan's side window, but his features are hidden behind dark glasses and a baseball hat.

"Sorry for being an ass after class. I was pissed Ben could ask you all those questions and you had to answer them," Ethan says.

"They were dumb questions."

"Yeah, but I've been trying to get more than your first name out of you for a week now."

"Well, I can tell you Ben would rather be Iron Man than any other superhero."

Ethan rolls his eyes. "Ben's a dumb-ass."

I can't quit looking at the man. He's just standing there. What is he doing—waiting for someone? Something about him makes me nervous.

Ethan leans over and flings the door open. "Get in. The bus sucks."

I hesitate for a moment. As much as I hate it, we were on the right track after health class. One ugly comment now and he'll back away for good.

And that's exactly what needs to happen, but for some reason I can't explain, I'm scared for him to drive off and leave me with that guy.

"Does that man over there look weird to you?" I ask.

He turns and looks out his window and asks, "What man?"

He's gone, just like that. I scan the school property, looking for where he went, but I've got nothing. He couldn't have just disappeared like that.

I'm being paranoid, I know, but I'm close to losing it, so I jump in the truck before Ethan takes back his offer.

"You okay?"

I look for the man again through the back window as Ethan pulls away from the school, but I can't find him. Was he really there to begin with? Am I completely losing my mind now? We turn the corner and the school is out of sight.

"Yeah. Fine."

"Where to?"

"Home."

As we make our way toward my house, the only sound comes from the radio, which is turned down low. It must be stress. That's why I'm seeing people who aren't really there—stress.

"Are you working tonight?"

"Yeah." I can't make this easy. I overreacted about that stupid guy, and now I've done the opposite of what I should have with Ethan.

"Do you always walk home from work or was it just that first day?"

I pick at the sleeve of my hoodie. "Walk. Mary goes with me at four, and my dad picks her up on his way home from work. It's not that far."

"It's supposed to be real cold again tonight."

Silence.

"I don't mind taking you home."

I rub one hand over my face. It would be nice to have a ride. It'd suck if a panic attack hit while I'm walking home at night by myself, but I answer, "No, it's only three blocks."

"What's Mary gonna do there all afternoon?"

"Homework."

More silence.

The air in the truck is warm and heavy with the scent of outdoors. I take a deep breath and let it fill my lungs. I like this guy and this is so not fair to him. "Don't take this the wrong way, but it's too much." My hands gesture to the truck. "All of this. Taking me home. Offering to pick me up."

His brow comes together, trying to understand. "I just want to be your friend. What's so damn wrong about that?"

Therein lies the problem. He has no clue what he's asking for. In one of our placements I had a boyfriend and it ended horribly. He was a nice guy, like Ethan. He was fun and cool to hang out with, and I thought it was no big deal to be in a relationship—until the suits came and grabbed us while I was waiting for him to pick me up. I still wonder how long Tyler hung around that night.

I can't do that to Ethan.

"Why me? Why are you trying so hard to be friends with me?"

Ethan cocks his head slightly to the side. "I don't know. There's something about you. You're different. And fun to be around when you're not so damn uptight." He stops talking and looks out his side window. A few seconds later he turns back to me. "I can see the second you put the wall up. You damn near cringe right before you do it."

"I've got a lot going on right now." I fiddle with the straps on my bag.

"So, you're blowing me off?"

Yes. Yes, I'm blowing you off. Don't talk to me again, and look in the opposite direction when you see me coming. "No, I'm not blowing you off. I just don't know right now, okay?"

God, I'm screwing this up. I should have never gotten into this stupid truck.

Neither of us speak until we arrive at my house. Mumbling a quiet thank-you, I give him a small smile and hop out of the truck.

I fold a cardboard sheet into a pizza box. It's dead at Pearl's right now, so she's got me doing busy work, which makes it a perfect time to work on The Plan. I need to come up with something concrete. Dad may be stuck in the program for the rest of his life, but that doesn't mean we have to be, too. I scroll through all the different scenarios that could make my life normal again.

We could leave Dad. Make him go through this all alone. We barely saw him before all this started, so it wouldn't be that different.

Where would we go? Some small town like this? Mom won't be able to work in the condition she's in now. I'd have to drop out and work full-time. Whoever's after Dad will still see us as something to use against him. That's not going to work.

When I turn eighteen, I'll leave and take Teeny with me. Go into hiding—just the two of us.

No good either. I have no money. No references. No work history. Bad guys will still try to get us.

My head falls onto the pizza box. No matter what it looks like in the movies, there is absolutely nothing glamorous about Witness Protection.

They took over our home, people everywhere, standing around talking like it was just some regular day at the office. Dad was in the corner, in quiet conversation with the head suit and two other men while Teeny cried in Mom's lap on the other side of the room. And I just sat there watching. Trying to understand how you could come home one day and find your entire life has changed.

"Meg, got customers!" Pearl yells from the kitchen.

Business picks up, and I push away all the half-baked plans that will never work out. About thirty minutes into the dinner rush, I notice Ethan strolling into the restaurant. He smiles and nods but doesn't come close. Instead, he walks to Teeny's booth and slides in on the other side. The customer in front of me has to repeat his order three times before I finally hear him.

Why is he sitting with Teeny? My mind jumps to the worst conclusion: he'll drill her with questions about me. Teeny's so fragile right now; what if she slips? Will I be able to hide it from the suits if Ethan finds out something he shouldn't?

Only one move that I know of was my fault. It was in our second placement. I tried hard there, fitting in and all that. I spent the night with Charlotte, a girl I'd become friends with, and it was the first time since all of this started that I'd stayed away from my parents.

We'd gone to a party and drunk a few too many beers. Once we got back to her house, Charlotte passed out. I lay in her bed, staring at the ceiling, and could swear her laptop was calling my name.

I snuck out of the bed and pulled the computer down onto the floor with me. Within seconds, I was logged into my old Facebook page. Before I could even think about what I was doing, I posted a message on my wall, tagging Elle and Laura. A single line—*Secrets always come out.* It was so stupid, and pretty cheesy, and I was drunk. Part of me wanted them to know that I knew what was going on behind my back, especially Laura, since she was the one who hurt me the most. But there was the other part of me that was just humiliated because some of what they said was true. That was the last time I've had any alcohol. Between that night and the last night at home, I obviously act completely stupid while hammered.

I shake my head and take a deep breath. I can't think about that right now—there's nothing I can do to change what happened. And I'm not sure I would even want to anymore.

I'd ended up passed out on the floor next to the computer and was woken up by Charlotte's mother. She was shaking me, telling me my dad was outside and there'd been some sort of family emergency.

It wasn't Dad but one of the suits. He all but threw me into the car, and the next time I saw my family was in a safe house. I had nothing but the clothes on my back. That's why I have the bag. That's why I never use the Internet.

The line at the counter is so deep, there's no way to check out what Ethan and Teeny are doing. I keep glancing to the back booth, but they don't look at me at all. After a few minutes they get up and walk toward the kitchen. Teeny's not exactly smiling, but her eyes look brighter and she's standing up straight, no hunched shoulders. She looks excited.

I track their progress across the dining room until they step through the kitchen door. Looking down the line of customers, I figure it'll be at least twenty minutes before I can see what's happening back there.

When I finally get back to the kitchen, I stand there stunned. Teeny and Ethan are making pizzas. They're both covered in flour and sauce, and Ethan is teaching her how to throw the dough in the air and catch it. Pearl is on them to get back to work, but she's all bark.

For the first time in months, Teeny is laughing.

Ethan finally notices me standing there. "Hey. You ready for some of these to go out?"

"Uh, yeah, sure." It's like my mouth won't work.

Ethan hands me two large pizzas and then follows me out of the kitchen carrying two himself. Teeny is right behind him, carrying an order of breadsticks.

With the food delivered, Ethan turns to go back to the kitchen. I tug on his shirt and he twists around so quickly, our heads bump.

"Oh!" I grab his arm to steady myself, and he does the same. His face is close, and I can't quit staring at one of those fat curls hanging over his eyes.

He leans in. "Yeah?"

"Uh, thanks for hanging out with Mary." I drop my hand quickly, but he doesn't move his. Or back up. We're very close.

Ethan breaks out in a huge smile and says, "She's cool. I hung out here all the time when I was a kid. Loved making pizzas."

I bite my lip. I should tell him to go away. To leave Teeny alone.

Ethan rolls his eyes. "There you go again. All good, then something changes in your eyes. They close off." He inches a bit closer and whispers, "It's driving me crazy trying to figure out what's going on with you. You told me she was coming to work with you, and it's more fun in the kitchen than out in the dining room." He leans in and I feel off balance again. "You look like you're about to freak out."

I can't speak. He's so close, and I'm trying super hard not to stare at his mouth. It wouldn't take much to close the distance between us.

I'm saved by the front door chimes, and within minutes the restaurant is full.

It's interesting to watch the crowd that comes here. No one is in a big hurry. Ever. This town is probably the most laid-back place I've been to. Most people ask me about my day or tell me about theirs while they wait on their pizza, and if it's ready before they're done talking, they hang around until they finish their story.

For the rest of the evening, we all work in an easy rhythm until Dad shows up at seven to take Teeny home. She cries when she leaves, begging me to let her stay. I try to assure her I'll only be an hour behind her, but she's inconsolable. I watch Dad drive off, thinking I've made a mistake by not giving in, when Pearl comes up next to me.

"She'll be fine. Let's get things picked up, and I'll let you cut outta here early." She turns to leave, but stops short. "You looking for another job?"

I check behind me to see who she's talking to. When I realize there's no one back there, I point to myself. "Me? No, why would I be looking for another job?"

"Some man called earlier, asking if you worked here and how long and all that bull. Figured he was checking your references." She shuffles back to the kitchen and misses the utter terror on my face.

I run to catch up to her. "Did he ask for me by name? Did he ask about Meg Jones?"

Pearl looks at me like I'm stupid. "Girl, you got more than one name? Yeah, he asked about you." She chuckles, which turns to coughing as she leaves the room.

I drop into the closest chair. Did the suits call? Would they ask questions like that? All the saliva disappears from my mouth. Surely it wasn't the bad guys. Wouldn't they just come get me?

Ethan walks out of the kitchen, shoving a huge piece of pizza into his mouth. He says something, but it's all muffled. Once he gets the food down, he repeats himself. "I think Mary had fun."

I force a smile. "She did. Thanks again for . . ." God, what do I want to say? Thanks for playing with her and making her laugh and smile and not worry about her drunk mother at home.

"No problem. It was fun." Thankfully, he didn't wait for me to finish, which is good because I can't think right now.

Pearl bustles in from the dining room. "Meg, go on and go. Make sure Mary's calmed down. I can finish the rest for tonight." She follows this up with a gruff, "But be back here on time tomorrow."

I grab my go-bag from behind the counter and follow Ethan to the door. Turning back to Pearl, I ask, "Did the man who called say what his name was or where he was calling from?"

She stops inside the kitchen door. "No, and I told him I didn't have time for questions since we were in the middle of our rush hour."

Ethan holds the door open and gestures to the truck. I hesitate for a second or so, then hop inside. The phone call has me freaked out, and there's no way in hell I'm walking home in the dark by myself now.

Chapter 8

RULES FOR DISAPPEARING
BY WITNESS PROTECTION PRISONER #18A7R04M:

If you have to get a job, do not make friends there. Don't ask your coworkers about their boyfriend, girlfriend, dog, cat, latest fad diet, thoughts on global warming, or anything else remotely personal. Because then you have to lie about your boyfriend, girlfriend, dog, cat, latest fad diet, and thoughts on global warming, and that really sucks.

ETHAN finds me in the courtyard at lunch, a weird expression on his face. He drops down beside me and fidgets with his Coke bottle.

"What's up?" I ask. Something is wrong.

He spins the cap on the moss-covered ground. "I don't know how to say this without pissing you off."

I want to yell, *"Well, don't say it then!"* I don't, but I'm nervous about what's about to happen.

"I don't think you're from Arkansas. Hell, I don't think you've ever been to Arkansas."

Uh-oh.

"I'm so sure. What makes you think that?" The sarcastic tone I go for falls flat.

"Gut, mostly. Things you say. Things Mary says." He shrugs. "Arkansas isn't much different from here, but you both look at us like we're from a different planet." He doesn't say this meanly, just matter-of-factly.

I run my hands over my face. I have to get out of here. I stand up quickly, jerking my bag up with me.

Ethan jumps up and grabs my arm. "Wait."

I yank my arm out of his grasp and whirl around on him.

"Meg, don't go." His hands are out in front like he's guarding himself from a wild animal.

I shove him. "What gives you the right to say this shit to me? Why do you care where I'm from? Why is anything I do or say any of your business?" With each question, I pound him on the chest.

I'm fuming by the time I finish. I knew he'd try to get info out of Teeny. She must have said something last night.

I all but run to the field behind school, looking for a place to sit and think. The marching band is walking through some sort of routine but without any instruments.

Scanning the field, I notice a pocket of people along the back fence. Smokers' section. There's so much smoke it looks like something's on fire. On the other side, I see several small groups of people walking toward school from the back parking lot. Obviously it's easy to cut out for lunch.

I plop down on the ground near the corner of the small building. What I am supposed to do now? Ethan's not going to let this drop.

I realize the waft of smoke coming from the smokers' section isn't from a pack of Marlboros. It would be so easy to join their little group. They wouldn't ask me questions about some stupid local legend or look for holes in my carefully fabricated background. They probably wouldn't even notice when I left. Maybe Mom has the right idea. I could finish out this placement in a haze, then move right into the same group at the next school. None of this would even matter.

And then Mom's frail body flashes through my head. Her greasy hair and bad breath. Her slurred words. I could never be like that.

I hear the bell ring and watch the fence line. None of them even flinch.

The thought of going to health class is more than I can handle. I can't be near Ethan right now, and there's no way I'm sitting through an hour with Emma either.

I don't really know where I'm going, but my school day is over.

This is the first time I've ever cut class. Even in my old life I never left campus without permission. As I cross the large open space between school and the road, I wait for someone to scream for me to stop, but no one does. It's easy; you just keep walking and don't look back.

I head toward cobblestoned Front Street. At least it's pretty warm this afternoon with the sun out.

The go-bag gets heavy as I walk, but I find the weight comforting. I've got about two and a half hours before Teeny will get off the bus, and I'm not going back to the house before I have to. It takes about thirty minutes to make it to Front Street, where I window-shop for a few blocks. Almost everything for sale has the fleur-de-lis symbol or a crawfish on it.

Mom would love this place. She's a sucker for all this touristy crap.

When she's not a sucker for vodka.

I keep thinking about Ethan and the bomb he dropped in the

courtyard. Who does he think he is? If I look at people around here like they're from another planet, it's because they are! Weird food and weirder animals. The gas station near our house has a jar of pickled pig's feet sitting on the counter. And people buy them. To eat. And part of the info they gave me at the safe house was how to identify poisonous snakes. I mean, we live near downtown, for God's sake. Why would I need to identify a snake?

On the next block I find a coffeehouse. It's fairly empty, so I choose a table in the back.

"What can I get you?" A young waitress walks up to the table—late teens or early twenties—and she has piercings in her lip, nose, and eyebrow. We have almost the same haircut, but I must admit, hers is cuter.

"Small chai latte."

"You want anything else? Scone, beignet, muffin?"

"No, thanks."

This place is like old meets new. The building itself is ancient brick walls and scuffed wood floors, but everything in here is state-of-the-art. On the back wall, flat-screen monitors and wireless keyboards line a long table, huge TVs fill every corner, and there's a sign offering free Wi-Fi. I've been terrified of the Internet, but I'm tempted now to take a peek. The problem is I don't know enough about it to know who can see what. If I search back issues of my hometown newspaper, will that throw up a flag to someone watching?

I'm torn. My need for information is equal to my fear of being picked up by the suits.

The waitress brings my latte.

"You okay?"

Not trusting my voice to speak, I nod.

She shrugs and walks off. Once she's behind the counter, she glances over several times. Maybe she's afraid I'm going lose it and go nuts in here. Maybe I should wear a sign: CAUTION: CONTENTS MAY EXPLODE UNDER PRESSURE.

Taking small sips of my latte and staring at the computers, I try to decide which Web site will be the safest to log on to.

"Don't even think about it."

I jump out of my seat, spilling the latte all over the table and nearly turning my chair over. It's one of the suits. The waitress runs over with a rag. She glances between the two of us, and I resist the urge to hide behind her. My body vibrates with tension.

This suit is young; no way he's over thirty. Military haircut, nice body, black jacket. I've seen him before, but I can't remember his name.

He pulls out the seat across from me. "Sorry about the mess. Will you bring her another cup? I'll take coffee, black."

The waitress throws me a look. I think she'd kick his ass if I wanted her to.

"It's fine," I mumble, and sit back down.

The suit calls out to her as she makes her way back to the bar. "Bring us an order of beignets, too."

I wait until she disappears into the kitchen before I ask, "Are we moving again?"

He shakes his head. "No."

"How did you know I was here?"

"You left school. We're one of your contacts. Apparently, your mom was unable to be reached."

I'm sure she was. I hide my hands under the table so he can't see them shake.

"But how did you know I was *here*?" There is something familiar about him, but I can't figure it out.

"Lucky guess. You don't have a car, so I figured you'd be on foot. Started looking through the windows once I hit Front Street."

I'm not sure if I buy that answer. The waitress comes back with the order, and he pushes a beignet in front of me.

"Am I in trouble at school?" I ask.

The suit stirs his coffee slowly. "No, I covered for you. Told them you had a doctor's appointment, and I forgot to call the school to let them know."

"Am I in trouble with you guys?" I pinch off a piece of beignet and pop it in my mouth. My fingers are dusted with powdered sugar, and the sweet fried pastry is delicious.

The suit lets out a quick laugh. "No. No more ditching, though. I may not be on duty next time."

The second I saw him, I thought we were gone. While it wouldn't hurt my feelings to never see Emma and the minions again, I'm sick of starting over. And as much as I hate to admit it, I'm not ready to leave Ethan behind.

I've never had one of the suits be so nice to me before. They're usually very distant and say the least amount possible. Maybe I can get him to talk.

"I'm so sorry. I don't remember your name."

"Agent Thomas."

"Oh, it's you. We talked on the phone."

He nods and sips his coffee.

"Can I ask you a question?"

"Sure, but I might not be able to answer it."

I take a minute, hoping to phrase it just right. "Why won't anyone talk to me about what happened? It's not fair that Teeny and I have to suffer through this without knowing why."

I sound like a whiny baby, but I can't help it. Maybe this is why most of the suits treat me like I'm seven, not seventeen.

"Well, from what I understand, your parents are trying to protect you. I haven't been with the agency long, but I do know you don't get offered protection unless the situation is dire. Your parents are coping the best way they know how, and I'm sure when the time is right, they'll answer all your questions."

"I guess it gets old having to move people around all the time. Making them start over, again and again."

He laughs and says, "Only when I have to chase down kids who skip school."

I lean forward, elbows on the table, chin propped up in my hand. "So, there's no way to talk you into telling me what's going on. Or why we have to move every month or so? Can you tell me that?"

"I wish I could, Meg, but I can't."

I'm frustrated now and I hope it shows. "Okay, what would happen if I decide to go home? Tell my parents to screw off, take Mary, and go live with one of my old friends?"

Agent Thomas comes close and whispers, "I would not recommend that. You may not understand who or what you are being protected from, but I promise you, it's nothing you want to deal with on your own."

"I just want some answers."

"I'm sure if you think hard enough, you can figure some of it out."

Thanks for the cryptic answer. Agent Thomas puts some money on the table for the bill. "Let me give you a ride home. School's almost out and you have work soon."

It totally creeps me out when the suits do this. They seem to know every little thing that goes on, yet we never see them. I wonder if he's the one that got Mom booze in the safe house.

"I'll walk. I have some time." I get up and grab my go-bag.

Before I can leave, Agent Thomas puts his hand on my bag. "I know it's tempting." He nods toward the computers. "But don't do it. You have no idea who is watching."

I jerk my bag out of his hand and storm out of the coffee shop.

Chapter 9

RULES FOR DISAPPEARING BY WITNESS PROTECTION PRISONER #18A7R04M:

Don't fall into a routine. Shake things up. Doing the same thing over and over makes you feel comfortable. And feeling comfortable is bad.

WEDNESDAYS at the restaurant are busy. Pearl says it's all those Bible-beaters eating early before church. I haven't stopped moving since I walked in at four, but I can't get Agent Thomas off my mind. When I got home from the coffee shop, I searched through my bag for some sort of tracker or bug or something. I hadn't been in that coffeehouse long, and it's freaking me out how fast he found me.

Ethan had the nerve to show up around six. His boots and jeans were covered in mud again, so I figured he'd been at the farm. He and Teeny have been in the kitchen ever since. Every time I hear them laugh, it pisses me off. He can't accuse me of being a liar and then waltz in here and win my little sister over. He's probably back there pumping her for more info. I've worked for months to make her happy, but two days making pizzas with him and she's back to her old self. So not fair.

Catherine and another girl from my homeroom come in to

Pearl's a little after Ethan. She seems surprised to see me behind the counter.

"Hey, Meg! How long have you been working here?"

"Not long. What can I get you?"

They order a seafood pizza and two drinks. Gross. The other girl, I think her name is Julie, heads to a booth, but Catherine lingers at the counter.

"So, how do you like Natchitoches so far?" she asks.

"It's fine. The people here are really nice," I answer.

"It's good to get new people around here. Livens things up."

Yeah, my family could certainly do that.

"Julie and I are heading down to Fat's after we eat. It's an old bar near the marina on Cane River, and they have some pretty cool bands come through there. If you want to go with us, we can wait until you get off," Catherine says.

This is so unexpected. And friendly.

"Oh, I wish I could, but I have to get home. I have a ton of homework."

"Okay, that's cool. Maybe we'll see you this weekend." She joins Julie at the table, and I try to keep busy and not think about how much fun it would be to hang out at some old bar down by the river.

Shortly after Catherine and Julie leave, Dad pulls into the parking lot, and I run outside to catch him before he comes in. I need to talk to him, and I'd rather not do that inside the restaurant.

"Hey. Teeny busy making pizzas again?"

"Yeah. Dad, we need to talk. Have you been home yet?" I grind my teeth, stopping myself from totally bawling him out on the sidewalk.

His whole body stiffens. "Not yet."

"Mom's bad. Every day this week, Dad." I pace around in small circles.

His fists are clenched by his side. "You think I don't know that?"

"She's gonna kill herself before long. Is that what you want?" My voice is too loud, and customers inside Pearl's are staring at us through the window, but I'm too pissed to stop.

Dad lets out a muffled curse and hits the car roof. "Of course that's not what I want. All I ever wanted was for this family to be safe and happy." He kicks a stone off the sidewalk.

I let out a snort of disgust. "Well, we don't seem very safe, and we sure as hell aren't happy." I turn to get Teeny, but stop when I get to the door. "Please tell me what you did. It's making me crazy. Maybe if I understood it—all of this would make a little more sense." And I could figure out how to get out of this.

His face turns several shades of red, then moves into the purple tones. Maybe if he strokes out, that'll take care of everything. I feel guilty the second the thought runs through my head.

"Leave Teeny here. I'll bring her home with me. Go take care of Mom," I say.

I walk back into Pearl's and run straight to the bathroom. There are two stalls, so I go into the oversized one and sit on the floor, pressing my fingers to my eyes.

The door opens, but I stay on the floor, silent. Two small legs appear in front of me.

"Pearl told me to check on you. Are you okay?" Teeny's little head pops into view from under the stall door.

I rub my eyes to make sure no water leaked out. "Yeah, I'm okay."

When I open the door, Teeny looks worried. I pull her into a hug. "It's all good."

She hugs me back, hard. "I saw Dad leave. Does that mean I get to stay?"

"Yeah. Just tonight, though."

Teeny looks up and smiles. "I'll go tell Pearl and Ethan." She sprints from the bathroom.

I walk to the sink and splash some cold water on my face. A pale-faced, dark-haired girl stares back at me from the mirror, and I wonder if the old me is in there at all anymore.

When I push through the door to leave the bathroom, I nearly run into Ethan.

"Everything okay?" His hand is on my arm. Whenever we're close now, he seems to find a reason to touch me. The rough texture on his palm sends tingly little shivers across my skin.

My mind goes blank and we stand there, staring at each other. And then I remember I'm pissed at him.

I step back. "Yeah, fine. Mary's staying."

"She ran back there to tell us." He shoves his hands into his pockets. "I shouldn't have said that in the courtyard. You're right. If you say you're from Lewisville, well then, you're from Lewisville."

"I don't know why you find it so hard to believe I'm from Arkansas."

He leans against the wall, and the dimple makes an appearance.

"It's the way you look at things around here. It's all new to you. And the way you said 'hick' that first day, like you wouldn't be caught dead near one. I mean, you're from Arkansas, right? Place is full of them."

He chuckles and I can't help but smile.

He steps in a bit closer. "And you sound different."

Good Lord, he's observant. And determined to invade my personal space. "My grandparents are from up north, and I spent a lot of time with them when I was little." I'm going off script here, but I've got to satisfy his curiosity. "Mom told me I never really found my place to fit in."

"You weren't in health class today."

The doctor's appointment answer is on the tip of my tongue when I realize this is my chance to see just how much the suits are watching. "Well, you pissed me off and I didn't want to see you. Why does everyone get to leave for lunch, but I get busted skipping Health?"

Ethan laughs and says, "Should have told me you wanted to cut. Lunch is easy; no one's looking for you. Knighton's a different story. He comes off pretty chill, but he's a tight-ass over attendance. Probably called it in when you weren't there."

Okay, maybe Agent Thomas's answer makes more sense now. "I was mad—I couldn't come ask you the best way to skip class."

"*Was* mad? Does this mean I'm off your shit list?"

I shrug. "Maybe."

"Knighton and Thurman are the only ones who care. You're safe cutting out on anybody else. Or you can always tell them you're sick, and they'll send you to the office. Duck out instead."

We stand there with nothing else to say, and it's awkward. It's hard to hold eye contact with him, especially since he's so close. "Well, I guess I better get back to the counter."

Ethan smiles, and I swear he knows he's getting to me. The next few customers whiz in and out, and finally business dies down. I peek into the kitchen, and Teeny is having the time of her life.

Maybe it was a bad move getting a job here. When we leave this placement, all the progress Teeny's made will be for nothing. But I need the money, and the little bit in tips I've gotten this week is really nice.

While I clean, my conversation with Agent Thomas rolls through my head over and over.

I'm sure if you think hard enough, you can figure some of it out.

As much as I hate to relive those last few months and weeks, I take Agent Thomas's suggestion. I think back six weeks before we moved, and there's not a single thing that wasn't normal.

Dad worked all the time. Check.

Mom skipped around from one charity committee to another. Check.

I go back months . . . nothing. My life was pretty damn perfect, at least until I found out my friends were frauds. My stomach flips, just like it does every time I try to think about that night. Everything in me wants to push this memory away, bury it where it can't hurt me, but I think about Agent Thomas and what he said, and I can't hide from that night anymore.

I close my eyes and I can see us—Laura, Elle, and me lounging poolside. We were at my house, painting our nails, discussing clothing options, and making plans for the night. Teeny had a friend over, and they were driving us nuts. They did cannonballs right next to us and soaked all our magazines. Elle screamed, "Teeny, quit being a pain in the ass," which is what she said to Teeny on a daily basis. And then Teeny turned around and shook her butt at her before doing another cannonball.

I open my eyes and glance toward the kitchen, watching Teeny with Pearl and Ethan. She's better now, but still miles away from who she used to be.

Moving to the tables in the front of the dining room, I struggle to bring the images back to my mind. Flash-forward a few hours, and I'm in Elle's house, headed up the stairs. Sophie, Elle's toy poodle, was snoozing outside her room, and I bent down to scratch her belly, just the way she liked it. And that's when I heard my name and the high-pitched laugh Laura reserved for when she was being flirty.

I push the memory away, scared to hear the words I know will slice me down the middle. Dropping down in the booth, I physically brace myself as I replay the conversation I've been avoiding for months.

"Brandon, I don't get why you have to go to those lame dinner parties. Just tell your dad you have other plans."

I peeked into the room. Laura was on the bed, phone to her ear, while Elle was leaning into the mirror over her dresser, applying mascara.

Brandon? Lame dinner party? My mom had another dinner party planned for the next night for Dad's boss, and I knew that's what Laura was talking about.

Laura laughed again, and the sound grated on my nerves.

"Brandon, you're terrible. She's liked you since freshman year. Just tell her you don't like her and put her out of her misery." And then Elle turned from the mirror and said, "Tell him to be nice about it. Don't hurt her feelings."

Laura laughed again (God, how annoying) and said, "Maybe we can hook up later. She'll be with us, but I'll get Elle to distract her so I can slip away. I can meet you at your house."

I can remember the fiery hands of rage creeping up my neck. And then the suffocating pain of my best friends' betrayal. I did have a huge crush on Brandon, and had since freshman year, and they both knew it and now so did Brandon. And Laura, sweet, nice, people-pleasing Laura, was hooking up with him behind my back. And Elle was covering for her. Those bitches.

I ran out of Elle's house. There was no way I was going to give them the satisfaction of seeing me so upset.

And then things get fuzzy. I remember seeing some girls from my school that I knew, but not well, and them telling me about a party at some sophomore's house. Did I want to go? Hell, yeah! I got in the car with them, and that's when the drinking started.

I sit in the booth at Pearl's and try like hell to remember the rest of the evening. There were lots of people, and the music was loud, but that was exactly what I wanted. I remember drinking a lot. And dancing. And kissing some random boy—I can't even picture his face.

By the time I made it home, cop cars had filled the driveway and the suits had made themselves at home. And that was the day I had my first ride in that van with no windows. It was like being on some sick amusement-park ride—feeling the speed and every bump in the road but no way to place where you were. It was the most claustrophobic I've ever felt.

That night was a disaster, but not for any reason that has to do with us being in Witness Protection. Agent Thomas was wrong—the only thing I got out of reliving that night was a depressing reminder of how completely my life has fallen apart.

"You about finished in here?" Pearl's turning off the lights in the kitchen, and Ethan and Teeny are getting their jackets on. I'm still in the booth in the front dining room.

"Yes. Just about done."

I gather my things from behind the counter, pull on the ugly gray hoodie, and look at Ethan. "Good night, Pearl. Ethan." I drag Teeny outside.

Both Ethan and Pearl get to the door at the same time.

"Good gracious, girlie, y'all can't walk home. It's almost freezing out there. I'll drive you," Pearl says.

"I'll take them, Aunt Pearl. My truck's right out front," Ethan says.

Teeny is almost clapping her hands together, she's so excited. Ethan holds his fist out, and she bumps it with hers. "I can't let my new friend walk home in the cold."

Teeny beams when she asks, "Can I sit in the front?"

I can worry and think about The Plan all day long, but I've already let Ethan slip into our lives. If for nothing other than seeing Teeny so happy tonight, it's worth the risk. "Yeah, that's fine."

Ethan and Teeny laugh and joke during the short ride home. I contribute nothing.

"Thanks for the ride, Ethan." Teeny's voice is higher than normal when she gets out of the truck. Does she have a crush on him?

"No problem. Do y'all ride the bus in the morning?"

Before I can even open my mouth, Teeny blurts out, "Yes, and it's horrible. It stinks and the kids on my bus are really mean to me. Meg said she hates her bus too, because they're all freshmen. She said she feels like a total loser."

My face is crimson by the time Teeny finishes. Ethan chuckles and looks at me. "Are you gonna get mad if I offer to come get y'all in the morning?"

"No." I'm humiliated.

Teeny jumps up and down next to the truck. "That's awesome!"

I let out a nervous laugh, but it quickly dies when I see Mom wobble out the front door. I grab Teeny's arm.

"Girls? Are you out there?"

No, no, no. Teeny stiffens when she hears Mom. Neither of us wants Ethan to see her like this.

"We gotta go. Thanks for the ride." Teeny and I both sprint up the front steps, pushing Mom back inside.

Dad helps Mom back into bed, and I get Teeny settled in our room with one of the books she brought home from her school library. It's been a few days since I've done any laundry, and we're both down to our last clean pair of underwear, so I grab our clothes, a small bottle of detergent, and my journal. Once I hit the steps outside, I hear a faint rumble in the distance and stop. This is a pretty quiet area, and there's usually no one out this time of night, especially with it so cold out. I start toward the laundry room, and the rumbling gets a little louder. It sounds like a car idling.

I glance around the lot and look for the smoky signs of exhaust fumes hitting cold air. A black Suburban in the far corner of the lot is backed into a spot, and smoke billows up from behind it.

Chills run down my spine and I can't move. Is someone in the car? I stare at it a few seconds but can't see past the tinted windows.

I take a deep breath and shake my shoulders. I'm letting Dad's craziness make me crazy. A ton of people live in these little cottages—it's not odd that someone is in the parking lot. It's only nine thirty.

The laundry room is dark, and it takes a minute to find the light switch. I feel better when the room floods with light. I load the machine, and as the wash churns I settle down in one of the chairs with my journal to write about how crappy my life is.

Before long, the buzzer notifies me it's time to put everything in the dryer. Just as I get comfortable again, I realize some loose change has made it in with the clothes. The rattling is annoying.

And then there's another noise. It's a metal sound coming from the window that stays open on the back wall of the laundry room. It's a grinding sound similar to a set of nails scraping down a chalkboard. And then everything goes dark. I'm frozen in my spot. The *clink, clink, clink* of the coins slows until it's completely silent.

I drop the journal and inch my way to the wall switch, flipping it up and down an absurd number of times. Nothing happens.

The only light in the room comes from a floodlight outside the back window. So the power is only out inside *this* building. Maybe some animal chewed through the wires, or maybe one of the breakers flipped. I strain to hear something, anything, that might help this make sense, but there's nothing.

Then the grinding sound is back, but this time it's closer. Louder.

Screw this. I haul ass out of the laundry room and run down the driveway to our little house. One glance at the parking lot before I bust through the door shows that the black Suburban is still there, fumes rising out behind it.

Everything is dark. A light flashes across the room. I can't get out. The light misses me by a few inches. I crawl on the floor in a haze until I hit something hard, don't know what it is. The flashing light is gone and the room is pitch-black. Voices, angry voices, but I can't hear the words. I'm scared and my heart beats so loud I'm afraid they can hear it. I peek to see who is there, but their faces are blurry. And then Laura's beside me. She doesn't move. Or talk. Or open her eyes. I shake her hard and then her face changes. It's Elle on the floor beside me now. I scream for someone to help, but nobody comes. Something breaks, sounds like glass. A huge noise. And then Elle disappears.

I stare at the ceiling and try to catch my breath. There's something warm next to me, and I look down to find Teeny cuddled up at my side. Her eyes are wide open and staring at me.

I'm soaked in sweat again and know it's the dream. I put my arm around Teeny. "Did I wake you up?"

"Yeah." Her voice is soft, scared. "I didn't know what to do. You were moving around and crying."

I kiss the top of her head. "I'm sorry; it's over now. You can stay here the rest of the night if you want."

I feel her head nod, and I pull the covers over us both. I didn't tell anyone about what happened in the laundry room, and I know thinking about Laura and Elle earlier somehow got them mixed in with my nightmare. It had taken me hours to convince myself that there were a hundred explanations for what happened. Buildings lose power all the time.

"What are you dreaming about that makes you cry?" Teeny asks.

"I don't know." It's hard to think about the dreams after I wake up, much less talk about them, which is why it's become important for me to write them down. "I think it's all the moves. And not knowing why all this is happening. It scares me."

Teeny snuggles in closer. "Yeah, it scares me too." It takes a few minutes, but Teeny finally falls back to sleep. I reach for the journal and realize I left it in the laundry room.

So stupid! I want to run back there to get it, but I can't make myself get up. I'm drained from the nightmare and not sure I could face that room again in the dark. It takes some time, but I finally drift off to a dreamless sleep.

Chapter 10

RULES FOR DISAPPEARING
BY WITNESS PROTECTION PRISONER #18A7R04M:

Remember your old life is dead and gone. Better it than you.

IT'S been a little less than two weeks in this placement, and it already feels like I've been here forever. The nightmare last night has left me exhausted, but I throw on my hoodie and run to the laundry room before anyone else gets up. I want my journal back.

When I yank open the door, every light in the room is blazing. My chair is overturned in the corner, but there's no journal anywhere.

It's gone.

I search the laundry room three times, including emptying out the trash cans.

Nothing.

"No! No, no, no!" I yell to the ceiling, pounding my fists in the air. I sink to the floor and want to cry.

This is a devastating loss. My neck hairs are standing up again, and I jump up from the floor. What if it was a person out there last night? What if they cut the power on purpose? Did they take my journal?

I run to the dryer and open the lid. All our clothes are still there, so I pull them out and run from the room.

Mom's up, sitting on the couch drinking coffee, when I rush through the door.

"Where've you been?" she asks.

"I had to grab our stuff from the laundry room." I drop everything on the table and start folding.

"You shouldn't leave things in there all night. It may not be there the next morning."

Gee, thanks, Mom, for the great advice. Maybe if you would step up and do the laundry for a change, I might not have lost the only possession I still cared about. Just thinking about all the personal things I wrote floating around out there for the world to see brings tears to my eyes.

Mom helps me fold the clothes, and it's hard to watch the train wreck she's turned into. The high this morning will fall around lunch, and she'll be stinking drunk again by the time I get home.

When it's finally time to leave for school, Teeny and I wait outside for either Ethan or the bus—whichever shows up first. Teeny can barely contain her excitement when his truck pulls into the driveway. She gets in the front seat, sitting between the two of us again. She's definitely got a crush on him.

She talks nonstop until we roll up to her school.

"He won't be able to pick you up. You get out a lot earlier than us," I say.

Teeny's face falls, and I see small hints of that sad girl again, but she nods and runs toward the school.

"Man, I feel bad. Are the kids on her bus really mean to her?" Ethan asks as he pulls away.

"I don't think it's that bad. She's exaggerating so you'll come get her. Riding the bus is fine. You really don't have to pick us up."

Ethan lets out a sharp laugh. The bruise on his cheek has mostly faded, but there's still a tint of yellow. His hair is slightly damp, and he's entirely too cute this early in the morning.

"You're gonna sit there and tell me you're happy riding the bus with a bunch of freshmen?" His grin will be my undoing.

"I didn't say I was happy about it. I just said it was fine."

"It's not that out of the way to pick y'all up. I don't live far from Pearl's; just a few blocks."

We pull into school and go our separate ways once we make it inside.

I trudge down the hall, dreading the day. Barely getting by in class, cleaning up Mom after school, and then working all evening at Pearl's, just to go to sleep and be assaulted by my dreams. The only bright spot will be my ride home with Ethan. I'm as bad as Teeny.

I get to my locker, and Emma is waiting nearby. She's alone, which is odd since she's one of those girls who travel in a pack. Before I get my locker opened, she's right next to me.

She doesn't look happy. Her eyes are squinted and her upper lip is curled.

"Do you need something?" I hope she hears the boredom in my voice. Whatever her problem is with me is so at the bottom of my list of things to worry about.

"What's the deal with you and my brother? I saw you get out of his truck."

I roll my eyes and get my books out of my locker. "Really?" I wait a few seconds then shift back toward her. "You're hanging around waiting for me this morning to ask me that?"

"Just answer my question."

I finish getting what I need for first period and slam my locker shut, spinning the dial on the lock. "Why do you care? You're with Ben. It's not like you're showing a lot of sisterly concern for Ethan by staying with the guy who beat the crap out of him."

"That is none of your business." Emma folds her arms across her chest and taps her foot incessantly.

"Whatever." I walk away.

When I get to homeroom, Ben is there waving me over.

Great.

I take a seat near him, but not right next to him. One of the minions is in my homeroom, too, and I have no doubt she'll report back everything she sees.

"Meg, we need to get together and work on that thing for Knighton."

Minion's head pops up. She's not even shy about eavesdropping on our conversation.

"Yeah, well, I have to work every day after school. Maybe we could work on it at lunch?"

Ben shakes his head. "No, no good. Can't do it. What's your number? I'll call you tonight and we'll figure something out."

Minion's phone is in her lap and she's furiously typing. I'm sure Emma is getting a real-time play-by-play.

"Call me at Pearl's. I'm there every day from four to eight." I'm sure this is gonna bite me in the ass somehow, but I don't know what Emma expects us to do.

The bell rings and the announcements play. I put my head down on my desk and resist the urge to cover my face with my hoodie. This is going to be a long day.

It took both Ethan and Catherine to convince me to cut out with them for lunch. I know they must think I'm some freak—I mean, who puts up a fight to stay at school—but they finally talked me into it. We pull up to Subway and everyone piles out, and I'm expecting Agent Thomas to jump out from behind the bushes at any moment.

The only people in the group I halfway know besides Ethan are Catherine and Julie. Although, I don't think Julie and I have actually spoken to each other yet. The guys with us, Trey and Will, I recognize from the Frisbee game by the river.

I'm standing in line to order when Catherine asks, "What's with the bag?"

No one else brought anything with them inside, but of course I have the go-bag on my back. "Just my stuff."

Catherine tests the weight by picking it up slightly off my back. "That's a lot of stuff."

Ethan nudges Catherine and says, "I've seen that monster bag you carry around. No telling how much junk you have in there." Catherine spins and begins justifying the contents of her purse. She's forgotten all about my bag.

Thankfully, the girl behind the counter asks what I want, so I move down the line picking toppings for my sandwich.

We take the two biggest tables in the back.

"So where are you from, Meg?" Will asks.

All eyes on me. "Arkansas."

"Really, what part?" Trey asks.

Coming to lunch was a bad idea. "Uh, Lewisville."

Will's head pops up. "Really? I have cousins who live up there. You probably went to school with them. Jack and James Horton?"

What the . . . Why couldn't he at least ask me about the Fouke Monster? Those questions I could answer now. I scrunch up my brow like I'm thinking about it. "Um, that sounds kinda familiar."

"I'm sure you know them. That school's not that big. They both play football," Will says before taking a huge bite of his sandwich.

Ethan pops a chip into his mouth and asks, "What positions do they play?"

"Jack is the quarterback and James is a running back." Will launches into their greatest plays and which college scouts have already come to watch them.

No one's worried about whether or not I know them. For the second time, Ethan has saved my ass.

Catherine and I stop in the bathroom before we head back to school.

I hesitate whether to ask this, but I'm dying to know. "So, what's the deal between Ethan and Ben?"

Catherine rolls her eyes. "Boys are so stupid. They used to be best friends and their dads were partners—the farm, the cows, all of it, but they split ways a few years ago, and Ethan's dad is now partners with Will's. I don't know what happened between Ethan and Ben, but they try to kill each other every chance they get."

"Then why does Emma still date Ben?"

Catherine puts her finger in her mouth and acts like she's gagging. "They've been dating off and on since freshman year. They're nothing but drama queens, both of them. It's like they try to see who can make the biggest scene in public."

On the way to the truck, Ethan hangs back, tugging on the go-bag for me to do the same.

"What?" I ask.

"You didn't know those guys, did you? The brothers at your old school."

Need some quick thinking here. "I do. They're just not that nice, so I didn't know what to say since that guy is related to them."

Ethan nods, but I can tell he thinks I'm full of it.

This is getting so old.

I drag myself up each small step to my house. It's time to pump my mother for information. I couldn't concentrate on anything today, and I'm still freaked out about what happened last night, so I'm throwing The Plan into high gear. It won't be pretty, but it's necessary. I hate talking to her when she's drunk, and I hate that it takes her being out of her mind to get any truth out of her.

Mom's on the floor in the kitchen—cleaning. Scrubbing it, actually. Just my luck: the one day I get up the nerve to work on her, she's sober. Or mostly sober.

My bag drops on the table with a loud thump, and Mom spins around. "Sissy! You're home." She hauls herself off the floor.

"Hey, Mom." I want to ask why she's sober today of all days, but I resist.

"You want a snack?" This is the first time since we've been here that she's worried about my dietary needs. She turns to the kitchen and starts looking for food. Dad went to the grocery store last weekend but only got a handful of things. She slams cabinet doors open and closed. She's just now noticing how bare they are.

"Well, there's soup. I can fix soup," she offers.

"I'm fine. I'll eat at Pearl's later." I sit down at the table. "Mom, can we talk?"

She takes the seat across from me. Her eyes are clearer than they've been in days, but her hands are shaky. "What is it?"

"I know I've asked this before, but I really need an answer this time. Why are we in Witness Protection?"

"Uh, that's, uh, not something . . . You need to talk to Dad." She gets up from the table and starts washing the dishes. I move to the counter next to her.

"He won't tell me. I've asked him a hundred times. I've asked you a hundred times. I have a right to know."

She scrubs a plate that has nothing on it. "I can't, Sissy."

"What did he do? Did he steal money? Sell drugs?"

Mom keeps scrubbing.

"I did some research in the school library. You're either in the program voluntarily because you witnessed something or because you did something wrong and agreed to be a witness against someone else. And it's mostly to do with drugs or money."

Scrub, scrub, scrub. I wait for her to say something—anything—but she's ignoring me.

"I think he did something wrong. If we're here voluntarily, why the big secret?" I ask.

Still nothing. I want to make her turn around and look at me, make her answer me.

"What did he do—sell drugs, launder money, what? I bet it's both, or these suits wouldn't be up our ass this bad."

Mom drops the plate in the sink, spins around, and slaps me. Hard. We stand there, face-to-face, both of us stunned. Mom looks at her hand like she doesn't recognize it, and then runs out of the kitchen to her room. The last sound I hear is the lock clicking into place.

Chapter 11

RULES FOR DISAPPEARING BY WITNESS PROTECTION PRISONER #18A7R04M:

Always act like you know what you're doing. Even if you have no idea what you're doing.

"SO, what are you doing this weekend?" Ethan asks after we drop Teeny off at school.

I freeze. This can be an innocent question or lead up to asking me out. It's cool spending time with him when Teeny's around, and she's almost back to her annoying old self. But a date is different. I can't let myself think about him like that. I'm desperately trying to keep some distance between us.

"Working tonight. I've got some stuff to do with my parents tomorrow."

I haven't seen Mom since she popped me yesterday afternoon. She's been holed up in her room. Dad's taking me to Walmart to get more food and other things, but I'd be humiliated to tell Ethan these are my big Saturday plans.

"Maybe we could do something after you're done at Pearl's. There's a party tonight we could crash." He smiles and his dimple cuts deep in his cheek.

"I'm sure I'd be the only one crashing. And you don't have to hang with Mary every night at Pearl's, by the way. I bet you love working for free."

He pulls into the school parking lot and parks the truck. "I pitch in at Pearl's all the time, always have. I usually eat there two or three nights a week."

Oooookay—now I'm mortified. I assumed he was coming by there because I was working. I'm obviously reading way more into his appearances there than I should.

Ethan and I walk side by side toward school. The parking lot is full, and people are milling around everywhere. No one is in a big hurry to go inside. I get a few odd stares, and I know it's because people are wondering what Ethan and I are doing together outside of class or Pearl's. We get closer to the front of the lot, and something's up with Emma and Ben. They're in the middle of a huge fight, both yelling and pointing fingers at each other. A small crowd gathers around them.

Ethan tenses next to me. His expression is hard and gets worse the closer we get.

He stops and stares at them. I'm torn. Do I keep walking? Do I stay next to Ethan? Are he and Ben going to fight again? Before I can bolt, Ethan barely touches one finger to my wrist. I'm taking this to mean he wants me to stay.

He looks to Emma. "You all right?"

Ben answers for her, "What the hell does that mean? Why wouldn't she be all right? She's the one who started this."

"I started this?" Emma pushes him in the chest with both hands, and he stumbles. He's got that look like he's not going to take too much more of this from her, and I hope to God he doesn't actually push her back.

Ethan's posture gets stiff. "Maybe you should walk away?" He says it as a question, but I can hear the fury in his tone.

Emma turns on Ethan. "I'm fine. And don't act like you have any say in this."

Ben moves next to Emma, a united front now against Ethan. "She's right, Landry. Be a good boy and move along."

Emma shoves him away. "Oh, no. You're not off the hook that easy."

I can feel the waves rolling off of Ethan. He's pissed and his fists ball at his sides. I'm sure the principal won't ignore two fights in two weeks. Without thinking, I grab his hand and pull. He doesn't budge at first, then finally he allows me to drag him away.

Once we get some distance from Ben, I try to drop his hand, but Ethan holds on tight. He's still mad and picks up the pace. We go through the back door of the school and then through another door on the right. It's a narrow space with barely enough room for a stairwell that I didn't know was here before.

"Wanna cut out of here today but not get caught?"

This makes me nervous. Do I want to sit through class all day? Hell no. Can I stand to spend the entire day with Ethan and not like him more than I already do? Double hell no.

I lean back against the wall. "I don't know, Ethan. I could get in a lot of trouble." What if the suits find out? The possibility of being relocated makes my stomach drop, and I realize I'm more attached to him and this place than I should be. "I can't. I really can't."

He looks disappointed. He's still holding my hand and rubbing his thumb over mine. It feels really good.

"I get it." He takes a step closer, putting his hands on my hips, and his head comes in close. He whispers, "Thanks for saving my ass. I was just about to knock the shit out of him, and that wouldn't have ended well."

I can't speak. He kisses the side of my neck, and I'm sure he can feel my pulse thumping. He moves away from my neck until his face is inches from mine. His lips are so close, but it's like he's waiting for me to close the gap between us. I hesitate for a second or so, then lean in just enough to make contact. It's all the invitation he needs. His hands leave my hips only to move to the sides of my face. Kissing him is as good as I ever thought it would be.

He breaks away, kissing me one last time on that really sweet spot on my neck, then pushes through the door leading back to the hall, leaving me alone in the stairwell. I sit down on the bottom step and put my head in my hands.

I should have cut with Ethan. Today sucks, royally. Ten minutes into Health and I want to take my book and knock Ben unconscious. We're in the library listening to a guest speaker talk about depression and suicide rates in college and how to recognize the signs. I'm trying to ignore the fact that it sounds like she's talking about my mother.

Ben started flirting with me the second he walked into homeroom and hasn't stopped yet. He's going out of his way to talk to me, and even walked me to the library. We didn't have to sit with our partners for this, but here he is. Emma is sitting at the table behind us with a few of her friends.

Ben crumples a note and flicks it toward me.

Sorry I didn't call you last night about our project.
What are you doing this weekend? Let's get together.

No. No, no, no. This is not good. I'm so not going over to Ben's house. And coming to my house is out of the question. We have two more weeks to finish—it's not due until Friday after next. I scribble back a reply.

Can't this weekend.
Maybe we can find a day next week.

I toss the note back. He reads it, puts it in his pocket, then winks at me. I want to punch him in the face.

He's using me to make his girlfriend jealous, and I know it. It's a combination of trying to piss her off because they're in some stupid fight and trying to screw with Ethan. If I'm really the girl he thinks I am—a nobody, new to this school, with no friends—he's assuming I'm falling all over myself right now because one of the most popular guys in school is showing me interest. But I know his game. In my old life, I played this game.

Time drags but finally class is over. I grab my stuff and sprint out of the room, not even bothering to put my books in my bag first. One more class to go.

The go-bag is a pain. It's stuffed so full of Teeny's and my things that I can barely get a book in, much less two or three, so I'm back to my locker between every class. Exchanging one book for another, I slam my locker shut. Ben's face is on the other side. Over his shoulder, I spot two minions watching.

Great. Surveillance.

"So, what's going on with you and Ethan?"

"Nothing."

Ben falls in next to me as I walk down the hall, the cheerleaders slowly stalking us from behind.

"He's not the guy you think he is. You can't trust him, and he'll turn on you in a second. Believe me."

I want nothing more than to defend Ethan, but I realize I don't know him at all. Or anything about what happened between them. I dart into my classroom, leaving Ben in the hall, and find a seat in the back. Throwing my head on my desk, I wonder if the teacher will notice if I stay like this for the next hour, because I don't think I have the strength left to deal with anything else.

When class starts, I raise my head to listen with half an ear. As the clock ticks toward the final bell, I picture Ben waiting for me after school and maybe even offering to take me home. Then Emma jumping me in the parking lot.

With fifteen minutes left, I raise my hand.

The teacher stops lecturing. "Miss Jones?" He's one of those goofy teachers who call everyone "Miss" or "Mister."

"I'm not feeling so well. May I be excused?"

He glances at the clock and says, "Yes, take your things. The bell's about to ring."

Well, that was easy. Once I clear the classroom I book it outside, toward the parking lot. There are a few random people scattered around, but no one I recognize.

I'll have to walk home, and while it's cold today, the sun is out.

I go one street over so I'm not on the main drag from school and walk at a semi-fast pace. I'm all alone now, hardly any traffic down this road, and it feels . . . wrong. I stop in the middle of the sidewalk—footsteps behind me. I turn around quickly and branches on a bush next to the sidewalk shake, and there's a snapping noise like someone stepping on dead leaves. Is someone hiding in the shrubs? I glance around. The street is deserted. No one to call for help if I need it.

Crunch, crunch, crunch.

I'm ready to run when an older man steps from around a tree. He's wearing overalls and carrying pruning shears and is completely oblivious to me freaking out on the sidewalk. He trims a few overhanging limbs on the front side, then wanders off to another part of the yard.

I'm turning into a paranoid basket case.

It's a harder walk down this street because the sidewalk has buckled in places from the roots of giant oak trees. I make it about three blocks before the traffic picks up. I check my watch—school is over.

I walk another block and stop. Ethan's truck is parked in a driveway up ahead. I'm guessing it's his house since I'm only a couple of blocks from Front Street and he said he lived near Pearl's. Moving to the opposite side of the street, I try to make it past without being seen. As much as I don't want to finish the walk home by myself, I don't want to look like stalker girl either. A loud whistle pierces the air, followed by a sharp bark. A big black dog catches something in its mouth midair in Ethan's front yard. The dog trots back to the porch and drops the tennis ball on the ground in front of Ethan, who's staring at me.

Great. This does not look good. Since this is not the most direct route home, it looks like I've gone out of my way to pass his house. Ethan jumps off the front porch and jogs across the street, the dog bouncing along behind him.

"Now I feel bad. You're walking home?"

I hold my hand up. "No, don't feel bad. I could've taken the bus, but I cut out of last period early. I took your advice."

Ethan chuckles. "Should have taken it earlier and come with me this morning."

Okay, heart really starting to pump blood, and I'm sure it shows in my face. Every time I look at him, my eyes go straight for those lips. "Yeah, maybe."

He kneels down and scratches the dog behind its ears. The dog drops to the ground in pure bliss, and Ethan looks up at me with those blue eyes. "You want me to take you the rest of the way?"

Say no. I should really say no. "Yeah, that'd be great."

Big smile, even bigger dimple.

He and the dog jog back across the street to his truck. Ethan's home is an old two-story house with a wraparound porch and lots of rocking chairs. It's charming, very fitting for the neighborhood. I follow behind them. "What's your dog's name?"

Ethan rubs his hands over the back of the dog's head. "This is Bandit." He lets down the tailgate of his truck, and the dog jumps in.

"He's pretty. What kind of dog is he?"

"Lab. Best bird dog there is."

I guess that has something to do with hunting.

We hop in and go about two blocks before Ethan asks, "So did Emma and Ben fight all day or what?"

His voice is tight, like he's trying not to still be pissed about what happened this morning.

"From what it looked like, he mostly ignored her." I'm not about to tell him Ben stalked me all day or what he said about not trusting Ethan.

"Oh, I bet she loved that." At a red light Ethan taps the steering wheel and asks, "Do you want to hang out later? After work?"

"Are you talking about going to that party?"

"Well, yeah, or we could do something else."

Decision time. That's all I really want to do in this town—hang out with him. But this is like jumping off the deep end. After the kiss this morning and going out on a date with him tonight, I won't be able to keep any distance between us. "Do I have to let you know right now?"

His forehead creases, and he stares at the road ahead. "No, you can tell me later."

I'm pretty sure that's not what he wanted to hear, but I can't help it. At this point I'm terrified to fall for him more than I already have.

We pull into the parking lot as Teeny is getting off the bus at the curb. She spots Ethan's truck and sprints toward his side until she sees Bandit in the back. She almost skids in the parking lot when she readjusts her direction to him. She climbs up on the back bumper and buries her head in Bandit's neck.

Ethan gets out of the truck and walks back to where Teeny and Bandit are. They both look at him with the same puppy dog eyes.

"I see you met Bandit."

"Is that his name? He is sooooo cute. Does he know any tricks?"

Ethan lowers the tailgate and Bandit jumps out. Bandit goes through his series of tricks: sit, lie down, play dead. Ethan grabs a tennis ball out of the inside of his truck and bounces it high on the concrete. Bandit catches it on the first bounce. Teeny is ecstatic.

Ethan throws Teeny the ball, and she starts bouncing it for Bandit. I watch from the tailgate, and Ethan joins me after a few minutes.

"You made her day," I say.

"I wish I would've known she loved dogs. I'd have brought him sooner."

"Mom's allergic, so we've never had a pet. That's all Teeny ever wanted."

"Teeny?"

Oh, shit.

I cannot believe I just called her that. Out loud. It's been three placements since I screwed up like that. I take a quick deep breath. "Oh, that's some stupid nickname Dad calls her. Don't tell her I told you or she'll be pissed."

Ethan laughs quietly and looks at Teeny. "She's not really small."

"She was when she was little. It just sort of stuck. Anyway, I guess I better get ready to go to Pearl's."

Ethan glances at his watch and says, "It's pretty close to four. I could hang out and then drive y'all over."

"No!" That was a little too loud and quick. I scoot off the tailgate. "I mean, Mary's gonna have to shower or Mom will have some sort of horrible reaction. So, I'll be busy getting her ready."

"She needs your help for a shower?"

I call Teeny over and totally ignore his question. She probably would be fine to get herself dressed today, but if Ethan waits, he would want to come inside, and that can't happen. He hops off the tailgate and whistles for Bandit to load up. Teeny brings him back the tennis ball, then acts ridiculous with Bandit for another couple of minutes before we can head up the stairs.

"Mary, I'm not gonna be able to make pizzas tonight, but Pearl will still let you help back there," Ethan says. "Okay?"

Teeny's bottom lip puckers slightly, but she says, "Okay." Then she turns and runs up the steps.

I grab my go-bag out of Ethan's truck and put it over my shoulder. Ethan tugs on it, and I turn around.

"I've got to go to the farm this afternoon, but I'll be at Pearl's to pick you up at eight."

I open my mouth to speak, but Ethan holds his hand up. "Loosen up. We're gonna go out. Have some fun. It's gonna be all right."

He links his hand in mine and pulls me in close. It almost looks like he wants to say something else, but he doesn't. I can feel his rough fingers on mine, and goose bumps shoot up my arm. I stare at his mouth, half open like he's caught in the middle of forming a word, and I want to kiss him again, right here in the parking lot.

But he drops my hand and walks to the driver's side of the truck. I let him go without another word. I hate being scared, but the last time I waited for a date, the suits showed up instead.

I have to remind myself—this isn't like the night I waited for Tyler. God, that night sucked. I was dressed up, waiting for him to pick me up for a Halloween party, when the suits yanked us out of that placement. I had to stay in that stupid costume until we got to the safe house.

I spent the next two placements being a total bitch to every boy who showed any interest in me. I never wanted to feel guilty for deserting someone who cared about me like that again.

And then I met Ethan.

Chapter 12

RULES FOR DISAPPEARING
BY WITNESS PROTECTION PRISONER #18A7R04M:

Most mistakes are made when you think no one is watching. And someone is always watching.

I tiptoe into the house. Mom's waiting for me on the couch. It's day two on the sober train. And she's been crying. Teeny's peeking from the hall, her eyes big.

"Sissy, I've been waiting for you."

I mouth the word "shower" to Teeny and motion her down the hall. I drop onto the couch next to Mom. She's got tissues bunched up in both hands and alternates between the two, mopping up her face. "I'm so sorry I slapped you yesterday."

"I'm sorry, too. I shouldn't have said that about Dad."

Mom waves her arms around. "We shouldn't be here. Dad may be close to working things out. We may not have to do this much longer."

I scoot closer and hold her hand. "What does that mean? Will we stay here? Or go back home?"

She shakes her head. "I'm not sure, Sissy. He won't tell me much, and he'd be really upset if he knew I told you anything." She pulls me in close. "Please don't tell him what I've told you." She lets go and runs her fingers through my short dark hair. "You and Teeny were the cutest little girls. I can't believe what they did to your hair."

I'm reeling over this bomb she just dropped on me, and she's upset about a bad dye job. "Mom, if all this may be over soon, please tell me what happened. I won't tell Dad you told me."

She picks at a lock of my hair and stares at it. "Sissy, there are a lot worse things than your dad finding out what we're talking about." Her voice is hard, bitter.

I'm applying lip gloss when Pearl sticks her head in the bathroom. "Ethan's outside." Pearl looks me up and down. "Whoa, girl. Look at you."

I can't help the smile that grows across my face. This is the first time in this placement that I've "dressed up." It's minor compared to what I used to do to get ready for a party, but it's about ten steps up from the normal towel-dried hair and gray hoodie. I took a break halfway through my shift and ran to a funky little clothing shop I saw on Front Street. I used most of my tip money but got a really cute distressed leather jacket that looks great over a plain T-shirt and jeans. I don't really have any other options for shoes, so these hideous sneakers will have to do. The jacket is a ridiculous waste of money, but it's been so long since I've splurged on anything for myself, I couldn't resist.

"Thanks, Pearl. Will you tell him I'll be out in a minute?"

"Sure thing, honey. Nothing wrong with making a boy wait."

Since my talk with Mom this afternoon, my mind is racing. There's a dangerous thing brewing in there—hope.

I haven't abandoned The Plan, but I am encouraged by my conversation with Mom. And as much as I try to push Ethan away, I'm already sunk.

Next week I'm going to try a new approach. I'll surf the Internet for anything I can find, and I may break down and call Laura or Elle to see what they know. Maybe something came out after we left—I don't know. It would be a hard thing to do, but that may be my only option.

I'll have to be smart about it, though—maybe take a bus to another town first. This will no doubt bring down the wrath of the suits, but I don't care anymore. Whatever Dad is working on can go one of two ways: we're out and free, or it blows up in his face. I still need to figure out what's going on, now more than ever.

But tonight is for me. I'm going to have one night to be a normal teenage girl who is going out with a really hot guy. If Dad and I both fail, my family could be running the rest of our lives, and then what? Someone could be right around the corner and kill us all dead! College is out when you move around like this. I'll be stuck finding some job like I have here and taking care of Mom and Teeny. Forever. So for tonight—screw it.

Pearl gave me a big-ass aerosol can of Aqua Net. It looks about twenty years old and is probably full of all the bad stuff they banned years ago. The bathroom fills with a cloud of sticky fog as I try to style my hair. I'm trying to mimic the hairstyle of the girl from the coffee shop, and the end product is actually pretty close. The only thing I truly despise is leaving the brown contacts in.

I throw my work shirt into my go-bag and head out of the bathroom. Ethan is talking to Pearl in the kitchen and actually gets tripped up in the middle of a sentence when he sees me. I blush to my hairline.

"Meg, you look great." It's said in a tone like, *Holy shit, you're not a total troll,* but I don't take it personally. I know I normally look like a war refugee. He looks down at the bag. "You want to drop that off first?"

I grip the handle a little tighter. "No."

Awkward silence.

In the truck I push the go-bag far under the seat. Hopefully, out of sight, out of mind. "So where's this party?"

"A friend of mine's house. His parents are gone. They live right outside of town. Shouldn't get busted."

I hadn't really thought of that. If I got picked up by the police at a party, I may as well pack the van myself. My screw-it bravado wavers slightly.

"Can I borrow your cell phone to call home?"

Ethan hands me the phone, and Dad answers on the second ring. "Hey. Get a pen and take this number in case you need me." There would only be two reasons why he would have to call: Mom or the suits. Ethan calls out his number digit by digit as I repeat it to Dad.

I hang up the phone and hand it back to Ethan. "Thanks."

He drops it into a cup holder. "No problem. I'm surprised you don't have a phone." He cranks up the heat in the truck.

I was really hoping for no questions so I wouldn't have to lie to him tonight. "Yeah, I had one but lost it. Dad refuses to buy me another one right now."

"Did it suck leaving your friends halfway through senior year?" he asks.

When I answer, I'm not thinking of the friends I made in the last placement, which was nowhere near Arkansas, but of Laura and Elle and how complicated it is. "God, more than you can imagine." Even though everything was so screwed up between us when I left, I still miss them. Miss my old life.

"I don't know. Sometimes I think it would be awesome to pick up and get out of here. Move off where no one knows you. Start all over." This surprises me. Except for the crap with Ben and Emma, he seems to get along with everybody.

"It's not all it's cracked up to be," I say.

Ethan pulls out his iPod. "Okay, getting too deep. What do you want to hear? I have it all." He cocks his head and looks at me sideways. "Let me guess what kind of music you like. Your favorite."

I turn sideways in the truck, facing him. "Go for it."

He chews his lip and looks back and forth from the road to me. "Not country."

"Good so far."

"Not Top Forty."

"Keep going."

"No heavy metal, headbangers, or big-hair bands."

I pull my feet up in the seat. "Getting closer."

"It's a toss-up. Depends on your mood. Every day you like alternative, indie pop, but on other days you're not afraid to bust a rhyme. You like a little hip-hop, a little Mary J. and even some Beyoncé, although she's Top Forty."

I'm shocked. He nailed it. "How did you know that?"

"Can't give away my secrets."

I lean forward and push his arm playfully. "Really. How would you know that?"

"So, I'm right?"

I shrug my shoulders and say, "Pretty close."

He fiddles with the iPod and says, "The first day when I found you outside singing, I didn't know what in the hell that was, but I finally figured it out. The Ting Tings."

The mention of my singing embarrasses me, and I'm glad it's dark in the truck. "You just figured it out, huh. It's not like they're mainstream."

"Emma was listening to them last night. Sounded familiar."

My upper lip instantly and uncontrollably curls up. "Shut. Up. There is no way we like the same music."

Ethan holds his hands up in a defensive posture. "I'm telling you what I heard."

"Fine. Okay, so how'd you figure out Mary J.? 'Cause I do love her. Beyoncé, too."

"Mary told me. I asked her what kind of music you liked. She said to turn on Mary J. Blige if I really want you to loosen up."

"That's cheating! And what did she mean loosen up? I'm loose."

Ethan starts laughing. Hard. "Loose. You're kidding, right? You're wound up tighter than a pissed-off rattlesnake." Mary J. fills the truck, and I smile. "I couldn't stand that Ting Ting shit or Beyoncé either, but I found a few Mary J. songs that didn't totally suck," he says.

I can't believe he downloaded songs for me. I wonder if he

would be surprised if I reached over and held his hand. My screw-it attitude is back in full force.

We pull up to the party and the yard is full of cars. I have a small moment of panic about what to do with the go-bag. I can't very well lug it around all night, but I hate the idea of leaving it in the truck. Ethan waits for me while I struggle with what to do about the bag. Leaving it is really my only option.

"Did you lock the car?"

He shakes his pocket and I hear the keys rattle. "Yeah, you need back in?"

"No. Just wanted to make sure it's locked."

Ethan grabs my hand and pulls me close. "Loosen. Up." He kisses me on the tip of my nose. It is so quick, but the contact leaves me with a warm, fuzzy feeling that goes all the way to my ears. On the walk to the house it dawns on me that I should be afraid of what's going to happen if Ben and Emma are here. Especially if Ben pulls that same crap he was doing at school.

I stop, forcing Ethan to stop, too. "Hold on. Promise me something."

Ethan takes a small step toward me. It's so dark, I can barely see his face. "Promise what?"

"Don't let Ben piss you off. That's what he's trying to do, you know. Piss you off."

His hand stiffens in mine. "I know exactly what Ben is trying to do. Don't worry, I can take care of him."

The closer we get to the house, the louder the music gets. On the front porch there's a guy from my homeroom doing a keg stand while a group of people watch. He flips over, lands on his feet, and everyone cheers. Ethan speaks to several people as we make it up the steps. Most do a double take when they see me, either shocked that I actually look decent or that Ethan brought me here. Or both.

We head to the kitchen, and I'm relieved to see that Catherine is here. And what's even better is she seems excited to see me too.

Ethan grabs two beers and hands one to me. "Everybody remembers Meg, right? Meg, I don't think you met Drew."

Everyone says hi except Julie and Trey, who are too busy making out against the counter to even notice we've walked in the room.

"What's up, Ethan? Didn't know if you were coming," Drew says.

"Yeah. I had some stuff to do at the farm before I could go out."

Will pulls Ethan into a headlock and messes up his hair. "Yeah, we're gonna catch hell tomorrow."

Ethan shoves him away, laughing. "Damn, boy, I worked hard on my hair tonight." He makes a big production of smoothing it back down.

Will laughs and says, "Dad says we're working cows in the morning. That son of a bitch is gonna make me get up at the crack of dawn." He punches Ethan in the shoulder. "Maybe I'll crash at your house. Your dad isn't as big of an ass as mine is."

Ethan turns to me and says, "Will's dad and mine are partners. They farm and have a couple hundred head of cows."

"Yeah, and they love to work the shit out of us," Will says. A few more drinks and he won't be worth anything tomorrow.

While the guys talk, Catherine hops up on the counter and sits next to me. Her dark red hair is curly tonight, but not in that awful beauty pageant sort of way that's common around here.

"Hey. I'm so glad you came. Ethan wasn't sure you could make it."

"Yeah. Me too."

Catherine's pretty in a different way, with tiny freckles across her nose and big brown eyes, but there's something else that really makes her stand out. It's her confidence—she wears it almost like a physical thing. It reminds me a little of Elle, but Elle's confidence had claws and was something to be feared.

"So, how are you handling the Ethan/Ben/Emma drama?" she asks.

I hesitate. What am I supposed to say? "Uh, not really sure."

"You just need to ignore her. She loves drama. She'll totally suck you into her cuckoo-crazy world if you let her. And Ben's not much better."

Since most people come into the house through the kitchen, it gets a little crowded. Will leans back into the counter where Catherine's perched, and she wraps her legs around his waist and rests her elbows on his shoulders. He keeps talking to the guys while she's talking to me, and it's almost as if they're unaware they moved into one another.

"I take it you're not a fan of Emma's?" I ask.

"P-lease. I learned my lesson with her years ago."

I hang with Catherine for a while, and it's nice to just girl talk. I didn't realize how much I missed this until now. Some guy comes through offering Jell-O shots, but I stick with beer since I don't trust myself to get tipsy or drunk.

Ethan has his back to me, talking to Drew, but he turns to look at me every couple of minutes, like he's making sure I'm still here.

Julie and Trey are still making out against the counter. They should find a room.

As the party rolls on, I get a running commentary from Catherine. "That's Sadie and Anthony," she whispers, and points to a couple who strolls through the kitchen, hand in hand. "They've got the record for breaking up and getting back together. It's like twenty-four or twenty-five times now. Ridiculous."

Another girl walks in and starts talking to Ethan and Will.

"That's Mary Grace. Watch out for her. Her favorite hobby is hooking up, and most times she doesn't care if the guy is with someone or not." Catherine leans over Will's shoulder and says, "Mary Grace, you've got to look somewhere else, sweetie—Ethan's with Meg tonight."

Maybe Catherine has a few claws of her own.

Mary Grace throws a fake smile at Catherine, then flips her off. Ethan laughs, and mouths the word *thanks* to Catherine. I try really hard not to blush.

Catherine fills me in on everyone who has the unfortunate luck to walk through the kitchen. She seems to know everything about them, most of it way more information than I need, but it's funny as hell.

As soon as a slow song starts, Ethan breaks away from the guys and grabs my hand, pulling me to the den. There'd been a steady stream of people dancing when the music was faster, mainly girls in a group, but there are only a few couples left once this slow song starts.

We pass the open door to the dining room on the way and see what looks like a very enthusiastic game of strip poker going on.

Most people are down to underwear, except one guy sitting at the table who is fully dressed. He's draped with what looks like all the clothes that other people have lost.

Ethan walks to an empty corner of the room and pulls me in close, one hand in mine and the other wrapped around my lower back. I used to love to dance. Would dance to anything, but I especially loved to slow dance. It was my favorite, being all cuddled up to a guy I liked and swaying with the music. This is the only time in all these months that I've even had a chance.

I'm still pretty nervous around him, so I bury my head in his neck. This way I won't have to look at him or try to find something clever to say. He smells delicious.

We move to the music and it's nice. Really nice. Warmth spreads from the contact on the small of my back, and the friction between his calloused hand and mine is making it impossible to concentrate. He feels strong. And safe.

The song ends and Ethan pulls back slightly. Everyone else leaves the dance area, but we're glued to our spot. His eyes are on my mouth. My heart is pounding. He moves back in, and I curl my fingers through his hair.

And then we hear sirens.

Chapter 13

RULES FOR DISAPPEARING
BY WITNESS PROTECTION PRISONER #18A7R04M:

Do not go to parties or any other non-school-related activity. It's risky hanging out with a bunch of amateurs.

THE entire house breaks out in pandemonium. I look out the window, and two police cars are roaring down the driveway with lights flashing. I freeze with panic. Can't move. It looks like my house did the morning the suits showed up.

Ethan pulls me from the window. "Gotta go, Meg."

He yells to the gang in the kitchen for them to follow us, then drags me through the house, and we explode out of a back door. He doesn't stop—just books it to the edge of the yard thick with trees and bushes. Different scenarios roll through my head, and none of them are good. My hands feel clammy.

Will, Drew, Catherine, Trey, and Julie are right behind us as we pick our way through the dark yard.

I squeeze Ethan's hand and whisper, "Where are we going?"

He pulls me in close. "We're heading to the front yard, to my truck."

Is he nuts? We're just gonna get in his truck with cops here? What does he think, they're gonna let us drive off?

Branches scratch my face and pull on my clothes. I do not like walking in the dark through a bunch of trees and bushy things. I'm scared some crazed animal is going to bite me on the leg or fall out of a tree and land on my head.

Catherine giggles behind me. I glance at her, and she has a scared expression, her hand over her mouth. She must be the kind who does that when nervous—so not what I expected out of her. Me, I feel like I'm one second from a full-blown panic attack.

Other people are running out of the house, too, but they all seem to be going deeper in the backyard. We're the only fools heading toward the cops.

A few vehicles become visible, so I guess we're almost to the front of the house. Ethan's truck is one of the farthest out and off to the side. We should come out of the trees just in front of it.

The front porch is full of people. Everyone who flew out of the front doors must have been quickly rounded up. There's a group huddled together on one side, where a policeman seems to be taking down names.

There are no other cops in sight. I assume they've gone into the house. We get to Ethan's truck as quietly as possible, open the doors, and climb inside. I take the middle spot.

We close the doors and sit there in the dark. I glance down at the go-bag and suck in my breath. It's open. The top is open, and I know I didn't leave it that way. I stare out into the yard, trying to make out shapes in the dark. I can't see anything. I grab the bag and dig through it quickly. It doesn't look like anything is missing, but I won't know for sure until I get home and pour everything out.

Ethan puts his key in the ignition. "Okay. I'm gonna crank it and we're hauling ass out of here. Everybody ready?"

Nervous energy runs through the truck, and Catherine starts giggling again.

"Hit it!" Drew calls out from the backseat.

Ethan starts the truck and quickly puts it in gear. We're moving. Fast. He takes out a few bushes since he threw it into drive instead of reverse. I turn quickly and peek out the back window. The cop on the porch watches us go. Ethan's idea suddenly makes sense—there's no way he can leave all those kids alone to chase us. They'd scatter like the wind. We hit the main road, and everyone starts cheering except me. I'm shaky.

Did I reapply lip gloss before we went in? Pop in a piece of gum and then forget to close my bag? No. My mind starts ticking off every creepy thing that's happened to me in this placement. I start second-guessing myself. Someone opened my bag. And I'm pretty sure someone cut the power to the laundry room and stole my journal.

"Close call by the po-po," Will jokes. He's sitting next to me, with Catherine in his lap. Trey and Julie are in the back with Drew. I'm almost in the seat with Ethan.

"What would totally suck is if you had been in that poker game," Catherine says. My freak-out cracks a bit. I can't help but laugh thinking about those half-naked people scrambling when the sirens rang out.

"You parked there on purpose, didn't you?" I ask Ethan.

His expression is cocky. "Hell, yeah. Rookie mistake to park close to the house."

I glance in the back, and Trey and Julie are making out again. We should drop them at the closest Motel 6.

Catherine glances across me. "Ethan, I wonder if Emma got out."

Ethan looks surprised. "Was she there?"

I never saw her either. Or Ben.

"They were there earlier. She and Ben were upstairs. Went up just before y'all got there," Will says.

Okay. Well, I can use my imagination as to what that means. Ethan doesn't ask anything else.

"I can't believe the cops showed up. There's no neighbor to complain way out there," Catherine says.

What if whoever is screwing with me called the cops?

"Where to now?" Drew asks. He scoots as far from Trey and Julie as possible.

"We can go to my place," Ethan offers.

There's a general consensus throughout the truck. I can't quit thinking about my bag. And everything else. I've got to get home and see if anything is missing. And then what? I lean into Ethan and whisper in his ear, "Can you take me home first?"

He looks at me quickly. "You're ready to go home?"

I nod. There's no good explanation to give him.

"Come to my house for a little while. I'll take you home whenever you're ready."

I shake my head. I can't tell him how terrified I am. It was a totally bad idea to go out tonight.

He looks frustrated. Everyone else in the truck is laughing and recalling our great escape. Catherine is texting and calling out the names of others who have gotten away as well. I sit quietly beside Ethan, looking at my hands in my lap. I feel funny, like something's not right. Sick almost.

We drive back into town, and Ethan heads straight to his house. Before I have a chance to say anything, he puts a hand on mine.

"All right, everybody out. Y'all go on up. I'm gonna run Meg home and then I'll be back."

Catherine stops in mid-motion from getting out of the truck. "You're not coming in?"

I shake my head. "No. I have to get home."

She looks confused. It's barely ten o'clock. "What the hell, Meg? It's early! Come up for a little while."

"I can't. Sorry." She's almost as hard to say no to as Ethan is.

"Okay, I'll see you later," she says, then hurries off to catch up to Will.

Everyone else gets out of the truck, and Ethan backs out of his driveway. I scoot to the passenger seat.

"No talking you into staying out longer?" He doesn't look at me.

"I can't."

We ride in silence. Ethan pulls into the parking lot and cuts the truck. I want to kiss him. I want to tell him everything. I don't want to go into that house.

But what I do instead is lean forward, peck him quickly on the cheek, and bail.

Sleep evades me, which is nothing new, but tonight it's different—not the usual stomach-churning thoughts of waking up the next day as someone else. Tonight I can't shake the sinking feeling I had when the cops showed up and when I noticed my bag was open. I searched through everything when I got home, but nothing was missing. It wasn't even rearranged.

I haven't told Dad anything. I have no proof: just crazy feelings and ridiculous stories about idling cars and power outages. If I tell Dad about any of this, he may go straight to the suits. And I'm not moving again.

Teeny's fast asleep. I can't roll around in this bed any longer, so I head to the kitchen for some water. I tiptoe out of our room, not wanting to wake Mom and Dad. I'm really not up to dealing with either one of them right now.

A muffled voice comes from the kitchen, and it sounds like Dad. He's whispering. I put my back against the wall and inch my way down the small hallway. When I get to the end, I slowly peek my head around.

Dad's on the phone. It's the wall-mounted kind, and he's stretched the cord across the kitchen and tucked himself halfway inside the broom closet. Whoever he's talking to, he definitely wants it to be private. This of course makes it crucial for me to know who it is.

I duck down and crawl to the table, which puts me very close to the closet. Hopefully he won't see me hiding.

I strain to hear what he's saying.

"No, we're not doing it like that." He sounds frustrated.

He's quiet for a few seconds and then says, "If you want my help with this, you will do it the way I say." I know that tone. He's getting pissed.

What are they talking about?

"You push me too hard on this and we'll disappear."

Holy shit! Can he do that?

Dad lets out a deep breath. "Yes, I'm aware of what can happen. The pictures you showed me made it very clear."

Pictures?

The *ticktock* of the clock echoes through the dark kitchen.

"No, of course I don't want to lose my family. I never wanted any of this to happen." His voice is different now. Resigned.

"As soon as I have it, I'll contact you. Do I have your word this will all be over?"

Over? What's over? And what's he going to have?

Dad backs out of the broom closet, and I'm frozen underneath the table. Do I confront him? Force him to spill it? I have more questions now than ever. He hangs up the phone and walks to the sink. Gripping the edge, he hangs his head and sobs. It's shocking, and my own eyes fill with water. He's been such a hard-ass since all this started. This is bad. Very bad.

I crawl quietly down the hall and back to my bed, forcing the broken-down image of my dad out of my head.

Hands are grabbing at me, pulling me in every direction. Voices talking fast but I can't understand the words. I feel nauseous. Bright lights. I can't see anything. Stone walls sprout up around me, trapping me. I bang on them until my hands bleed. I fall to the floor and watch the blood drip down the wall.

My eyes pop open. My heart races, but hopefully I didn't scream out loud this time. Focusing on the big piece of chipped-off paint that looks like the state of Texas, I work on slowing my breathing. I try to lick my lips but my mouth is so dry, my tongue gets stuck to them.

I think of everything but the nightmares that torture me. Dad and the one-sided call. The close escape from the police. The total disaster I've become. I ache to write all of this down, and mourn the loss of the journal all over again.

Teeny pokes her head into our room some time later. "Dad made breakfast. You want some?"

"Maybe in a little while." The words come out in a soft croak.

She comes in and sits on the bed next to me. "Are you sad? You look sad."

Yes, I'm a complete failure. Everything I wasn't going to do, I did. I've fallen for Ethan. I love working at Pearl's. I even like this crazy little town. And Ethan's friends last night were really cool to me, especially Catherine. Whatever Dad is working on to get us out of Witness Protection, he's doing from the broom closet in the middle of the night. That's the worst part—he must have done something really horrible to get us in this, and I don't know if I can ever forgive him for that.

But I can't tell Teeny any of this. I shake my head. "No. Just tired."

"Are you working this weekend?"

"No." I'm dreading the next two days stuck in the house with my parents and nothing to do. Especially with all the questions rolling around in my head.

"Oh." Teeny sounds as disappointed as I feel. "Dad says we're going out later. Do you think Mom will come?"

I shrug my shoulders. "Who knows."

Teeny grabs her book out of the go-bag and leaves the room. I stare at the ceiling a little longer. It's like I'm sapped of energy. Those few carefree hours last night sucked everything out of me.

After hearing Dad on the phone last night, something is gonna change. And whatever it is, we're waiting around for it.

There's a knock on the door, and Mom sticks her head in. Her eyes are red and puffy, and she looks tired. And old. "Can I come in?"

I nod, and she sits at the end of Teeny's bed. She looks sober, but it's still early. Her hair is wet and combed back. At least she showered.

"Just wanted to check with you about school this week. Have you gotten settled? Made some new friends?"

Is she kidding? She's been drunk for two weeks and now she wants a little mother-daughter time?

Do I want to tell her there's a cute boy who seems to like me, but his sister is a total bitch and her boyfriend is making it increasingly likely that I will get my ass beat by a gang of cheerleaders? No.

I guess I should be glad she's been sober for a few days and is trying to stay that way, but I can't muster the energy for that, so I describe the school on the surface. What it looks like, names of teachers, and what classes I'm taking. Once I'm done, Mom tries to keep the small talk going, but it falls flat.

I sit up in the bed. "Mom, don't start drinking again." I may get another whack across the cheek, but it needs to be said.

She picks at her nails and then raises her head. "I know. I'm trying." She stands to leave. "Dad wants to get to Walmart soon."

"Are you coming?" I ask.

"I think I will." She escapes the room, and I almost fall out of bed, stunned by her good attitude this morning.

The Aqua Net has left my hair feeling plastic and crunchy, and I can barely get a hand through it. It'll take shampooing it twice to get all the gunk out.

By the time I'm dressed, my family is assembled in the kitchen, waiting for me. Dad's finishing a list of some sort. We'll probably be there all day. I grab my go-bag and open the door.

The phone rings.

We all stare at it a moment. The suits never call us—they just show up—and we're all here. I look at Dad quickly. Could it be the person he was talking to last night?

Dad answers it and holds the receiver out to me. "It's for you." There's relief all over his face.

Ethan. I called home from his cell last night. He's the only possible choice. I look at Dad, and then I look at the phone and walk slowly to get it.

"Hello."

"Meg, it's Ethan."

"Hey." My family is standing inside the open door, watching me.

"What's up?"

"Not much."

Silence.

"What're you doing later?" he asks.

"Not sure."

Silence.

"Are you gonna be around? Can I come by?"

"No. That's not a good idea."

Silence. Family still staring.

"Can I meet you somewhere?"

"I don't know. Maybe."

Silence. Most awkward conversation. Ever.

"Is this not a good time to talk?"

"No."

"Take my number and call me later. When you can talk."

I look down to the notepad sitting by the phone and see Dad's scratchy writing. "I've already got it from last night."

"Okay, cool. Call me later, then."

"Okay, bye."

I hang up and look at my family. "What?"

Dad shakes his head. "Nothing. You ready?"

I tear off the sheet of paper with Ethan's number and shove it in my bag.

Who would have thought we could walk out of Walmart with two full carts when we're scraping by on what the suits give us? Dad got his paycheck from the factory yesterday, but he'll have to pay some bills with it. I'm shocked we loaded up on so much food when we could get pulled out of here any day, but maybe Dad is planning on our being here a while.

Dad gave Teeny and me twenty bucks each, and after adding it to some of my own money, I replenished some of our personal items from the bag. I got a new crossword book I thought Teeny would like, and some lip gloss and mascara for me. All in all, we spent almost three hours inside the store, including having lunch at the McDonald's in the back. Dad has never let us splurge like this; forget that Mom used to spend this much every week just getting her hair and nails done. I wonder again if this has anything to do with the call last night.

Teeny's happy. She got a new book and a Monopoly board game. She's decided that tonight is game night and everyone has to play.

Mom looks even more tired, if that's possible. Pretty shaky, too. I really hope she can power through it and not drink.

Despite Mom looking so terrible, Dad actually seems pleased. This is the longest amount of time we've spent as a family in months. Inside the store, we got each item on the list in the order it was listed, even if it meant leaving the produce section to walk across the store for a cleaning product, then back to produce. I'm pretty sure he planned that on purpose to draw the trip out.

When we get home, Mom tries to help with the groceries, but she looks beat down. Dad suggests she take a hot bath and grab a nap. His smile is gone, and all three of us spend about twenty minutes putting everything away. When we're done, the kitchen actually looks like people live here.

I convince Teeny to open the game, and the three of us start playing. Teeny's bummed since we're technically having game night at two o'clock in the afternoon, but she goes along anyway. This used to be our favorite game to play. She's a master, buying up everything she lands on, no matter how measly the rent it is.

We play until Dad and I are both out of money and Teeny's sitting on the whole bank. I haven't been back to the laundry room since that night, but I can't put it off any longer. Plus, it's the middle of the afternoon and I have Teeny with me, although what good she'll do, I don't know.

Teeny brings her new book, and I bring the piece of paper with Ethan's number and a handful of quarters.

Once the clothes are going, Teeny settles down in one of the chairs to read, and I walk to the pay phone that I spotted earlier in the week. I wonder if Dad knows about the phone down here. I drop the coins in the slot. Ethan answers on the third ring.

"Hello?"

"Hey. It's Meg."

"Hey. Where are you?"

"Mary and I are doing laundry. I need to stay with the clothes so they don't disappear."

"Cool. I'm glad you called. I was hoping maybe we could go see a movie tonight. Or hang out. Something low-key. Nothing that will involve running from the cops."

I laugh and take a minute to think. I remember my regret this morning. Say no or say yes? Say no. Every time I say yes, I wish I wouldn't have. Definitely say no.

"A movie sounds good."

"I'll pick you up at seven."

"Okay. Bye." I want to bang my head with the receiver. Can't I say no even once? I turn around just as Agent Thomas walks into the laundry room.

Chapter 14

RULES FOR DISAPPEARING BY WITNESS PROTECTION PRISONER #18A7R04M:

Educate yourself on what you plan to lie about. It sucks when you say your family is from Arkansas and then you can't answer a damn thing about Arkansas.

SHEER panic runs through my entire system. I left the go-bag in the house. How friggin' stupid can I be? The color drains from Teeny's face. She curls into a ball in the chair and starts screaming. I sprint to her chair, dropping down beside her and repeating, "It's okay," over and over.

Agent Thomas holds his hands up quickly. "No, it's not what you're thinking. Came by to check on you."

What? Check on us? He about gave me a heart attack just so he can check on us? I take a deep breath and count to ten. Then twenty.

Still pissed.

Agent Thomas kneels down and whispers to Teeny, "I didn't mean to scare you. Just came by to check on things. Your sister is right: it will be okay."

I move in front of Teeny and ask, "What do you want?"

Agent Thomas motions for me to step outside. I hesitate, not really wanting to be alone with him, but it's probably better not to include Teeny.

I turn to Teeny. "It's all good. I'm going out to talk to him."

"Don't leave me!" Her voice cracks and her hands shake.

"No, I won't leave you. I swear. You heard him: he's just checking in. If he was gonna take us, we'd be gone by now." I hand her the book she dropped on the floor. "I'll be back in a minute."

Agent Thomas is leaning against the building, waiting for me. "I really didn't mean to upset her like that."

I cross my arms. "Whatever. You guys normally don't just come check on us."

"Well, we're afraid things are getting out of hand."

"What do you mean 'out of hand'?"

"Your mother. The drinking. We tried talking to your dad, but he's not being very cooperative."

"She's better. She hasn't had a drink in three days. Why did my mother have your number? There's a hotline we can call if we need help."

He cocks his head toward me and waits a moment before answering. "I'm worried about her. I was trying to see if she needed any help."

I roll my eyes. "Yeah, right. Do the other suits know you're contacting her?" I really don't know the protocol here, but I seem to have caught him off guard, so I'm rolling with it.

Agent Thomas pushes away from the building. "Are you ready to move again? Are you so tired of this placement already? How do you think your sister will handle another move? If your family has to be relocated again, for any reason, it will be to a permanent safe house situation until it's time to go to trial. No more identities, Meg. You understand what this means."

I understand there's no way my family can handle being stuck in a safe house, day after day, being watched by suits 24/7. I pace around in a small circle, forcing down the urge to run away or vomit. Then I remember Ethan and all his questions. He has no idea what his curiosity could do to us.

"Things aren't that bad. And how can you really say my dad isn't cooperative? We're here, aren't we?" I taste bile in the back of my throat.

Agent Thomas gives me a look that says *I'm not a dumb-ass.* "Meg, tell me how bad it is. Do you think she's going to do something to jeopardize your placement here?" His voice drops and he truly looks concerned for us. "Is there anything I can do to help? We're on your side in all this."

"No. Mom doesn't like moving any more than the rest of us. She'll be fine. Is that all?" I need him to leave. Now.

"For now." He pulls a white business card out of his pocket. "Call me if something happens. If you need any help."

I shove the card into my back pocket. "Nothing's gonna come up."

Agent Thomas walks away. Once he's completely out of sight, I turn and puke my Big Mac and fries into the bushes.

Teeny cries when she finds out I'm going to the movies with Ethan. I'm not sure if she's mad because she can't go with us, or if she's a little jealous I have a date with him.

"Teeny, let's go out to dinner. You pick the spot. Just you and me," Dad says.

The more normal Teeny is, the better Dad handles her.

Teeny's sitting on the arm of the couch, pouting. "I want to go to Pearl's."

You'd think she'd be tired of pizza.

"Great. Pearl's it is. But only if you make my pizza." Dad is teasing her, trying to cheer her up.

She rolls her eyes. "Fine, let's go." I'm kind of glad to see her upset like this. It's the old bratty upset she did back home when she didn't get her way.

Dad and Teeny leave, and I wait on the steps for Ethan. It took me a long time this afternoon to get over Agent Thomas's visit. I debated whether or not to tell Dad, and thought it might be the perfect way to bring up the phone call last night. If he's got some way out of this already in the works, I don't want to screw it up. I'm almost scared to know who he was talking to.

I'm so confused. I don't even know what I want to happen anymore. When we first started running, all I wanted was to go back home. Even though that meant dealing with Laura and Elle, I couldn't imagine being anywhere else.

Now I don't know if I could go back there. Or if I even want to anymore. The way we live now is so far from how we lived before. It'd be hard to go back and act like none of this has changed me, like I'm still the girl whose biggest concern is what I'm wearing to the next party.

Lights flash across the parking lot when Ethan pulls in. I jump up and run to the truck.

"Hey," I say once I'm inside.

"Hey." He looks at my bag. Then at me. "I know some girls who won't go anywhere without their purse, but I've never seen anyone drag around their luggage."

The one thing I was hoping he wouldn't mention is the first thing he says to me. "Ha-ha. It's stupid, I know, but it's coming with us."

"It's huge. Why do you carry it everywhere you go?"

I shake my head. "Just forget the bag," I beg. "So what movie are we going to?"

He glances at the bag once more, then lets it go. "Well, there are two new ones out. One looks scary as hell, and the other is about some girl and a guy and I think a dog."

God, he is so cute. He's trying to make it sound like he wants to see a romantic comedy. But I'm cool with the scary one. I don't necessarily want to see some happily-ever-after movie. Too depressing.

"Let's go with scary. But I have to have a big bucket of popcorn because I eat when I'm nervous."

He looks like he got a stay of execution. "That's awesome. Girls don't usually like scary movies."

"Yes we do. But we force you to sit through the chick flicks so maybe you'll get some idea of how you're supposed to act."

He laughs. "You know the exact opposite happens. Those guys usually look like total dumb-asses."

We pull into the cinema parking lot and walk up to the box office. Ethan holds my hand like he did walking into the party last night, and I want to lean into him, snuggle up close, but I chicken out. I remember how cozy Will and Catherine were, and I'm jealous. That's what I want—something natural and comfortable. Not what I thought I had with Brandon, which was me flirting and constantly devising ways to be with him. And it wasn't what I had with Tyler either.

Ethan buys the tickets, and we head to the concession counter. We load up: popcorn, candy, drinks, and even hot dogs. We can barely get the doors to the theater open with our arms so full.

We find two seats in the back row and try to get comfortable with everything spread across our laps.

"We may have overdone it. I don't know how we're gonna eat all this," I say. We barely get ourselves settled before the room goes dark.

About halfway through the movie, I have no food left. I'm petrified about what comes next. I push all the empty containers onto the floor and lean closer into Ethan.

"Are you scared?" he whispers to me.

I look at him with big eyes. "Are you kidding me? Of course I'm scared. This movie is crazy. Who even thinks up crap like this?"

Suddenly, some crazy *thing* jumps out from behind a door with a hatchet. I scream and push my face into Ethan's shoulder.

Ethan leans his head close to mine. "This is why guys like to take girls to scary movies."

I punch him in the arm. "You may be sorry you brought me when I tear out of here screaming."

He puts his arm around me, and I watch the rest of the movie from the corner of my eye. Maybe we should have gone for the chick flick.

Once the movie is over, I feel kind of gross. We ate all that food, and then my nerves almost made me throw it back up.

Ethan holds my hand as we walk to the car.

"Where to now?" he asks.

"Oh. I don't know." I glance at my watch and it's only quarter to ten. "What are you thinking?'

We get to his truck and Ethan leans me against the door. "I'm thinking I don't want to take you home yet."

I can feel my cheeks getting warm. "Oh."

He kisses me lightly on the lips. "Do you have to go home now or can you stay out a while?"

At this moment, I can't even remember what my fake name is. "I need to call home first."

He grins big and hands me his phone. Dad answers on the second ring.

"Dad, I'm going to stay out a little longer."

"Where are you?"

"Just leaving the movies. I won't be long."

"Do you think that's a good idea?"

"Yes. Bye." I hand Ethan back his phone, and we climb into the truck. "Where are we going?"

"I thought we could go to my house."

No. No meeting parents. No crazy sister and no crazy sister's boyfriend who may or may not be present. "Is that our only choice?" I try to keep my tone upbeat, but Ethan catches something in my voice.

"You didn't want to stop by last night either. Something wrong with coming to my house?"

Yes. Everything is wrong. "No."

We're still sitting in the parking spot at the theater. Ethan stares out the front windshield. "Tell me what's going on."

"What do you mean?" I don't like where this is going.

He throws his head back against the seat and closes his eyes. "I wasn't going to do this."

Definitely not good. "Do what?"

He leans forward and opens his glove box, pulling out a piece of paper. He toys with it for a second, then shoots those baby blues at me. "Is your real name Avery Preston?"

Ho-ly shit! My mouth is open, but no words will come out. Ethan unfolds the paper and produces a picture of three girls with a news article below it. I know what it is instantly. I got my ass chewed out over that article by one of the suits. In our third placement, I was on my school's dance line. I placed in the top three for the high kickers contest, and we made the local paper. Avery Preston was my name when we lived in Naples, Florida.

I grab the article from him.

"I wasn't sure it was you until I printed it."

Printed in black-and-white, the blue eyes and the blond hair fade away. It looks exactly like me now, except my hair is long. How in the world did he find this?

I crumple up the paper and stuff it into my bag. I can't look at him.

"That's you, isn't it?" He nudges my leg.

"How did you find that?"

He shrugs. "Mary and I were talking the other night about fishing. She said Paradise Coast was the best place to catch fish. The second she said it, she clammed up. Wouldn't hardly talk to me for twenty minutes. I've been to Paradise Coast. It's around Naples, Florida. I know you're not from Lewisville, so I Googled the area and found that article."

I want to get out of the truck and run. Far away. But we're nowhere near my house, I wouldn't know how to find my way back.

"Take me home."

"Not until you talk to me." He cranks the truck, and the heat blasts all over me. "Is that you in the picture?"

Pulling my legs in, I drop my forehead on my knees. If the suits find out Ethan knows this much, we're gone. And after my conversation with Agent Thomas, it'll be some safe house crawling with suits. I roll my head toward him. He's watching me. "Yes," I whisper.

"Let's go somewhere we can talk." He throws the truck into reverse.

We drive for a while, country music playing softly in the background. He parks at the end of Front Street, close to the Vistor's Center. All the shops are dark and the street is deserted. I wait by the side of the truck, unsure of why we're here.

He comes around to my side. "I thought we could sit by the water. It's not too cold tonight."

I look down the hill toward the river that runs through town.

He grabs an extra jacket from the backseat, and I follow him down a set of stone steps that curve around a rock waterfall and lead to the river. There's a small dock just over the water, and Ethan spreads the jacket out. We both drop down on it, side by side, facing the water.

We're silent for what feels like forever.

"You can tell me anything. You should know that," Ethan says.

"How would I know that? I've been here for what . . . two weeks?" I spin around to face him. "And why so nosy about me? Have you been drilling Mary for information this whole time? You're acting like her friend, but you're using her!"

I'm so pissed right now.

He faces me. "No! It's not like that. Nothing about you made sense. You're always so nervous. You wouldn't talk about your family, your friends, your old school, nothing." He snatches his cap off his head and throws it on the dock.

I turn away from him, but he pulls me back around, holding my hands. "You got in my head. It's driving me nuts not being able to figure you out. Talk to me."

I shake my head. "I can't." It's hard to stay mad at him. He moves his hands to my face and inches me closer.

"I can keep a secret. Whatever you tell me stays right here." He's so close our noses almost touch.

Oh my God, I want to tell him everything. I'm almost bursting with it. And that little niggling thread of hope that Dad's going to fix this is almost the push I need. If we get out, I can stay here—as long as I want.

I could be with Ethan—as long as I want.

"That was me in the picture. My name is Avery Preston. My dad moved us here because he got into some trouble in Florida. You can't tell anyone." I'm going to hell for lying. I've done it for so long now it flows right out of mouth even when I want to tell the truth.

"What happened?" He squeezes my hands.

I shake my head. "No, I can't tell you. Just promise me you won't tell anyone what my name is."

He leans back and looks at me funny. Does he believe me? Can he tell I'm full of crap? He shakes his head and his forehead scrunches up. "Does this have something to do with that bag you haul around?" he asks. He's not going to let this go.

"Kind of." I put my hands on his cheeks and pull him back to me. "Don't ask me anything else."

He opens his mouth, I'm sure to ask another question, so I do the only thing I can think of to get him to stop talking—kiss him.

And he kisses me right back.

My hands explore his chest while his wander to my hips. We fall back until we're lying on the dock, the coat little protection against the cold wood. But it doesn't matter.

Ethan's hand edges up the hem of my shirt, and the rough pads of his fingers skim across the tender flesh at my stomach before moving around to my back. Every spot he touches sends tingles through my body. I move my hands up his neck to the back of his hair, wrapping my fingers into his thick curls.

As our legs intertwine and our hands wander, all the worries and the plans fly away. I could stay here with him, like this, all night. And then I realize I want to stay here with him, in this town, for as long as possible. And that feeling scares me more than anything else.

When we pull into the parking lot near my house, I spot Dad heading into the laundry room. Ethan offers to walk me to the door, but I turn him down, kissing him quickly before hopping out of the truck. I have to find out what Dad's doing. I'm pretty sure it's not laundry.

I'm praying someone didn't close the window along the back wall that's usually open, or there's no way I will be able to hear what he's doing in there.

I make my way around the side of the building, my feet crunching loudly on the dead leaves. It will be a miracle if he doesn't hear me coming.

I use the go-bag as a stool to peek in the high window, which, thankfully, is still open.

Dad has discovered the phone in the laundry room. It's right next to the window, so he's got his back to me. I work my toe into a spot where a brick is missing and hitch myself a little higher.

"This is bullshit. I said I'm working on it." Dad is pacing, but the cord is keeping him on a short leash.

Three tight circles later, he says, "If I can get it, I'll need some guarantee that my family will be safe."

Oh. My. God. Who is he talking to?

"I don't believe you." His voice is controlled, but his movements are jerky.

Five more circles. "What happens if I can't find it?"

He leans against the wall. "No, you've made that very clear." He slams the phone in the cradle, and I almost fall off the wall. I grab my bag and haul ass to the house, praying I make it there before Dad sees me.

Chapter 15

RULES FOR DISAPPEARING BY WITNESS PROTECTION PRISONER #18A7R04M:

Know what you're getting into before you get into it.

ETHAN calls after lunch on Sunday, and I meet him at the coffee shop on Front Street where I first met Agent Thomas.

"I want to take you somewhere tonight."

I sip my latte, and those blue eyes watch me until I put my cup down. "Where?"

"To the farm."

I shake my head. "I don't know. . . ."

I'm really nervous today, and it's probably due to Dad's mysterious late-night phone conversation. I couldn't look at him this morning. He was probably talking to the assholes looking for us, and it sounded like he was making some sort of deal with them. That's his way of getting us out of this—work with whoever got us into this to begin with? I'm totally disgusted.

Ethan works his magic on me, and like the weak-ass I am, I agree.

The entire afternoon I try to work up the nerve to call him and cancel. I just can't do it.

It's dark when Ethan picks me up. He's dressed in camouflage, and Bandit is loaded up in the back of the truck. He doesn't tell me until we're halfway to the farm what we'll be doing.

Hog hunting.

In my old life, I would have laughed if anyone ever suggested this is how I would spend my evening. Apparently hogs rut through all the fields, tearing them apart and eating everything in sight.

Who knew?

And they are the only animal you can hunt legally at night, all year round. So I now have more knowledge about a hog than I ever thought would be necessary.

"So are we going to ride around in the truck to look for these hogs?" I ask. Ethan gave me some "hunting clothes" to wear over my own stuff. Looking at everything he handed me, I don't think there'll be an inch of skin showing once we're all suited up.

Ethan chuckles. "I'm almost afraid to tell you too much. You may bolt on me."

I pick at the fingers on my gloves. "You're right, because this seems crazy to me." I look up at him. "Just tell me what I've gotten myself into."

"We'll be on four-wheelers. Main reason you need all the gear is it'll be cold. The dogs do most of the work. We follow them to the hogs."

My eyes get big. "What do you mean the dogs do all the work? Are you talking about Bandit?"

Ethan scrunches his forehead. "Hell no, he'll just ride along with us. I'm talking about the dogs we keep at the farm. The hog dogs."

And he wonders why I look at everyone here like they're from another planet. I lean back against the door of the truck. "How are we supposed to follow the dogs in the dark? And if these hogs are so big and bad-ass, how are the dogs not going to get hurt?"

Ethan just laughs. "You'll see."

At the farm, we make our way back to one of the big sheds that houses all the tractors and equipment. There are a few men hanging around, all dressed like us.

"You came!" Catherine calls out to me from the shed.

She comes jogging over to where we are, Will following close behind her.

"Hey! I didn't know you'd be here." This makes me feel so much better. I was really worried about being the only girl and possibly, no, probably, embarrassing myself.

"Yeah, what could be more fun on a Sunday night than riding around in the dark looking for wild animals? Even with them here." She points to another truck that Emma and Ben jump out of. Great.

They keep their distance, and Catherine pulls me in the opposite direction, saying, "You've got to see this."

I get my first glimpse of the dogs. They look like biker dogs, with black vests and collars with metal pointy things. "What are they wearing?"

Ethan comes up behind me and says, "Armor. The dogs are outfitted with Kevlar vests, chest armor, and extra-wide collars. It'll protect them from major injury."

It's official. I have left planet Earth. "Is that enough?" I don't know how I feel about this. It seems cruel. "Do you have to use the dogs?"

Ethan puts his arms around my waist and pulls me in. "I promise this isn't as bad as you think. The dogs love it. They love the hunt. We rarely have an injury, and when we do it's usually just a cut or gash that needs some stitches."

He moves his mouth close to my ear. "If at any point you want to stop, we'll stop. Have you ever been hunting before?"

I shake my head. I look at Catherine and ask, "Is this your first time, too?"

"No, I've been a few times. It's insane but fun."

"Whatcha talking about?" Will asks. He's carrying a crate full of small electronic devices.

"Meg's a little nervous," Catherine answers.

Will laughs and says, "Don't feel sorry for those hogs. They can destroy a whole field overnight. If we can't get a handle on them we won't have any farmland left."

"And this has to be done at night?" I ask.

"Yeah, that's when they're on the move," Ethan answers, then reaches into the crate and hands me one of the devices. "These are transmitters. They fit on the dog's collar. We'll have a GPS unit that tracks the signal. That's how we follow the dogs in the dark."

This whole thing is bizarre, but it's also pretty sophisticated. I watch as Ethan puts transmitters on all the dogs. We walk to a row of ATVs, Bandit following us closely, and I climb onto one behind Ethan. Bandit jumps on the back and settles in on the rack behind me.

"Can he ride like that?" I ask.

"Yes, he's been riding there since he was a puppy. He's fine."

Will and Catherine jump onto the ATV next to us.

"Glad to see it's not just you and Bandit tonight, Ethan. I was starting to worry about you," Will jokes.

"Ha. Ha. You're just jealous my dog actually likes me."

Ben and Emma walk toward us, and the ribbing stops. There's a definite change in Ethan's mood when Ben gets near.

I lean in close and whisper in Ethan's ear. "Why is he here?"

"His dad's farm borders ours. Hogs are equal-opportunity nuisances—they don't care whose property they're on. Ben's dad can be an asshole. If we invite him on the hunt, he won't bitch about us riding across his land to catch one or get our dogs back—forget we're doing him a favor by getting rid of them." Ethan points to two men near the dog pens. "The one on the right is my dad, and the one on the left is Ben's."

They have a map out and are studying it by flashlight. Ben's dad is loud and moves his arms while he talks. A lot. The light from his flashlight dances through the night sky. Ethan's dad shakes his head and points at the map, and then Ben's dad stomps off.

"I guess I don't understand. Do your dad and Ben's get along?" It sure doesn't look like it.

Ethan shifts toward me and says quietly, "Used to. It's a long story and one I'd rather not get into right now." He squeezes my hand to soften the brush-off.

"Where's Will's dad?" I ask.

Ethan laughs and points to a rather large man with the biggest beer belly I've ever seen. He's leaning against a truck with a bottle in one hand and a cigar in the other.

Ben and Emma get on the ATV one over from us just as the men let the dogs out. Before I can grasp what's about to happen, the dogs are gone and the little light on the GPS unit starts blinking. Ethan cranks up the ATV and turns to me. He's excited and pulls me in close. "Don't freak out on me."

And then his lips are on mine. It's a quick kiss but enough that I feel it in my belly.

The ATV takes off, and I feel the urge to hold on to Bandit before he falls, but he's standing on the back rack, feet firmly planted, and seems to be enjoying the ride. I glance behind and see that several others are following us. I lean forward and shout in Ethan's ear so he can hear me over the roar of the engine. "Are we tracking all the dogs?"

"No, we're tracking the bay dogs. They go out and find a hog and corner him. Then the dads come in with the catch dogs. They'll pin the hogs down."

"So what happens after that?" My voice sounds hysterical, but I can't help it. We're flying down the side of a field; empty raised rows on one side and woods on the other. Before Ethan can answer me, we turn into a break in the woods where everything is pitch-black except for our headlights. I look behind us and see that one other ATV has turned off, too.

"Once the catch dog has the hog, we go in and tie him up. Mouth closed, feet together."

I wait for him to finish, but he doesn't add anything else. We're moving slower now that we're in the woods, but still quicker than I'm comfortable with.

"Then what?"

Ethan maneuvers the ATV over a log, and adrenaline pumps through my system. I'm terrified and excited at the same time.

He gets us back on somewhat flat ground and says, "We put them in a cage. Cart them off. We donate the hogs to a local group, who butcher them and distribute the meat to people who need it. It's a win-win for everybody."

We ride through the woods for a while with the moon full above us. Once my eyes adjust to the darkness, I can see a break in the canopy of trees around us. It's almost bright out here. Every little part of me feels alive.

There's no telling how many miles we've gone. The light on the GPS screen stops, and so does Ethan. It's amazing how quiet it is once he cuts the engine. The other rider pulls up close and turns his ATV off, too. It's Ben and Emma. We all look around, no one really wanting to make eye contact.

I can hear the dogs barking in the distance, although I can't see them. I finally whisper to Ethan, "What's happening now?"

"The dogs have found some hogs, but they're circling around, probably trying to figure out how to get to them."

"How many will there be?" I ask.

Ethan shrugs. "You never know. Sometimes one, sometimes two or three."

Ben yells out to Ethan, "I'm going to check it out." And they're gone.

It's just us, alone in the middle of the dark woods. Bandit jumps off and goes sniffing around. "Is he okay?"

"Yeah, probably just stretching his legs."

It's silent again except for the howling in the woods. My hands are on Ethan's hips, and he pulls them forward so I'm hugging him from behind. He leans back, and I lay my chin on his shoulder.

"Are you sorry you came?" he asks quietly.

"No. Not yet, anyway," I whisper in his ear, and bury my face against his back. Faster than I can think about what he's doing, he spins me around until I'm straddling him and starts kissing me. I lock my legs around his waist and kiss him back. Our heavy coats make it hard to get too close, but I try anyway. He pulls my scarf off, and his lips find the spot on my neck I like so much.

The rumble of an approaching ATV has me squirming back to my seat, but Ethan's reluctant to let me go. I win in the end, just as Will and Catherine pull up to where we're parked.

"Where are the dogs?" Will asks.

Ethan points to the patch of woods in front of us. "In there. Dumb-ass went to check it out."

Will and Catherine laugh while I struggle to get the scarf back on. Ethan keeps his hands on me—my leg, my arm, my hands. All this touching is so distracting.

Ben and Emma fly out of the woods, and Ben yells, "I'm calling the dads."

Ethan picks up the GPS screen, studying it. "You need to make sure they got them first. Looks like the dogs are still circling around."

Ben's phone is out and he's dialing. Ethan seems pissed but doesn't say anything else.

"They're gonna be mad if you call them too soon," Will says in a low singsong voice.

Ben shuts his phone. "I gave them our coordinates. They're on their way."

We hear the approaching vehicle, and I move away from Ethan. I haven't met his dad yet, so I'm not crazy about him catching us all cuddled up.

Mr. Dufrene and Mr. Landry pull up on a larger all-terrain

vehicle that has a small truck bed on the back that says RANGER on the side. Behind them are two kennels with dogs in them.

Mr. Dufrene turns to Ben. "Where are they?"

Ben points to the heavily wooded area in front of us. "In there."

"Are they pinned yet?" Mr. Landry asks.

Ethan glances at the little lights on the GPS. "Not yet, still circling around."

"Why on God's green earth did you call us if they weren't pinned? The other group is closer to having one ready than y'all are." Mr. Dufrene hits the steering wheel with his hat, then whips the vehicle around. Ethan's dad throws us an apologetic look before they head back the way they came.

Will leans forward on the handlebars of the ATV. "Told you not to call him."

Ben cranks his ATV and slams it into gear. His vehicle jumps, and he and Emma head into the wooded area. Emma glances back for a second—the look on her face shows she's scared.

"What the hell." Ethan cranks our ATV and hollers to Bandit, "Load up." The dog lands on the back of the ATV in one move, and we chase after Ben and Emma.

Once we're moving, I lean forward. "Is this bad?" I say, trying not to panic.

"No, it's fine. Ben's an asshole. The dogs will get them, but Ben wanted to be the one to call the dads in. Everything's a friggin' competition with him."

It's darker in this section—almost no light from the moon down here. I can hear the dogs ahead and the rumble of Ben's ATV, but I can only catch a glimpse of his lights.

The dogs go crazy. They're yelping and howling, and then I hear another sound. It's a loud grunting noise.

"What is that?" Catherine asks.

Ethan starts driving a little faster. "It's a hog." Our lights flash over Ben's ATV, and we stop. Three bay dogs surround the hog, and they're barking so loud it hurts my ears. Ben shifts around and I get my first glimpse of a feral hog.

Oh. My. God. It's huge.

If I were standing next to it, it would come up to my hip. Its tusks are long and it's jabbing at the dogs, but they seem very good at staying just out of range of the tusks.

Ethan jumps off. He grabs something from a compartment on the back of the ATV and turns to me quickly. "Don't move." Will follows him, and Catherine starts her nervous giggling behind me.

Now I'm really freaking out. They walk toward the hog, and I glance around nervously. What if there's another one they don't see and it comes after us? I look for Emma across the clearing and see she's crawled up on the back of their ATV. She looks as scared as I feel. Ben's on the phone. I'm assuming he's called the dads again.

Ben hangs up and shouts commands to the dogs, and Ethan starts yelling at him. I can't make out any of the words over the barking dogs.

The hog lunges in the direction of Ethan, and Bandit is off the ATV.

"No, Bandit! Come back," I scream. I chase after him, and Ethan yells something in my direction. I can't make out the words, but I catch a glimpse of what he's got in his hand. It's a gun.

Chills race down my back, and everything sounds like I'm underwater.

I feel someone grab me from behind. Hands on my arms, pulling at me. I twist around and it's Catherine. I yank free and start running.

The hog lunges again, and there's a gut-wrenching yelp. Will and Ben run toward Bandit. He's lying on the ground, not moving. Ethan raises the gun at the hog, his body seeming to move in slow motion, and fires, the loud crack vibrating through me. It hurts as it travels through my body.

Something wet sprays my face, and I wipe it off. My hand is covered in blood. The hog drops, and the smell of blood and gunpowder hover in the air. I fall to my knees in the dead crunchy grass. This is wrong. This shouldn't be happening.

My mind spins so fast, it makes me dizzy. Images start firing through my brain, but I can't sort them out. I squeeze my eyes closed to make it stop, but it doesn't work. I hold my head in my hands as every horrible image from my nightmares now plays in vivid color.

Ethan drops down beside me. His mouth is moving, but I can't understand the words, and the features of his face start to blur. The trees spin around me, and I can taste bile in my throat. I look at the gun where Ethan dropped it on the ground, and then at Bandit. Will is trying to stop the flow of blood. This is wrong. Catherine and Emma shout at each other, but I can't hear them either, and Ben is back on the phone. There's a humming in my ears that drowns out everything else. I shove my fingers into my ears, trying to make the sound go away.

And then everything is black.

Chapter 16

RULES FOR DISAPPEARING
BY WITNESS PROTECTION PRISONER #18A7R04M:

Confine yourself to your living space as much as possible, especially at night. Remember, nothing good ever happens after midnight.

I'M trapped in the room again. The voices are loud but distorted. There's blood everywhere. I look down. It's coming from me.

I wake with a start. There's a crowd over me, and Ethan helps me up to a sitting position.

I lean back from everyone and ask, "What happened?" My throat feels rough and scratchy.

Ethan's brow scrunches up. "You started screaming and then passed out. How do you feel?"

I'm looking at Ethan's face, but that's not what I see. I'm back in that room from my nightmare. I'm behind something. A couch. It's leather. It's so real, it's like I'm actually there, right now. I reach my hand out to feel its buttery softness, but all I hit are dead leaves. My jaw gets tight like I'm going to vomit. This isn't real. This can't be real.

"Meg, are you okay?" Ethan twists around and screams, "Dad, I need to get Meg out of here."

Now there are sounds. Screaming, loud, angry ones. My head vibrates with the noise. I sink back down to the ground, but Ethan picks me up and helps me into the Ranger I saw his dad riding in earlier. I curl up in the seat, and every time my eyes close, I'm back in that room. I open them quickly, scared of being sucked into that dream. Mr. Landry is at my side. I look at his face but I see Mr. Price, Brandon's dad, instead. And there's blood pouring from his chest. I dig my palms into my eyes, hoping to erase the image.

"Take her home, son. We'll see about Bandit. Will's got the bleeding stopped, and they're wrapping him up now."

"You want me to come with you?" I hear Catherine ask.

"No, stay with Will. Help get Bandit back to the truck."

I want to tell Ethan to stay, to take care of Bandit, but I have to get out of here.

We drive fast through the woods, and Ethan keeps one arm across me the entire time. Every dark shadow from the surrounding woods looks like it's trying to close in around me and suck me in.

I drop my head against Ethan's shoulder, and my eyes drift closed. Brandon's face fills my mind, but it's not the tanned beautiful face I remember. His eyes stare past me in a lost sort of way, and then there's blood. Everywhere.

"No!" I scream, and shake my head, hoping to erase the horrible things there.

Ethan slows the Ranger and pulls me to him. "Meg, are you okay?"

"Yes, I'm fine." I'm so not fine. Not at all.

We make it back to his truck and he helps me into the passenger seat, handing me a bottle of water.

"I'm so sorry, Ethan. Is Bandit going to be all right?"

"Yes, he'll be fine. Just a gash in the shoulder. They gave him a shot to help with the pain. I'll take him to the vet first thing for a few stitches, but other than that, he'll be good as new. I probably won't be able to pick you up in the morning."

We leave the farm, and I fight down the images forcing their way through my head. I focus on the white center line of the road and try not to think about anything else.

"I'm worried about you. Are you okay?"

I take a deep drink of water and wipe the back of my hand over my mouth. "I can't talk about it right now."

I don't want to talk about it. I don't want to even think about it. The nightmare scrolls through my head, and it takes every bit of determination I have to keep from falling apart.

"Are you taking me home?"

"I can't decide if I need to take you home or the hospital."

"Home. Please take me home," I beg.

Ethan is quiet but keeps looking over at me.

"What about the hog?" I ask.

"Dead. It was either him or Bandit." I can hear the heartbreak in his voice.

He really should have stayed with his dog rather than having to deal with me. I pick at a dried flake of blood on my hand, and then I realize I'm covered in it. Once I start, I can't stop. I rub my hands together, hoping to get rid of every piece, but it's not working.

Ethan leans across the truck and puts his hand on top of mine, stopping me. "I can take you to shoot targets. Let you get comfortable with a gun. They're not near as scary once you learn how to use one."

My jaw gets tight. "No. It's fine."

"Have you ever been around guns before?"

The image of a hand with a gun fills my head, but it's not Ethan's. It's a man's hand. And I'm in that room. I shake my head, hard. Can't think about the gun. Or the blood. Or the sound.

"Well, if you change your mind, let me know."

"I won't."

We ride the rest of the way in silence. I stare at the dashboard, letting myself zone out.

Ethan moves to get out once we pull in the parking lot, but I stop him. "I'm so sorry about Bandit. Please go check on him." He starts to argue, but I put a finger over his lips. "I'll feel so much better if you do."

I jump out of the truck before he has a chance to say anything, then tiptoe into the house. It's late, sometime around midnight, and all I want to do is get into bed and process what happened tonight and why I'm flooded with visions from my nightmares. I'm startled when I see Mom at the kitchen table, her head in her hands, with an empty gin bottle beside her.

"Mom?"

She looks up and her eyes are red and swollen. "You're back."

I sit down at the table. I need to ask her what's happening to me, but she's stinking drunk. Just when I need her the most. "I thought you stopped."

She shakes her head and looks back down. "What happened? You've got blood all over you. Are you hurt?"

"I had some sort of panic attack. I think I'm going crazy." I drop my head on the table. I have to talk to someone, even if it's my hammered mother, who won't remember a single thing I say come morning. "Something is wrong with me, but I don't know what it is. I've been having nightmares for months, but tonight I had one while I was awake. I've got things in my head I can't get rid of."

Mom turns toward me and almost falls out of her chair. "You're not crazy." She puts both of her hands on my face and pulls me close to her. This is why I hate being around her when she's like this. The smell of gin is overwhelming. "They said it'd happen like this." She drops her hands back on the table, then her eyes flutter closed.

I nudge her shoulder. "Mom, what are you talking about? Mom?"

She opens her eyes about halfway. "It's not your fault. Don't feel bad." Her words are slurred, but I can make them out. I don't understand them, though.

"What's not my fault? And who are 'they' and what did *they* say?"

She rolls her head to the side. "Can't tell you. Dad will be mad at me." She lets out a sharp laugh. "Ha! Dad's always mad at me."

I lean forward, closer to her face. "Please tell me. I think something is really wrong with me."

She props herself up on her elbows, eyes squinting like she's trying to focus on my face. "It's not your fault, baby. You weren't supposed to be there." Her head falls again.

"Mom, talk to me. Stay awake. Not supposed to be where?" I get that tingly feeling I had in the woods, and I break out in a sweat. "Tell me, Mom. What's not my fault?" I pull her head up and turn her face to me.

One eye cracks open, and she spreads her arms wide. "This. All this. You're why we're here. You're the one they're after."

Chapter 17

RULES FOR DISAPPEARING
BY WITNESS PROTECTION PRISONER #18A7R04M:

Always stay one step ahead. Then when things go to shit you won't be one step behind. And things always go to shit.

MY mother's words ricochet around my brain. The room. The blood. The gun. Pictures flash across my eyes, and I squeeze them shut. My palms get a little sweaty and my mouth goes dry.

"Dad did something. We're in this because of Dad, not me." Not me, not me, not me.

Mom is drunk. And out of her mind. But the words echo through my brain, and the images get a little sharper. That room with the stone walls and the giant dark furniture.

"No, baby girl. It's you." She falls backward in the chair. I grab her shirt, pulling her back up.

"Don't say that!" I shake her hard, and her eyes open.

"You saw him. That's why we're here. But you forgot. You froze up and now you don't remember."

Mom starts crying as her head falls back down on the table. I sit there stunned. Minutes go by while I watch her cry. My mind is numb, like someone threw an ice-cold bucket of water over my head.

I get up from the table and run outside, down the steps. Don't know where I'm going but I can't stay in that house. *It's got to be Dad, not me. . . . Dad, not me . . .* plays in my head like a broken record.

The parking lot is deserted. As much as I hate to go there, I run to the laundry room. I have nowhere else to go. I fling open the door and flip every switch, flooding the space with light.

I plop down in a chair against the wall. I'm terrified to dig deep in the hazy memories, scared to death of what I'll find there, but all I've wanted to know since this started was the truth, so I close my eyes and let my mind go.

A light flashes across the room. There are two men. Arguing. Everything is blurry around the edges. Their screams mix with the sounds of the hog and Bandit. I rush to the trash can and throw up.

At the laundry sink I douse my face with water and rinse my mouth. Dried blood still covers my hands. I rub my skin until it's raw; the smell of the blood with the water makes me vomit again, but nothing's left in my stomach.

The blood is all over my shirt, too. I have to get it off of me. I jerk it off, leaving me in a tank top. It's cold in here, but I can't stand all that blood. I fall to the floor.

The two men. They're still yelling but also shoving each other, like they're one step away from a full-out fight.

I focus on one of them. It's Mr. Price, my dad's boss. Brandon's father. Concentrating on the details of the room, I know where it is. The Prices' house—I've been there a million times, but not often in this room. It's Mr. Price's office.

The other man—he's tall and big with short dark hair. He's got a thin scar that starts above his eyebrow, slices through his left eye, making it sag, and continues down the side of his face. It's hard to look at him without flinching. They circle around each other like caged animals, yelling. Something about ledgers. "Give me the ledgers . . ." over and over. The nightmare with the books crashing around me fills my head. Books are everywhere. All over me. Every time I touch one, they multiply. I'm drowning.

I lie on the cold concrete floor, pressing every part of me to the ground, hoping to separate what really happened in that room from the nightmares that have plagued me for months. My breathing steadies and the images become clearer, like someone adjusted the focus. The man with the scar lifts his hand; he's holding a gun. Mr. Price lunges for it, and they both fall to the floor.

The noise in my head is like a freight train. It's coming closer until it's so loud I can't hear anything else—no screaming, nothing. And then the gun fires. The sound vibrates through my body, and superfast images of Mr. Price with blood gushing from his chest explode in front of me.

I drive my palms into my eyes, not sure I can take much more of this.

Then I see Brandon.

My heart stops the moment he walks in the room. He's just a few feet away, but doesn't see me behind the couch. I want to scream at him to run, hide . . . anything to keep him safe. But before I get the chance, another shot stops me cold. Brandon, beautiful Brandon, drops to the floor. From behind the couch all I can see are his feet, and they aren't moving. I look down. I'm covered in blood—Brandon's blood.

Then the noise dies down, and it's finally quiet. All I can hear is the rhythmic dripping from the sink. My face is wet, and I realize I've been crying.

Drip . . . drip . . . drip. . . .

I can't move. Or think. Brandon's dead. Mr. Price is dead. The movie in my mind fades to black. That's it. That's the last thing I remember.

I don't know what to do. I feel sick again. Those were not just nightmares. They were memories. My memories.

Oh, God, I can't believe he's dead. And I'll never see him again—he's gone.

I curl up on the floor and stuff my fingers in my ears. I can't take this. Brandon's dead and now someone wants me dead, too. I'm close to passing out again, just like I did in the woods.

I start humming.

Anything to drown out Mom's words rolling through my head. *"It's you they're after. . . . It's you they're after. . . ."*

My head hurts. It feels like ten thousand needles are sticking in my left arm. I try to get up, but the arm buckles underneath me. There is a soft light filtering through the windows of the laundry room. I check my watch. Dad will be up soon.

I suddenly realize how horrible I've been, blaming him for getting us into this, when it was me this whole time.

Throwing my bloody shirt away, I stagger to the door. In no time, I'm flying down the driveway to the house. Mom's still passed out on the table, and Teeny's still sleeping, but I hear Dad starting to stir. He's probably figured out that Mom never came to bed.

I lock myself in the bathroom, then turn on the shower, strip, and jump in before the water gets hot. I slide to the floor and pull my knees in close. Questions roll through my brain so fast it hurts. What am I going to do? What does it mean that I remember? Obviously someone is after us because of what I saw. Is it the man with the scar? And why is it a secret?

Brandon is dead.

The thought pops into my head and I begin to cry. Hard. I've gone this long blocking out his death, and now the only thing I can think of is his crumpled body and the obscene amount of blood that splattered out of him. I try to think of a time when he was alive and happy, but I can't picture him any other way.

Why was he there? Why was I there? There's so much that's still fuzzy.

I hear the shouting match between Scar Face and Mr. Price in my head again.

Where are the ledgers?

That's what he kept screaming. I squeeze my eyes shut, trying to remember. I think there was a book. I can see Mr. Price with something, but what was it? Every detail I try to focus on retreats out of my head. Like my mind is playing a game with me.

Arghhh! This is so frustrating.

Dad said earlier that going to trial doesn't mean we're getting out of Witness Protection. And he's kept this from me all this time. Why? Will I have to testify? That man didn't even hesitate before he killed Brandon. Every time I think about Brandon, my eyes swell with tears and I wonder horrible things, like if he knew what was about to happen to him. Or if it hurt when the bullet ripped through his body. I don't think I could ever be in the same room with Scar Face again.

I scrub my hair and body as if I could wash away the last twenty-four hours. I have to get out of here. There's no way to face Mom this morning after our conversation last night. I run from the bathroom in my towel and get dressed in record time. I wake Teeny, rushing her to get dressed, too. I'm scared to see Mom. I'm afraid she's going to remember what she told me. The only thing I know for sure is I'm not ready to let anyone know I have my memory back until I can figure some things out. I can't shake the feeling there's something missing.

We get outside early to wait for the bus. Teeny's pouting, walking around the lot kicking loose rocks. I don't know what has made her madder—that I got her up so early or that we're back on the bus. I sit on the bottom step and wait. My entire body is in a state of tension I didn't know existed.

The bus drags down the street. Just as it stops at the curb, Ethan pulls into the parking lot. Teeny lets out a yelp and tries to get in his truck before it even stops. I walk toward him more slowly. After last night I don't even know what to do.

Once I'm in the truck, Ethan says "Morning" to Teeny, then looks at me. "You okay?"

True concern is written all over his face. He's worried about me and what happened, and, God, how can I let him be anywhere near me right now? I'm a target, the reason my family lost everything we had and are living with fake names. And Ethan thinks I'm just some girl who freaked out over a dog getting hurt and a hog getting shot.

"Fine," I answer.

Teeny starts jabbering about something. She'll take care of all the conversation until we pull away from her school.

"I totally creamed them in Monopoly. You should have seen it. Meg was the first one out and then I went for Dad."

Ethan's laughing. They're sitting here talking about regular life, and I'm one step from full panic mode.

Scar Face killed Brandon just for walking into the room. Ethan could be next. Or Teeny.

The enormity of this is finally sinking in.

The entire trip to Teeny's school, I watch the side mirror. I'm close to hyperventilating by the time we drop Teeny off. Every dark-haired man I see makes my heart stop.

"Man, that girl can talk," Ethan says once Teeny's gone. "Are you sure you're okay?"

Hell, no.

I nod. "I'm fine. I thought you'd be with Bandit this morning."

"I was. Dad and I took him over around five this morning. He's all stitched up and sleeping it off at the vet's." Ethan looks at me closely and says, "Maybe you should've stayed home today?"

I shake my head. "No, I'm fine, really." I'd go crazy trapped in the house with Mom and my thoughts all day long.

We pull into school and walk toward the building. Lots of people in the parking lot this morning, but I zero in on the perimeter. Is someone out there, right now, looking for me? Would he kill Ethan just for being with me?

Before we part to go to our lockers, Ethan says, "Meet me in the parking lot at lunch. We'll get out of here for a little while."

I nod, then stand there watching him walk away. There's no chance of a relationship with him now. I won't go to lunch . . . or ride to school with him . . . or anything else. The best thing I can do for him is stay as far away as possible. Anyone close to me is in danger.

I should have stuck with The Plan. Distance. No relationships. No friends. Definitely no boyfriends. The Plan was in place for a reason.

More and more details from that night at Brandon's house have been flooding in. One minute I'm staring at the chalkboard, the next I'm back in that room. I'm remembering weird things, like the vase of flowers that flew off the desk when Mr. Price and Scar Face started fighting.

I still can't figure out why I was even there that night. That's bugged me all morning.

While my English lit teacher drones on about *Macbeth,* I squeeze my eyes shut and start at the beginning: walking up the steps at Elle's house, petting the dog, and Laura's high-pitched laugh while she made fun of me to Brandon. Oh, God, Laura! She told Brandon she would meet him at his house. Was she there?

I rack my brain, but I can't pull up a single memory of Laura at his house that night.

I know I went to that sophomore's party and wanted nothing more than to get drunk and forget about what happened.

I run my hands through my hair as the party gets a little clearer.

After downing a few beers I decided to confront Laura and Brandon. I didn't care anymore what they thought of me. I knew they'd be at Brandon's, so that's where I went. I remember stumbling across the lawn, tripping over the garden hose by the back door. I wanted to surprise them, so I didn't knock, just tiptoed in through the kitchen. The house was dark. And quiet.

But they weren't upstairs, so I expanded my search downstairs, wandering into Mr. Price's office, and saw him behind his desk. After that, my memory gets hazy. He was doing something. Lifting something big, or maybe moving it—I can't remember. I heard someone coming down the hall, so I dove behind the couch. Everything seemed wrong all of a sudden—like I knew I shouldn't be there—so I hid. A few minutes later, Scar Face entered the room and he scared the crap out of me. No way was I coming out after I saw him. I decided to wait them out.

And then all hell broke loose.

The bell rings, ending class, and I'm happy to be pulled out of my thoughts. I have to shut my mind down for a while. I'm overwhelmed with the influx of information over the last twenty-four hours and completely numb at this point. I slide a note into Ethan's locker and hide in the deserted stairwell when the bell rings for lunch. I need to end things with him—push him away to keep him safe—but I can't handle that right now. And I can't act like everything is fine either.

Catherine finds me after lunch and drags me into the girls' bathroom with her.

"What happened last night? I checked in late to school and then you were a no-show for lunch. Girl, you had me worried."

"I don't know. Just got a little scared."

She steps up to the sink, digging around in her purse. She pulls out three different tubes of lip gloss before deciding which one she wants. She hands one of the other tubes to me. "This one will look great on you."

I take the tube from her and stare down at it. "Thanks."

Catherine applies the gloss and smacks her lips together a few times. "You looked great Friday night. Ethan couldn't keep his eyes off of you. And you should have seen him at lunch—lost without you. So what's up with being Mrs. Frump at school?"

I blush slightly, shrugging my shoulders. I know how bad I look today. I spent half the night riding through the woods and the other half sleeping on the cold concrete floor of the laundry room.

I hand the gloss back to Catherine without ever applying any. I've got to push her away, too—Ethan isn't the only one in danger just for being with me.

"Meg, he's all yours if you want him, you know," she says.

I nod. Wanting him is so not the problem. But after last night, I don't believe there's a chance in hell there could ever be a future for us, at least not while Scar Face is after me.

Chapter 18

RULES FOR DISAPPEARING
BY WITNESS PROTECTION PRISONER #18A7R04M:

You can only disappear successfully if you know who you need to disappear from.

I scrub the counter at Pearl's, trying not to glance at the clock. Fifteen minutes to eight. Ethan didn't come in today. He told me in Health that he was going to check on Bandit, then head to the farm. He was more worried than pissed that I stood him up for lunch, and his concern for me is going to make what I have to do that much harder.

I've been plagued all day with thoughts about how to break things off with him, and there's no way to avoid it any longer. I have to do it tonight. But that doesn't solve the more serious problem I have—someone wants me dead.

Assuming Scar Face is the one after me, these are my main questions that I can't work out:

1. Why did my parents hide the reason we are in Witness Protection?
2. Why didn't the suits force me to get some sort of help to get my memory back?

3. Who is Scar Face and what are the ledgers he kept screaming about?
4. What's in the ledgers that is so important that Mr. Price and Brandon had to die?
5. Who was Dad talking to in the laundry room? He asked *"What happens if I can't find it?"* What is *it*? Is *it* the ledgers? Is he helping Scar Face now?
6. What about all the crazy things that have been happening to me lately? Feeling like I'm being followed, that night in the laundry room, my missing journal, my open go-bag, the man who called Pearl's . . . Is someone out there screwing with me or am I completely losing my mind?

"Meg, you're gonna rub a hole in that counter you keep scrubbing it like that." Pearl is watching me.

"Sorry," I mumble.

"We're done for the night. Let's shut 'er down."

Since I've already cleaned the front dining area, I only have to close up the register and turn out the lights.

Pearl's fumbling with her keys. "Forgot to tell you. Ethan called earlier. He should be here any minute."

As soon as the words are out of her mouth, he pulls up to the curb.

I prepare myself for what needs to be done, and hope to hell it doesn't hurt as bad as I think it will.

I meet him in the doorway and he grabs my go-bag. It's not lost on me that he's the only other person besides Teeny that I've allowed to carry this bag.

Once we're in the truck he says, "I checked on Bandit. He's doing great. One more night at the vet and he's home."

He grins at me. I look at that dimple and those blue eyes, and it kills me knowing I have to let him go. My nerves turn to gripping tension in my back and neck.

It's now or never.

"Stop the truck. Pull over."

Ethan glances at me with a weird expression, but pulls the truck over. We're halfway between Pearl's and my house.

"What's wrong? You have that look."

I turn to face him. "I can't do this."

He throws his head back against the seat in disgust. "I've been waiting for this." He blows out a deep breath.

"Waiting for what?" I'm surprised by his reaction. I was all geared up to pick a fight—to be rude to him—but he's frustrated with me?

"For *this*. For you to find some reason to push me away. Like you did when we first met. I've seen this brewing ever since I found out your real name."

"You don't know what you're talking about." Okay, obviously I'm the easiest person to read.

He turns and pulls me in close. "Look, I get it. You've got some serious shit going on. I promised I wouldn't say anything, and I haven't. I like you. I like being with you. You can trust me."

Dying to say the things I can't, I bite my tongue, and as hard as it is, I pull away from him.

"You know what? I can't do this anymore either," he says.

I suck in my breath as if I've been punched. Even though this is what needs to happen, I wasn't expecting him to be the one to do it. He hears me but goes on anyway. "When your guard is down, you're the coolest girl I've ever met. It makes me feel good just to be with you, even though there's a ton of shit you refuse to tell me. But then I'm worried all the time that I'm gonna push you too hard, too fast, and you're gonna run the opposite way."

I grab my bag off the floor of the truck and yank open the door. "Well, great. That makes this easy, then." I dart from the truck, not stopping until I reach my house. I collapse just inside the door, breathing hard after running with my bag, and every inch of my body hurts. I'm exhausted. And scared. And all alone. I got exactly what I wanted, but it still hurts like hell.

I do not want to see my parents. I tiptoe in and notice the light on in our room. My parents' door is shut, but I hear them fighting from behind it. Teeny's on her bed, reading.

"Hey. You're home."

"Yeah. Is everything okay?" I nod toward Mom and Dad's room.

"They've been fighting since Dad brought me home from Pearl's. What's wrong with your eyes?"

"My contacts are messed up." I don't want Teeny to know what happened between Ethan and me. In the bathroom, I hear my parents through the wall, but can't make out what they're saying.

I turn the shower on to drown out the sound, then close the door and lock it. I can't handle hearing anything else right now. I wish I could forget everything again. It's all so screwed up.

Ethan's face fills my head. Images from the last week—at Pearl's, when we slow danced, at the movies. Next to the river when he told me I'd gotten in his head. Kissing him on the ATV.

I cut the water off and head back to our room, dress, and grab my go-bag.

"Sissy, where are you going?" Teeny looks worried.

"I'll be right back."

"You're leaving?" Her tone turns hysterical.

"I'm going down to the laundry room for a minute. I need to wash something for school tomorrow. I'll be right back."

I'm going to the laundry room but not to wash clothes. I have a call to make. I'm still scared shitless of that room, but I need to make a call in private. I grab a can of wasp spray from the kitchen, just in case someone is down there again, and head out the door.

I take a deep breath and feel along the side of the wall for the light switch. My fingers brush against it and I flip the lights on. Bright industrial light floods the room, and it blinds me for a moment.

I try not to think too hard about what I'm about to do. I need to talk to him. I dig in my bag for the number and head to the pay phone. I throw some quarters in the slot.

He answers on the second ring.

"Agent Thomas, we need to talk."

Chapter 19

RULES FOR DISAPPEARING
BY WITNESS PROTECTION PRISONER #18A7R04M:

Don't forget who is a friend and who is a foe. And don't forget, sometimes a person can be both.

THE wait for Agent Thomas to show up is excruciating. The only sound in the laundry room is the constant *drip, drip, drip* from the leaky faucet. I'm nervous about what I'm going to say to him, but not enough to back out. The door opens slightly and he walks in.

"I was surprised when you called. Do your parents know you're down here?"

He picks up the chair next to me, moving it so we sit facing each other. Even at ten at night he's dressed in a suit, without a wrinkle on him.

I ignore his question and ask my own. "Who's after us?"

His forehead creases. "I don't understand." He has an odd expression. His arms cross as he leans forward in his chair.

"Who's. After. Us? It's not a difficult question. We are in Witness Protection for a reason. Someone wants my dad dead. Who is it?" There's no way I'm telling a suit I have my memory back before I have a chance to talk to Dad, but I also want to know how far I can push Agent Thomas to talk.

"That information is unavailable to you."

"So what happens if I leave the program? Will someone try to get me?"

"I thought we discussed this in the coffee shop."

"No. In the coffee shop I asked a hypothetical question, and you answered it. Right now, I am asking you point-blank: what happens if I leave the program? Big difference."

"What's happened?"

I sit up straighter. "Nothing."

"Nothing. You just decide in the middle of the night to call me to talk about leaving. I'm not buying it. Did something happen with your mom?"

"No. She's fine."

"Did you figure out what happened to get your family in Witness Protection?"

Shaky ground. My heart is pounding.

"No. I still have no idea what he did." This is such bullshit. I try to keep the emotion out of my voice. It all boils down to who can bluff who better.

Agent Thomas sits back in his chair. He's assessing me.

"Have you thought about it like I suggested?"

Oh, shit. He wants me to figure it out. "Yes. I thought about it. I thought back months before we left. Nothing. I got nothing."

"Why do you want out? I will not even consider discussing this until you tell me what's going on."

I lean my head against the wall. "I'm tired." Tears roll down my face and I can't make them stop. "I'm exhausted. I don't want to lie anymore. I don't want to act like someone I'm not. I want to stop running. This is killing my family." This is all true, no matter what else I know about the situation.

Agent Thomas hands me a handkerchief from inside his jacket. Who even carries those anymore? I take it from him and mop up my eyes.

"You have no idea what kind of trouble you'll be walking into if you leave on your own. We don't open this program to people unless it is absolutely necessary to ensure their safety and well-being. I cannot tell you who is out there looking for your family, but I can tell you it is no one you ever want to meet."

I let all the air out and slump down in my chair.

"Remember what we talked about. If you have to be relocated again, it won't be to another identity. I don't know what's running through your head, but that means no more school, no more job, no more parties or movies."

My blood runs cold when he says parties and movies. They're watching me closer than I realize.

"After the trial, we won't force you to stay. But I wouldn't recommend going off on your own at that point." Agent Thomas leans forward on his knees.

"What if Dad decides not to testify? What then?" Maybe if I refuse to testify, no one will want to hunt me down.

Agent Thomas is tight-lipped for a moment. "That's not really an option."

I pull my knees up and lay my head down on them. We sit in silence another few minutes.

"Is this about a boy?" Agent Thomas asks, his tone much softer.

My head pops up. "No. This is not about a boy."

Studying me, he sits back. It's like I'm something under a microscope.

"I see this often in girls your age who are in the program. They meet some boy and they're ready to give it all up. You're young. This will pass."

I roll my eyes. I hate nothing more than a condescending adult. "Whatever. If that's all the help you can give me, then we're done here."

"Don't forget to put your contacts back in if you leave the house again."

I want to flip him off, but instead I grab my bag and storm out of the room.

I crack the door to my parents' room and tread softly to my dad's side of the bed. He jolts up after I tap him on the shoulder.

"Sissy, what's wrong?"

"I need to talk to you," I whisper.

He stumbles out of bed. Once we're in the hall, I motion for him to follow me. There is no way I can make any sort of plan without knowing the full truth of what happened that night.

We step outside and sit on the steps.

Dad rubs his eyes a few times, then lets out a big yawn. I clench my jaw, fighting the panic rising in me.

"Dad, I remember."

His head snaps up.

"We're here because of what I saw. I remember about Mr. Price." I take a deep breath and say, "And Brandon. Is that why we're being protected?"

His face goes pale and his shoulders slump. "I never wanted you to remember. I wished you thought it was me forever, just so you didn't have to remember."

Seeing him deflate is like a knife to the gut. I move up the stairs and throw myself in his arms. "Daddy, I'm so sorry. I'm sorry I've been so horrible to you. I'm sorry I was there. That I saw it."

He hugs me tight. "No, don't be sorry. You had no idea what he was involved in. None of us did." He moves me to the step under his. We sit facing each other. "Tell me what you remember."

The flashes set off in my brain once more. I tell him everything, about hiding behind the couch, Scar Face shooting Mr. Price and then Brandon. That I can't remember anything past watching Brandon's body hit the floor.

His forehead pinches together. "Are you sure there's nothing else? Nothing at all you remember while you were in that office?"

"No, Dad, that's it. Please tell me what you know. I'm ready."

Dad lets out a deep breath. "I don't know, Sissy."

"This is about me. If you know something, then tell me. You may have thought you were doing the right thing, keeping me in the dark, but you weren't. I need to know everything I can."

He waits forever. "I only know what the agents have told me. The man with the scar is Eduardo Sanchez. He's a big client of our accounting firm, and Price was his CPA. The FBI tells me that they've been watching Sanchez for years. On the surface, he has some import/export business, but they say he really works for a drug cartel out of Mexico, smuggling drugs into the States and laundering their money through his fake business. Price was helping him do it."

"But why would Sanchez kill Mr. Price if he was helping him?" This is insane. I can't believe Brandon's dad was into something as horrible as this.

"Because Price was close to making a deal with the Feds—immunity for turning over all accounting records that could convict Sanchez of money laundering, and also showing them how the cartel moved the drugs and money. But Sanchez must have figured out what Price was doing—Price called one of the agents earlier that day saying he was scared Sanchez was on to him. Price agreed to meet with agents the next morning, turn over the evidence, and enter protective custody."

Dad takes a deep breath before continuing. "But that night a neighbor called nine-one-one saying they heard gunfire, so officers were sent to his house. Price was dead. So was his son. And you were a wreck, hiding behind the couch. The police who showed up on the scene said you were mumbling things about a man with a scar, the ledgers, the fighting, the gunshots . . . The Feds couldn't find any accounting information tied to Sanchez, and they couldn't connect Sanchez to Price and Brandon's murder. But they had you and they knew you witnessed what happened in that room so we were the ones who entered protective custody instead."

My stomach drops.

Dad's face looks grim. "The man with the scar, did he see you? From what you were saying to the police at Price's house, they believe he knew you were in the room somehow."

I take a second to search the foggy parts in my brain. "Uh . . . I don't *think* so. No."

Dad runs his hand over my head. "Sissy, I've been dealing with these agents for months. At first they weren't sure I wasn't involved. I've pored over every account the firm had, looking for anything that may help them."

I shake my head, still confused. "There has to be something, other than me, to get this guy. What about the gun? Surely he left some fingerprints or something?" This can't rest solely on me. It just can't.

Dad's voice gets rough and he puts his hands over his face. "They never found the gun, and they went over every inch of that house. It was clean."

This is a nightmare.

"I don't get it, Dad. Why did I forget all of this? Why can I only remember part of it now? Why is everyone just sitting around waiting for me to remember? Why not hypnotize me or get me into counseling?" A million questions form on my tongue.

"By the time they brought you home from Price's house, you were like a zombie. Counselors came in and they talked to you for hours, trying to get you to open up but—nothing. There was just a blank expression on your face. They called it dissociative amnesia. It was too much for you to handle, so you blocked it out."

I must look completely freaked out, because Dad starts squeezing my hands. "Sissy, why were you there that night? If one thing has been killing me this entire time, it's wanting to know that." I tell him about what happened with my friends, leaving out some of the more humiliating details. And the drinking.

"But I still don't understand. Why didn't they do something to help me remember?" I try to keep the hysteria from my voice. Dad watches me for a few minutes.

"Because I wouldn't let them," he says finally.

My dad's a hard-ass, but I'm pretty impressed he could hold off the FBI. My eyes get huge, begging him to keep going.

"I didn't want you to remember. If you could testify, you would have had an even bigger target on your back. The case's head FBI agent is on my side. Agent Williams said the courts are throwing out testimony from witnesses when their memories had been restored through hypnosis or any other therapy like that. They're saying it's too easy to place false memories in that kind of situation. He didn't want to risk this case on that argument, so the Feds are waiting you out. The counselors said your memory should come back."

Small beads of sweat break out on my forehead, and my stomach is rolling. It's getting hard to breathe. "So what does this mean now?"

Dad shakes his head. "I don't know. We don't have to tell them you remember. The prosecutors keep pressuring me to at least put you back in counseling. I can hold them off a while longer, but I don't want you to testify. Sanchez is connected to some pretty dangerous people. The Feds want Sanchez bad. If they can get him on the murders, they've got something to work with. They'll offer to take the death penalty off the table, or something like that, if he supplies them with all the ins and outs of the cartel's drug-smuggling operation. Right now, he's not talking."

"So who are the suits protecting us from? Sanchez?" I ask.

"Not him, personally. The Feds have men watching him back home. It's probably someone who works for him. Or someone who works for the cartel in Mexico. They have as much riding on your silence as Sanchez does," he answers.

I stare out into the darkness, wishing there was some way to go back and forget everything I learned. "So if they know I can testify, they may come after me even harder to shut me up."

Dad pulls me in close, hugging me hard. "They've been trying to make a case with the drug smuggling and money laundering, but they're not having much luck without Price. I've been through the books a thousand times, and I can't find anything. I told them Price was a paranoid bastard. Didn't trust computers. Didn't trust anybody." He beats on the step with his fist. "Price had to keep a set of books, something that tracks where the money goes. A list of dummy accounts or fake fronts. Bank account numbers. Overseas transfers. It's too complicated not to have a record of that. There has to be a paper trail somewhere. But I can't find it. The Feds tore the office apart and even his house. They found nothing."

The ledgers! I flash back to the night at Mr. Price's house. My head starts spinning. "Dad, there was something about ledgers. Sanchez and Price were arguing about it."

"I knew it! Did you see them? Do you know where they are?"

"No." I feel helpless.

He pulls my face up to meet his. "Are you sure? This is really important."

His expression is freaking me out even more. "No. That Sanchez guy kept screaming, 'Where are the ledgers?' at Mr. Price. But he wouldn't tell him."

"Promise me, Sissy, if you remember anything about where the ledgers are, you have to tell me right away. Come to me first, okay?"

I take two quick breaths. "Is that what you were talking about on the phone in the laundry room the other night? The ledgers?"

He drops his hands. "Were you listening to me?"

I nod. "I saw you go in. I went around back."

He leans against the step.

"Dad, who were you talking to?"

Dad pulls me in close. "No. You shouldn't have been listening. You let me worry about this." He leans back. "Just promise you'll tell me if you remember anything at all. No matter how small it is."

"Are you trying to find the ledgers so you can turn them over to Sanchez? Because that's what it sounded like."

He looks pissed. And guilty, so I know I'm right. "You have no idea how ruthless these people are. I'm scared to death every day that something will happen to you or Teeny." He looks away from me. "The Feds and their case are not my problem. He killed Price's son, for God's sake. This man is an animal. All I care about is this family, and I know the Feds can't protect us. The man I was on the phone with called me first. I was at work." Dad bangs his hand against the railing of the steps. "They know where we are. They've always known where we are. He said he'd let us go if I hand over any evidence the Feds could use against them. Said if I told the Feds, he'd know and he'd kill us all."

I feel dizzy. "Why do they think we have any evidence to turn over?" I ask, my voice cracking.

Dad's shoulders slump and all of a sudden he looks old. And tired. "I don't know. That's what's been driving me crazy ever since we got to Natchitoches. The man on the phone is *convinced* you know where the ledgers are. I keep telling him you don't remember anything, but he doesn't believe me. But I'll promise you this—if I did have any evidence, I wouldn't give it to the Feds. I'd use it as leverage to get this bastard to leave my family alone."

I slump back against the stair railing and can't breathe. I feel like I'm falling. Dad shakes me and hits me on the back until I'm finally able to suck in some oxygen. His worried face looms over mine, and it's a few minutes before I'm able to speak.

"Oh my God, Dad, I think I know what he's talking about." I take a few deep gulps of air and say, "That man—Sanchez—he did see me. After he shot Brandon, he must have heard me cry out or something, because all of a sudden he was there. Standing over me. With the gun in his hand."

These new memories come rushing in as fast as the ones last night. And just like that—I'm back in that room. Brandon is dead. And I know I'm next. It's quiet, so I hold my breath, praying he won't find me. I hear footsteps—they echo off the hardwood floor—and I brace myself for what's coming. And pray it doesn't hurt.

I clear my head, bringing myself back to the present. God, I was terrified. I knew I was dead—there was no way he would let me live—not after what he did to Brandon.

"Sissy, calm down. Think. You have to tell me what you remember." Dad is shaking me, probably harder than he realizes, and I put my hand on his to make him stop.

"I lied to him. And now he believes me and that's why he's after me." I break down and sob against Dad's chest. He holds me close, stroking my back.

"You're not making sense, Sissy. Tell me what happened."

I hiccup and use his shirt to wipe my eyes. "He didn't say

anything at first. He pointed the gun at me, and I just blurted out, 'I know where the ledgers are!' He must have believed me, because he lowered the gun and asked where they were."

Dad leans back and asks, "Do you? Know where they are?"

"No!" I'm crying again. "I just said that so he wouldn't kill me. I knew that's what he wanted, so that's the first thing that came out of my mouth. Then we heard the sirens. He just looked at me kind of funny for a few seconds, then ran off."

Dad brings me back into the house and rubs his hands across my back in a calming rhythmic motion and says, "I'm so glad you said what you did. That's probably the only reason he didn't kill you that night, and the only reason you're still alive today. He needs the ledgers more than he needed you dead."

"Maybe we should tell the suits." I'm shaking. This is so much worse than I expected.

"Sissy, if I thought that would make us safe, I'd have gone to them the minute that man called the factory." He waits a moment before continuing. "He knew every town we'd been to and every name we used. We're going to keep this to ourselves until I can figure something out. If you remember anything else—come to me immediately. This is the only way."

I lay my head on his shoulder, and he holds me while the tears pour out.

Chapter 20

RULES FOR DISAPPEARING
BY WITNESS PROTECTION PRISONER #18A7R04M:

There's a time to cut and run. There's a time to stay and fight. The most important time is to know when to make this decision.

THE nightmare was horrible last night. It's worse because now I know it's real. Now the colors are more vivid. The noises are louder, the dark is darker, the fear is stronger.

In our tiny bathroom, I stare at my reflection. I look like death. My eyes are puffy and red, and my nose is stopped up. I sound as terrible as I look. It's been almost a week since I've left the house. I haven't gone to school. I haven't gone to Pearl's. I haven't gotten dressed.

I wet a washrag and hold the cold cloth to my eyes. I barely sleep anymore, instead I try to remember every detail of that night at Brandon's house. Some parts are still blurry. Every time I feel like I'm getting close, my thoughts scatter. I can't shake the feeling I'm missing something.

Teeny won't go to school either. She doesn't know what's wrong, but she's scared if she leaves me at home like this, I won't be here when she gets back. And she's sunk back into that same horrible quiet shell, just like when we first got here.

I've single-handedly ruined this family.

I'm starting to think I didn't tell Sanchez I knew where the ledgers were just to save my ass. So I have a new plan: find the ledgers. And that plan rests solely on my stupid friggin' memory. The ledgers are the key, but where are they? Every time I think about it I get this pattern in my head. Different shapes—all fitted together. I have that feeling like it's on the tip of my tongue but I can't pull it up. I'm determined to find them, and when I do, Dad and I will have to figure out what to do with them. We just have to make sure we have some guarantee that this is over.

I break it to Teeny that we're going back to school this morning. I must really look bad, because she doesn't complain.

She gets onto her bus just as mine pulls up behind it. I step inside, and Teeny's right: it totally sucks riding the stinky bus to school. I take a seat in the back and resist crying again. A few freshmen look at me, and I want to growl at them.

The bus stops in front of school, expelling us along with a cloud of smoke. I'm second-guessing my decision to come back to school, but I can't feel sorry for myself any longer. The pity party is over.

It doesn't take long for Catherine to spot me. She, like Pearl, has been calling the house every day, but I've brushed them off, telling them my entire family got the flu. She grabs my hand and pulls me to the nearest bathroom.

"Oh, hell no." She digs through her bag. "I don't know what happened to you, but you're not walking into school looking like Mrs. Frump's ugly half sister." She gets out a brush, a clip, and a bottle of hair gel and lines them up on the counter next to the sink. She then unloads a fully stocked makeup bag. "Especially if you and Ethan are over."

"How'd you know?" I shouldn't be in here with her—no one is safe around me—but it feels so nice to have a *normal* moment.

"Ethan told Will. Will told me."

"What did Ethan say?" I don't know why I'm doing this to myself. The sooner I get over him, the better off everyone will be.

Catherine manages to kick my short hair up in the back and pulls the front part to one side in the clip. "Will wants to rent a limo for the Mardi Gras Ball. He asked Ethan last week if y'all wanted to go with us. Ethan said it wasn't working out between y'all. And then you disappeared."

Even now, he's still protecting me.

Catherine keeps working on me, and I get the full face treatment with the makeup, finishing up with a little gloss. She eyes my clothes and shakes her head in disgust. "It's like you're trying to wear the ugliest shit out there."

She pulls the hoodie over my head and has to fix my hair again. "Here, shove this in that big-ass bag of yours."

She digs in her bag and pulls out a soft, black, V-neck sweater. "Put this on."

She also grabs a red-and-black scarf and puts it around my neck, forming it into a low hanging loose knot.

She stands back to survey her work. "Much better. So what happened with Ethan?"

"It's all my fault. I freaked. Everything was kinda moving fast, ya know?"

Catherine looks at me like I've lost my mind. "No. That's the craziest thing I've ever heard. Do you like him?"

I roll my eyes. "It's not that simple." God, if it were only that simple.

"Yes. It is." She holds up her hand when she sees I'm about to protest. "I don't mean to get all up in your business. If you don't want to be with Ethan, fine. But I'm not going to let you walk into this school looking like some bag lady."

I turn and look in the mirror. Unbelievable. And what's even crazier is I feel better. The makeover was like a slap in the face. No more poor, pitiful me moaning and groaning about how sucky my life is. I want a regular life. I want my family safe. I want to be with Ethan. I want to stop running. I even want to stay in this crazy-ass town. And Catherine is right: Mrs. Frump's ugly half sister is not going to be able to accomplish that.

But the old me will.

We both look at the door when it opens. It's the girl with pink stripey hair, and I get a funny feeling. Like déjà vu or something, but I usually only catch her when she's leaving. I never see her when she first gets here.

The girl throws all her stuff down on the floor and starts picking at the wall. I glance at Catherine in the mirror. Catherine mouths the word *loser* and shakes her head. The girl goes about her business, unconcerned that the two of us are watching her. She wiggles a brick out of the wall. It's slow going, and I can't tear my eyes off of her. The brick wall blurs and the pattern makes me dizzy. My mouth gets dry.

Once the brick is loose, she balances it in one hand while shoving a plastic bag into the hole. She turns back and looks at us for the first time.

"If my stash disappears, bet your ass I'll come after you," she says.

Catherine turns around with her hand on her hip. "If I really wanted your stash, I'd have taken it years ago. Everyone knows that's where you hide it."

I lean against the wall near the sink and feel my knees get weak. I stare at the girl as she shoves the brick back into place. But that's not all I'm seeing. Price's image is superimposed on top of hers. I can see him . . . shoving something into the stone wall behind his desk.

The bell rings and the girl flees the bathroom.

"What a freak." Catherine stuffs her things back into her bag. She turns to me and her expression changes. "Are you okay?"

I'm close to sliding to the ground, but I manage to hold myself upright. I don't want to fall apart in front of her.

"Yeah, fine. Not feeling a hundred percent yet," I manage to squeak out.

Catherine's face scrunches up. "You look pale. Are you sure you're all right?"

I nod. "I'll see you in class."

Catherine leaves the bathroom only after looking back at me a few times first. The second the door shuts, I hit the floor.

Oh. My. God. I know where the ledgers are.

I squeeze my eyes closed and focus on that night. I start at

Brandon's house, combining all the pieces I've recalled over the last week. After I search upstairs, I step inside Mr. Price's office. He's facing the back wall, shoving some thin books inside a small hole, then picks up a stone from his desk and stuffs it into the wall.

Just as the stone slides into place, I hear footsteps and jump behind the couch.

I open my eyes and stare at the bathroom wall where the girl stuffed her drugs.

The ledgers are probably still in the wall in Mr. Price's office.

I sprint out of the bathroom and quickly get to homeroom before the second bell rings. I need time to think, to plan. I slide into a desk in the back, and Ben moves to sit near me.

"I hear you broke poor Landry's heart." And then he bursts out laughing.

I hold up a hand. I'm so done with this. "Quit being an asshole. Whatever it is you've got against Ethan, drop it. Or don't. I don't really give a shit. Just leave me out of it. And leave me out of your little games with Emma. It's getting old."

Ben's eyes get big. He's trying to stutter something out, but nothing makes it past his lips. I glance behind him to the minions watching. "Did you get all that?"

They look shocked, too.

Good.

I turn back to Ben. "About the project. We can get together either tomorrow night or Thursday at Pearl's. You pick. I'll have the packet." I couldn't care less about this, but I've got a plan brewing and I'm hoping in the end we can stay here. At some point, I'll have to salvage what's left of senior year. And hopefully there's something between Ethan and me that can be salvaged, too.

Ben shakes his head and goes back to the seat he was originally sitting in.

I'm on fire. I can't tell Dad I know where they are. He'd never let me go with him. And then, what if the ledgers aren't in there anymore? No, Dad needs to stay with Mom and Teeny. I got us into this, so I'll get us out.

Chapter 21

RULES FOR DISAPPEARING BY WITNESS PROTECTION PRISONER #18A7R04M:

Avoid conflict at all costs. Even if that means letting some bitchy cheerleader get the best of you.

TEENY heads straight to the kitchen when we get to Pearl's. It feels really good to be back. Grabbing a phone book and the cordless phone, I pick a booth close to the front. It's pretty dead this early in the afternoon, so I figure I have a little time to start putting my plan together before we get too busy.

How will I get to Scottsdale? Car, bus, or plane? I call the bus station and the airport to find out how much a ticket back home will be, and how long it will take to get there.

Okay, first problem: no airport or bus station in Natchitoches. I have to get to Shreveport. And then I would have to get back here from Shreveport if, I mean *when*, I recovered the ledgers.

Second problem: Greyhound doesn't require an ID to buy a ticket, but the airlines do. Showing an ID is the sticky part. I don't have a driver's license, but I do have a state-issued ID in Avery Preston's name. I told the suits I lost it when they yanked us out of Florida. I'm a little nervous about using the ID even though a plane would be tons faster. Do the airlines run the name and ID through some system? Will it flag someone in the marshal's office?

It'll take forever to get there by bus. More than a day. I drum my pen on the table and go through my options. I don't have a car. I can't take the station wagon because I have no intention of telling my parents what I'm doing. I hoped to leave on Friday and possibly be back by Monday with ledgers in hand. This is a very ambitious plan, but it's balls to the wall time.

Pearl spots me in the booth when she comes out of the kitchen. I give a ridiculous little wave, and she scrunches her forehead. I'm sure she's wondering why I'm sitting here. She finally walks back to the kitchen.

Third problem: Either by bus or plane, a ticket round trip is over three hundred dollars. I have maybe a hundred and twenty-five in my bag—that includes the paycheck Pearl just gave me. I'm really regretting the splurge on that jacket. I can get some money from Dad, and maybe ask Pearl for an advance on my next check. That won't leave much for when I'm there. I could call Elle or Laura once I get there, but that is a last resort.

Fourth problem: This plan doesn't even take into consideration what I need to do when I actually make it to the Price house. It's not like I can walk up and ring the doorbell. Mr. Price was remarried—would his wife still be living in the house her husband and stepson were killed in?

I drop my head on the table. Every time I think about Brandon and the fact that he's dead, it hurts. Moments later someone slides in the booth in front of me. It's Catherine.

"So, I'm dying to know if Ethan's jaw dropped when he saw you. Dish. I want to know everything."

"Nothing. He hardly looked at me today."

"This is bullshit—y'all belong together." Catherine rubs her hands together and smiles. "We'll figure out a way to work this out. We just need a plan."

She's got no idea.

Catherine claps her hands quickly. "And then we can all go to the ball together."

"I don't know about that. He's pretty pissed off at me." I cringe. I may not even be here next week, much less by the time the ball comes around. And then a lightbulb goes off. "Catherine, do you ever go shopping in Shreveport? Maybe we could cut out early on Friday and have a girls' day."

"Only if we look at dresses, too. I have complete faith y'all will work it out!"

She seems really excited, and we make plans. If there's somewhere we can shop close to downtown, I can get to the bus station. I don't know if I'm gutsy enough to use the ID at the airport. I'll have to tell Catherine something before I ditch her, so she doesn't have the police out looking for me, but I'll cross that bridge when I get to it.

I hate doing this to her, but if everything does work out, I can make it up to her later.

Okay, so I have half of problem one sort of worked out. This is going to take a miracle.

Catherine leaves once customers start walking in. Luckily, a steady stream of business keeps me from obsessing over everything that I haven't figured out yet.

In the front dining area, I spot Teeny cleaning up a table,

unaware of the group of businessmen headed her direction. God, she's been so skittish lately—I hope she doesn't freak when she sees them. She picks up her rag and the cleaning spray bottle, takes one look at the businessmen, all dressed in dark suits and overcoats, and runs out of the back of the store, crying.

Shit. I knew it! She must have thought they were here for her instead of just looking for a place to sit.

Pearl sticks her head out of the kitchen. "What in the world was that?"

I'm in a panic. Teeny is gone, and I need to go get her. I've got a fistful of money from one customer and another couple waiting to place their order. I clear the line in front of me as quickly as I can, then call to Pearl as I run and push open the back door. "I'm sorry, Pearl. Mary ran away; I've got to find her."

"Of course, girlie. Go," she says, concern etched all over her face.

The cold air slams into me. The alley behind Pearl's is empty, and I listen for a moment for Teeny's footsteps, or crying, or anything, but there's nothing. She's only had a few minutes' head start—she's got to be close.

Picking a direction at random, I run toward Front Street. It's dark and cold. And I'm really scared for Teeny right now.

I cover almost all the streets near the river, calling her name. By the time Ethan's truck turns the corner, I can't stop myself from running to it.

"Mary's gone! She ran out of Pearl's and I can't find her. She doesn't have her coat."

I don't realize I'm crying until Ethan brushes a few tears from my cheek. "We'll find her. Hop in."

We cover some of the same ground; I don't know what else to do.

"You don't think she went home?" Ethan asks.

"No." If she thinks those men were agents and she ran from them, there's no way she'd go to the cottage.

"What happened?"

Deep breath. "She got scared. You know things didn't end well for us in Florida. She got upset over something tonight and ran."

Ethan doesn't ask any more questions, and we continue to zig-zag through downtown, yelling her name from the windows.

"There she is!" Ethan yells, then pulls off the street.

Teeny is down by the river, sitting in an empty canoe that's been pulled up on the bank. I don't know how Ethan spotted her; all you can see is the top of her head poking out.

I run to the canoe and pull her out, crushing her in a hug. "Why did you run away? You had me worried to death."

Ethan keeps his distance, and I'm thankful. I need to talk to her without worrying about what he'll hear.

She's shaking and buries herself in my arms. "I saw those men and I thought they would take us away." Her teeth are chattering, so I wrap my coat around her. "You and Mama have been so weird. I thought something bad was happening. I don't want to leave. I like it here," she says.

I drop to the ground and hold her tight, rocking back and forth. I don't know how long we sit here, but Teeny cries it all out, then falls asleep in my arms.

Ethan wanders over and sits down beside me.

"Is she okay?"

I nod and stroke Teeny's hair. "It's just been really hard for her lately." I move my hand to his and squeeze. "Thank you so much for helping me tonight. I don't deserve it."

He lets out a strained laugh and says, "Maybe not, but you know how much I like Mary."

Being with him here, down by the river, makes me ache for the way things were before. It's still not safe for him to be with me, but there are only a few days left before this is over—one way or another. And I'm about to be the most selfish person on Earth, because I want him in my life—even if it's just for a little while.

"I'm sorry, Ethan."

Ethan nods and looks down.

I drop my hand from his. "You know I'm not Meg Jones. There are things going on with . . . my family. Hopefully, very soon I can tell you everything about me. Until then—could you just bear with me? I really want to be your friend."

"Friend? That's it?"

I dare to smile. "I'd actually like to be more than your friend, but I'm afraid to test my luck with you right now."

Ethan scoots in close. "I get it. You've got things going on—things I can't understand—but you have to stop pushing me away. And let me know if you need help. I had to hear about Mary tonight from Pearl."

I squeeze my eyes tight and open them again. "Yes, but no questions about my family. Or anything crazy we may do."

"Okay. So are you gonna get that panicked look when I suggest we go somewhere, like my house?"

I shake my head. "No, but I'm terrified of your sister."

Ethan laughs. "She's all bark, no bite."

He leans in, and I can feel what's coming. He braces himself on his hands, hovering over Teeny's sleeping form, and kisses me softly. It's the sweetest kiss I've ever had.

I struggle with the last thing I want to say to him. It's important I get it right. "If there is ever a time when you are really . . . confused, I want you to know it's out of my control."

"I've been confused since the day I met you."

It's necessary he understands this. "You'll know what I'm talking about when it happens."

He hears the seriousness in my voice and edges closer to me. "You can tell me anything."

I shake my head. "No, I can't. Not right now. But it's not because I don't want to. I just can't. And that has to be okay."

He nods. "Okay. But I have a condition of my own. Loosen up. Whatever's gonna happen is gonna happen."

I smile. "I'll try." He's asking a lot, but he's right. The plan that's ticking around in my head will either work or it won't, but one way or another, this shit is about to end.

Teeny sits on the counter, legs swinging, and waits for Dad. She's clung to me since we found her in that canoe last night, but the last few hours at Pearl's seemed to have loosened her up.

"I don't see why I can't stay and ride home with you," she says.

I finish writing up a to-go order and hand it to her to take to Pearl. "Because you didn't do any of your homework yet. And Dad will want to see you before it's time for bed."

She hops off the counter and takes the slip of paper to Pearl. I'm so worried about her—one minute she seems fine, then the next she's a total mess.

By the time Dad shows, Teeny is less pouty and seems okay with going home. It's probably because Dad told her he picked up some Blue Bell ice cream, her favorite flavor, chocolate chunk, and it was waiting in the car for her.

Ethan comes in right before closing. "Hey."

"Hey." I feel silly. All I want to do is pull him across this counter and kiss him. "Are you hungry?"

His eyes linger on my face. "Starving."

It's been twenty-four hours since we declared peace. And it's been nice, really nice. If I can go through with the plan to retrieve the ledgers just right, this is the last week I will live a lie. After this weekend, no matter what, Ethan will know who I really am and anything else he wants to know about me.

I call his usual back to Pearl while he glances around the room. "Can you come sit with me?"

"Yeah, let me close up back here."

I finish with all the chores that have to be done before we close just as his pizza is ready. Most of the traffic this late is for to-go orders, so the dining area is deserted.

I bring Ethan's pizza out. "Pearl says we can go as soon as you're done."

"Is Mary still here?"

I pinch a piece of crust off. "No, she left with Dad a little while ago."

"Can you hang out, or do you have to go home?" Ethan says, shoving a piece of pizza into his mouth.

I lean against the booth. "I can stay out awhile. What do you have in mind?"

He wiggles his eyebrows. "Wanna go back to my place?"

I giggle at his cheesy line and hit him with one of my own. "Why? Wanna make like a fabric softener and Snuggle?"

He falls back, laughing, then says, "If I told you that you had a great body, would you hold it against me?"

My cheeks get warm, and I rack my brain for another line. He's smiling, dimples and all, and waiting for my comeback. *Oh! Got it!* I move in closer, trying hard for a serious expression, and say, "If I could rearrange the alphabet, I'd put U and I together."

He braces his hands on the table and is inches from my face, eyes twinkling, and asks, "What's a nice girl like you doing in a dirty mind like mine?"

Oh my God. I'm probably blushing to my hairline—my face is on fire. He puts a hand under my chin and pulls me in for a quick kiss, then says, "Let's get out of here. We can hang out at my house. Watch a movie, whatever."

It's the way he says "whatever" that really gets my heart racing. Ethan packs up his barely eaten pizza while I call home to say I'll be late. We're both rushing to get out of here.

All the warm and fuzzy feelings evaporate when we pull away from Pearl's and I spot a black Suburban in the side mirror. I don't know if it's the same one from the other night. Cars in Louisiana don't have to have a license plate on the front, so I've yet to see a number. It stays behind us all the way to Ethan's house but doesn't seem to slow down—it just continues to drive down the street. I hate this! Is it real or all in my head?

I try to shake it off as we walk in the back door of Ethan's house. His parents are sitting at the kitchen table, going over some paperwork. My palms sweat, but I resist the urge to dry them on my jeans. The last time I saw Mr. Landry I was lying on the ground in the middle of the woods. After being in school all day and then working all evening, I'm sure I look rough. Probably stink like pizza, too.

"Mom, this is Meg Jones. Meg, you know my dad."

Ethan's mom stands up quickly and walks toward us.

"Meg, so nice to meet you." She holds her hand out to shake mine.

Mr. Landry shakes my hand after I finish with his wife's. "Yes, Meg, nice to see you again. I hope you've recovered from the excitement the other evening."

I force a laugh and say, "Yes, I'm much better."

Mrs. Landry playfully slaps her husband's arm. "Meg, you're a real trouper for going out there with that group. I've been once and that was enough to last me a lifetime," she says, her accent very soft and very Southern.

"We're gonna go watch a movie, so we'll see y'all later." Ethan drags me through the back door of the kitchen as I mumble a goodbye. We follow a cobblestone path through the yard, which leads to a small building in the back, then walk up a set of stairs on the outside wall that leads to a single door. Inside is a large room. It has a bed against one side, a couch in the middle, and a ridiculously big flat-screen TV mounted on the wall. There are clothes everywhere, covering almost every surface.

"Sorry it's so messy in here right now. I guess I should have cleaned up before I asked you to come over."

"Do you live up here?" I turn around in the room and see another table against a wall that has a minifridge, a microwave, and a small coffeepot. There's an open door on the other side of the table leading to the bathroom. How cool is this? It's like Ethan has his own apartment.

"Yeah, my parents let me move up here at the beginning of the school year."

He pulls me to the couch, and I sink down on it with him. I want him to kiss me again, but he looks down at the go-bag, which I dropped at my feet.

"Is your backpack one of those off-limits topics?"

I nod and change the subject. "Why do you and Ben hate each other now? Catherine told me a little about it, but I still don't get it."

We lay side by side with my head resting on his upper arm. "So, you get to ask me personal stuff, huh?"

"Yes, new rule: I can ask you anything, and you have to answer." Teasing him, I poke him gently in the ribs.

He rubs his hand up and down my arm. "Everything got screwed up a few years ago. Our dads used to be partners, but they had a falling out. My dad wanted to update all the equipment, change the way some things are done—ya know—catch up to modern day. But Ben's dad is old school. Doesn't like change, so they decided to split ways. It was fine at first, until my dad partnered with Will's dad. They feel the same way about that stuff, and it was a good fit. Plus, Will's dad has the farm on the other side of us. Ben's dad didn't like that."

"So this is why you and Ben fight?" It seems like the dads' problem, not theirs.

"Things were weird at first, but it wasn't until last summer that it got bad with Ben. His dad is about to go broke. He never had to handle the money or take care of any bills—my dad did all that stuff. He'll probably have to sell his farm, and we're the only ones around who could buy it. Ben blames us, says we cheated them. Says Dad split ways knowing this would happen and we would end up with their land." He plays with my fingers.

"Where does Emma fit in with this?" I lock my fingers in his.

"She doesn't believe Dad did anything wrong, but she also isn't trying to convince Ben he's wrong either. What sucks is we were so close before all this shit happened. I know she feels like she's caught in the middle, but she could make things easier if she tried to talk to Ben about it."

I brush a fat curl away from his eye. "My sister and I are close. It would suck if that changed." I bite my lip, hesitating to take this close to home. "I have another question."

Ethan turns his face to mine. "Shoot."

"How far can you get from one of those collars you use for the bay dog and still have the GPS work?" I know this is out of the blue, but I couldn't think of any way to randomly bring it up.

He leans back, looking at me funny. "Where'd that come from?"

I shrug. "Just curious. Been thinking about it."

He looks up to the ceiling like he's trying to figure it out. "I don't know—maybe a mile and a half."

I slump down in my seat. "That's all?"

He looks at me with a confused expression. "Yeah, with those, but Dad's got a tracker. You can stick it on anything and pull its location up on the computer."

This perks me up. "From anywhere?"

"Pretty much. He has a bay dog that would damn near run to Texas looking for a hog. He'd get too far ahead of us, and we almost lost him once. Dad uses the tracker for him."

"How long does the battery last?" I hope I'm making these questions seem somewhat conversational.

"Depends on what it's set for. On demand recall, the battery could last maybe a week."

This is the hard part. "Can I borrow it?"

He turns so we're facing each other on the couch. "What's this about? What's going on?"

I lick my lips and take a deep breath. I want to bring the tracker with me. I really don't have a death wish. I'm hoping if something goes wrong, Ethan can lead the suits to where I am. I'm going to have to involve him more than I want, and I hate that. "I want to find out where my mom goes during the day. She's not going to work, and I think she's drinking too much."

Ethan runs a hand through my hair. "Sure. If you had a smart phone, I could download the app for you. Do you have a computer at home?"

I nod and answer, "Yes." Another little lie. "Can anyone track it, or do I need something special?"

"You need the code for that transmitter. What are you gonna do, drop it in her purse?" he asks.

"Yeah. Or her coat pocket."

He runs his thumb over my lip. "Tell me one thing about you. Just one thing I don't already know."

I want to tell him something real, not something written on the sheet I've got in the safe house.

"I have a small tattoo on my left shoulder. It's tiny."

Ethan wiggles his eyebrows. "Well, you know I have to see it now."

I roll over on my side and he pulls my shirt down to expose my shoulder, uncovering a small, single daisy on a stem. This makes the list as one of those things the suits don't want me to share with anyone else, because it's an "identifying marker."

Well, screw them.

"Why did you pick that flower? Does it mean something?"

"The daisy? Not really. Back home, a bunch of my friends and I decided to get tattoos. I was really kinda hoping everyone would chicken out, but they didn't. There was a huge board with thousands of designs to pick from. It was almost more than I could take in. But my eye kept coming back to this little daisy. It was so small and cute and was surrounded by all of these other really weird things. I don't know, I just liked it."

Ethan leans down and kisses the daisy. Then moves up from my shoulder and kisses the curve of my neck. Then moves a little higher to the underside of my jaw.

Every time his lips touch my skin, chills rise through me. We haven't kissed, really kissed, since that night in the woods on the ATV. The anticipation is killing me. By the time we're face to face, I don't know who moves in first, but we're fused together, his hands in my hair, my hands curled around his back, and it feels good. Really good.

With him, like this, I hate all the secrets. I pull away, and we stare at each other. I am going to tell him. Everything.

I open my mouth, ready to spill it all, when the door to his room flies open. We're both startled, and I would have fallen off the couch if Ethan hadn't had his arm around my waist. Archenemy is standing in the doorway.

"I was hoping like hell it wasn't her when Mom said you had a girl up here. I mean, my God. She's friggin' everywhere I go now." Emma has both hands on her hips, fuming.

Ethan jumps up from the couch and walks slowly to the door. Emma starts backing up, tripping over clothes on the floor. When he gets to the door, he doesn't say a word—just slams it shut in her face. He stares at the door for a moment before turning back to me.

"I'm sorry my sister is such a pain in the ass."

"It's fine. I'm an easy target." I stand up, grabbing my go-bag. "If you think she's left already, could you go ahead and take me home?"

Ethan puts his arms around me. "I'm really sorry."

"I know—we can't help how our family acts." How well I do know this. "She's not the only reason I need to go, but it's late and I have to start all over tomorrow. I'm exhausted."

The truth is I'm glad Emma busted into the room. I was seconds from telling Ethan everything, and that would have been the stupidest thing I could have done.

He grabs my go-bag and we head out of his room.

Chapter 22

RULES FOR DISAPPEARING BY WITNESS PROTECTION PRISONER #18A7R04M:

Be paranoid. The best way for the bad guys not to get you is to think the bad guys are always just about to get you.

I feel better this morning than I have in months. I take extra care with my hair and makeup and wear the cute jacket I bought on Front Street. I loathe putting in the contacts. I'm really resenting the things that aren't the real me.

Mom is up surprisingly bright and early. She's making eggs and bacon when I walk into the kitchen.

I eye her warily, not trusting the change in her this morning. I have no faith in this bout of sobriety.

"Good morning. Can I get you some breakfast?" She's making me nervous with the Martha Stewart act. At least she hasn't shown any indication that she remembers spilling the beans.

"No, I'll grab a granola bar."

Teeny laps up her attention this morning. Part of me wishes Mom wouldn't have these moments. It makes it so much worse when she does fall off the wagon again. Mom and Teeny chat awhile at the table as I watch from the counter. All Teeny can talk about is Pearl and the pizza parlor.

Mom looks toward me. "I'm here when Teeny gets home. She doesn't have to go to work with you every day."

She's jealous, listening to Teeny go on and on about Pearl.

Before Teeny can speak, I answer, "No, she likes coming up there. We have a good routine going." I gesture toward the door. "Let's go, Teeny. Ethan's probably waiting outside for us."

Mom stands up from the table. "Who's Ethan?"

This time Teeny beats me to the answer. "It's her boyfriend." She says this in a singsong voice, hoping to embarrass me with the word "boyfriend."

"Really, you have a boyfriend?" Pure sadness is etched all over Mom's face.

"Yeah, I guess you could call him that."

I grab my go-bag and Teeny's backpack as we leave. Ethan is waiting in the parking lot, and Teeny runs to the truck. I must look like a fool, but I can't help the huge smile plastered across my face.

"Hey, Ethan!" Teeny squeals when she hops inside. "I told my mom that you're Meg's boyfriend." She dissolves into laughter in the backseat.

Ethan tickles her. "You did, huh? But I thought *you* were my girlfriend."

Teeny laughs even harder. I love to see her like this.

I have butterflies when we pull into the parking lot. Things feel different today. Good, but different. We walk with our hands locked together. A few casual glances, but nothing I'm not used to.

I part with Ethan and walk into homeroom. Ben plops down in a seat near me, smirking. "Emma said she caught y'all together last night."

My cheeks burn. "I'm sure she made it sound a lot worse than it really was."

He laughs. "Look, Meg, We've got to work on that stupid project tonight. Coach moved practice, and this is the only free time I've got."

"Okay. Let me see what I can work out with Pearl."

Ben scratches his number on a piece of paper, then hands it to me. "Call me when you know what time will be good." This Ben is so much better—I should have told him off weeks ago.

I meet up with Ethan in the hall, headed to first period. "Ben and I have to work on the project tonight. He has practice tomorrow. I guess I'll get him to come to Pearl's. Do you think she'll care if we work on it there?"

"Why don't you talk to Pearl, see if you can get off early? Then y'all can come work at our house. Emma and I haven't done ours either."

I'm relieved. I can't say I was really looking forward to hanging out with Ben alone. "That sounds great."

Ethan pecks me on the cheek. "See ya after class."

Pearl's is packed. Ethan arrives just before the rush and offers to help out before we need to leave for his house.

Teeny's busy in the back. She's gotten so good at making pizzas that customers are requesting the girl who makes pictures with the toppings.

I ask Pearl if I can talk to her in private.

She shuts the door once we're inside her office and asks, "Whatcha need, girl? Got pizzas in the oven."

"I have two favors to ask. I would like Friday off, and I was hoping I could get my paycheck early. My friend Catherine and I want to go shopping in Shreveport to look for dresses for the school dance."

"Girl, you coulda asked me that in the kitchen. That's fine. I'll have your check ready tomorrow."

I look at the ground. "I didn't want to mention it in front of Ethan because he hasn't officially asked me to go with him yet."

"You kids are crazy." She chuckles, then asks, "Is that it?"

"Oh, can I get off a little early tonight to work on a school project?" This third request may be pushing it.

"I reckon," she answers and heads back to the kitchen.

I leave the office without making eye contact with Ethan. Even though it's all a charade going to Shreveport, I feel guilty for lying about the dance.

I stop dead when I see Agent Thomas at the counter. I glance back at Teeny, but she's oblivious to his presence. Thank God! I couldn't handle another meltdown from her tonight.

Forcing my feet to travel the remaining distance to the counter, I ask, "Can I help you?"

"One large pizza with everything. To go." He hands me the money, and I ring up his order.

"I wanted to check on you. Make sure you were feeling better after you missed so many days of school."

I glance behind me one more time to make sure Teeny hasn't noticed him yet. "What's there to feel better about? My life sucks. It will always suck as long as I have to live like this." I lean toward him, not wanting anyone else to catch our conversation. "I will tell you this: I'm not gonna hide forever. And if that gets me killed, so be it. At least I won't have to spend the rest of my life being scared of what might happen."

I'm not sure what possessed me to tell him all of that, but I feel better actually saying it out loud to another human being.

And surprisingly, Agent Thomas lets out a soft chuckle. "All that nerve and courage. Both are good in small doses. I hope you don't do anything impulsive." He puts his change in his wallet. "You remind me of someone I know."

I check around me before I speak. "Who? Some other pathetic girl stuck in a fake life?"

He shakes his head but doesn't answer. It feels like it takes forever, but finally his pizza is ready. I breathe easier once he's out the door.

Six o'clock comes around, and I hesitate at leaving Pearl all alone.

"Get on out of here, girl. I handled all of this before you, and I can handle it when you're gone," she says.

Pearl likes to come off like a grump, but it's all a bluff. I may as well add her to the list of those I will be devastated to lose if this plan doesn't work.

Since Dad doesn't get off until seven, Ethan and I have to run Teeny home. I'm nervous about what I'll find, and hope I don't have to cancel working on the project. It's all gonna depend on the shape Mom's in. When we get inside, I talk to her for a few minutes and she seems pretty sober. I leave Ethan's cell number for Teeny and race back to the truck. It's really cold tonight, colder than it's been the last several days.

"You okay?" Ethan asks.

"Yeah, yeah, fine. Let's go."

He hands me a small black pouch. "There's the tracker. It's fully charged and set for 'on demand,' which will give you the longest battery life. There's a sheet in there that tells you how to use it."

I put it in the go-bag. I'll mail him a letter on Saturday that says something like, *If I'm not home by Monday afternoon, give the tracker information to my parents.* I'll come clean with him one way or another.

Emma and Ben are already hanging out in the family room of the main house when we get there. Emma is sitting practically on top of Ben on the couch, and she rolls her eyes when she sees me. "God, I thought y'all would never get here. Let's get this over with already."

Ben removes himself from her so we can work at the bistro table in the back of the room. I put the packet on the table. Ethan and Emma take the couch and coffee table.

"So, where are we?" Ben asks, once he's seated on a stool.

I open the packet and read the top of the project sheet. "It looks like we were supposed to do this over an eight-day period, so we're gonna have to fib some of this."

"No problem here."

We figure out how to sum up an eight-day project in one hour. I agree mainly because I really don't care. I turn to Ethan and Emma, who are going through their packet. "What'd you get?"

Ethan says, "We were supposed to keep track of what we ate for the last week and measure it against the food pyramid to see if we eat healthy."

"Yours sounds easier to re-create than ours."

We finish our project around the same time they finish theirs. I'm putting everything back in the envelope when Ethan comes up to the table. "Can you stay awhile?"

"Yeah, that should be fine." I may need to make one more call to Teeny, though.

"Good. My mom's got every movie ever made. Let's pick one out and head to my room."

We walk to the built-in cabinets under the flat-screen, and he opens a drawer that has hundreds of movies in slots. Going down the titles one by one, we look for a movie we both want to watch.

About halfway through the search, I hear Emma behind me. "What the hell is all this? You carry around five pairs of underwear in your bag? Are you afraid you're gonna crap all over yourself or something? There's even little-girl panties in here. Look, here's some little kids' books. This is what you haul around every day? Are you into kids or something, freak?"

Before I can even think about what I'm doing, I launch myself across the room and push Emma off the couch, away from my bag. "Get out of my stuff!" I start piling everything back inside. I'm mortified.

Ethan bends down to try and help me pick up my things, but I push him away. He starts yelling at Emma, and Ben starts yelling at him. I don't even hear the words; I just finish getting everything back in my bag. I'm up and racing out the front door, not stopping even when Ethan calls my name. I'm halfway down the block when his truck brakes next to me. He hops out and physically restrains me from going any farther.

"Meg, I'm sorry. Emma is such a bitch. I know those are Mary's things. Who cares what's in your bag?" He pulls me into his arms. I don't return the gesture.

I'm so embarrassed, I don't want to be around him right now. But it's too cold to walk all the way home.

"Please take me home," I mumble into his chest, my warm breath puffing out in front of me. I can't even look at him. He stands frozen in place, and I repeat, "Please, just take me home."

He lets me go, and I get in the truck. Ethan slams his hand down on the hood before getting back inside.

"Can we talk about this?"

"No."

The ride to my house is a quiet one. Once we're in the parking lot, Ethan pulls me to him. I bury my head in his shoulder and cringe as I recall Emma's expression when she was going through my bag. It *would* look ridiculous to someone else, my carrying around all that stuff. But these are my only possessions in the entire world right now, and she pawed through all of them, making fun of my things. Teeny's things.

We stay this way for a few minutes until I pull away. Ethan reaches for the door handle. "I'll walk you up."

I glance at my house and see a dark figure lying on the front steps. My breath sucks in.

It's my mother.

Chapter 23

RULES FOR DISAPPEARING
BY WITNESS PROTECTION PRISONER #18A7R04M:

Don't be afraid to get down and dirty.

BEFORE I can get my paralyzed body to react, Mom moves. Slightly.

I grab Ethan's arm. "No! Don't get out of the truck."

He looks out the front windshield and sees her, too. "Let me help you."

I don't want him to know my mother like this. If he could have known her before Witness Protection, he wouldn't recognize the woman on the ground. "No. Please don't stay when I get out of the truck. Promise you'll drive away the second I close the door." My voice is strained.

He squeezes my hand. "Are you sure?"

"Please," I beg.

Flinging the door open, I jump out of the truck before I change my mind. My mind races with thoughts of my mother. The temperature is so cold tonight, and there's no telling how long she's been out here. I hear the truck back out of the spot, but I don't turn around to watch him go. I race toward the steps.

Mom looks blue when I get to her on the steps. She's only wearing pajama bottoms and a long-sleeve T-shirt. The smell of alcohol and vomit are almost more than I can handle.

I try to get her to put her arms around me, so I can wrap mine around her torso. They slip off my shoulders each time I try.

I grab under her armpits and struggle to lift her. She's deadweight.

"Mom, can you hear me? Please, Mom, help me get you inside." I'm sobbing now, but just as I lower her down so I can go get Dad, Ethan's truck screeches back into the parking lot. He jumps out of the truck before it comes to a full stop and runs up the steps.

Choking on words that will get him back in his truck, I let out a scared cry. I can't bear for him to see this.

"Meg, I can't leave you like this. I'm going to help you. You won't be able to lift her. I'll go once she's inside."

He's pure determination as he puts one hand under Mom's knees and the other under her back. I hop in front of him to open the door as he carries her up the remaining steps. He takes her straight to the couch, where he puts her down gently.

We look at one another for just a few seconds, and then he's gone.

I rush to her on the couch and slap her face a few times. "Mom! Mom! Open your eyes."

Her skin feels like ice. I run into my room and pull my comforter off my bed. I look quickly to Teeny's bed, and I'm relieved to see her in a deep sleep. I throw open the door to Dad's room. Even in the dark I can see the bed is empty. My stomach drops. I stand there a moment before running back into the den.

Once the blanket covers Mom, I sit down on the floor. "Mom, please open your eyes. I don't know if you're okay or not. I don't know if I need to call an ambulance. Please, Mom."

I slap her face a few more times, and her eyes flutter. "Mom! Mom! Open your eyes. Try to talk to me."

"What, what? Tooooo early. Sleeping." Her eyes roll back in her head.

"Mom, you have to wake up." I shake her almost violently now. "Mom, please.

"Mom, sit up. I'm going to call nine-one-one if you don't sit up." I glance at the phone in the kitchen. It's shattered to pieces. What happened here?

"Nooooo," she moans. "I can't move anymore. No more names. I want to go home."

"I know, me too." *Where's Dad?*

I hear the door handle turn. I'm terrified. Dad walks in, and my vision blurs with tears.

He steps into the living room with the suits right behind him. Not now!

He races to Mom. "What happened?" He's got a bloody lip and blackened eye.

"I d-d-don't know," I stutter. "I came home and found her passed out on the stairs outside."

He sits down in the chair next to the couch. "She needs help. She's going to kill herself at this rate. They're going to take her to a treatment facility."

My eyes get huge. "They're gonna lock her up somewhere? What happened to your face?"

"She hit me."

Oh. My. God. "What about us, do we get to stay here?"

Dad glances at the suits, but they watch me. I recognize one of them—Agent Parker, the one who cut all my hair off. I wish Agent Thomas was on duty tonight.

Dad looks back to me. "Mom called the agents earlier and told them you had your memory back. We went to look for you at Pearl's since you didn't come home after work. They're moving us to a safe house for a while. We're not in the normal rush this time, so we can have a chance to pack first. We'll leave first thing in the morning."

"Did she remember talking to me about that night?" I say, trying not to panic.

Dad won't look at me. "I let it slip," he whispers.

I'm so screwed.

He moves some of the hair out of Mom's face, then takes a washrag and cleans around her mouth. He's so sweet and gentle, it's almost hard to watch. He glances up at me. "Come help me pack for Mom."

I follow him down the hall. The Feds know I remember. We can't move. Not now. I'm leaving on Friday, but that won't happen if we're stuck in some safe house God knows where. And they'll start drilling me about that night. Get me ready to testify. I was working out a plan, and now this.

Dad shuts the door, and I move to the dresser, pulling Mom's clothes out.

"Sissy, have you remembered anything? Do you know anything about where the ledgers would be?"

I want to tell him, but I can't. He'll never get out of here unnoticed, and he'll end up doing something crazy. And his plan is so stupid—handing them over to Sanchez won't solve anything.

I turn from the dresser. "No, Dad. I'm sorry but I don't." I rush up to him, putting my arms around him. "Do we have to leave?"

"That's what the agents want to do. I've tried to reason with them, but I didn't get anywhere. They're insisting. This changes things drastically now that you remember."

I don't like the way he says "insisting." I'm tempted to tell him my plan, but he'll never let me go alone. The best bet I have is to get the ledgers and make copies or something to use as insurance against these guys. That's the only way we'll be truly free.

I pull away from Dad, and together we pack Mom's stuff.

While Dad gathers the last of her toiletry items together, I rush back to the living room. My mind is racing, running through possibilities. The room is empty except for Agent Parker. Mom's gone, as well as the suit who was on his cell phone.

"Where's my mother?" I ask.

"She's been taken to a hospital. Her condition seemed serious enough that she needed to be examined." Agent Parker stands in front of the door with her arms folded.

"You couldn't come get us before they took her away?" I pace around the room.

"We thought it best for it to be done as smoothly as possible."

Never a scene with these guys.

The suit watches me. She seems nervous, like she's afraid I'm about to attack.

Time to get out of here.

It takes a second to alert Dad that Mom's gone. He barrels

down the hall, yelling at the agent, and I make a big production of crying and telling them I'm going to my room. That should keep them out of here for a while.

Within minutes, all my things, including the tracking device, are transferred to a Walmart bag I saved from the store. As fast as Agent Thomas found me in the coffee shop, I'm not a hundred percent sure my bag's not bugged, so I'm leaving it behind.

I need to leave a note for Dad. I panic a moment, thinking of where I can put it so the suits don't see it first. Dad is still in the living room arguing with the suit, so I tiptoe to his room and open the closet. I ball the paper up and stuff it inside his tennis shoe. He'll feel it the second he puts it on. There's money on the dresser, and I take it. I hate stealing from him, but there aren't many options at this point. Since I haven't gotten my check from Pearl yet, I'll only have enough money for a one-way ticket. But I can't worry about that right now.

Back in my room, I shrug on my hoodie and grab my heavy coat, glancing every other second at Teeny to make sure she's still asleep.

I run to the window, throw it open, and look one last time at Teeny before I leave her.

Once outside, I wish the plastic bag wasn't white, because it's shining like a beacon.

I step around the building toward the back parking lot. I'm afraid to go past the front of the house. I've got to figure out how I'm going to get to Shreveport, and I won't get far if I'm stuck on foot.

God! I had a plan. Maybe not the best plan out there, but it could've worked. And now it's ruined. I run toward Front Street. Maybe I can get a cab to the interstate and then try to hitch a ride to Shreveport.

I walk one street over from my normal route. This section of town is deserted this time of night, as most stores and restaurants close early. It's about eleven, and now I'm afraid I won't find anyplace open where I can use a phone. I hit the cobblestone street and walk in the direction of the interstate. Hopefully I'll come across a gas station soon.

A vehicle pulls out of a driveway, the lights sweeping the street.

I duck into an alleyway next to a souvenir shop and try to cram myself into a corner.

The vehicle stops right outside the store. God, I haven't been gone twenty minutes and they already caught me.

"Meg? What are you doing?"

It's Ethan.

Chapter 24

RULES FOR DISAPPEARING
BY WITNESS PROTECTION PRISONER #18A7R04M:

Lay a false trail. Make it look like you're going this way. Then everyone looks that way. Then when they're going that way, you really go the other way. When everyone gets to where they thought you were, you're somewhere else. Pretty simple, huh?

I throw myself at him. "What are *you* doing?" I should be pissed he's here, but I'm not.

"Meg, what's going on? I've been watching these dudes come in and out of your house for the last twenty minutes. I checked that tracker and about freaked when I saw it heading down Front Street. After seeing your mom tonight, I knew it couldn't be her. I never even saw you leave."

"I'll tell you what I can, but we have to get out of here first." I run to his truck.

He gets in and throws the truck into drive.

"I'm gonna ask a big favor. You can say no. I need you to drive me to Shreveport."

Ethan slows down. "You have to tell me what's going on."

"I can't, but don't stop." I wave my hands, urging him to keep going forward.

He stops the truck on the side of the road. "Bullshit. I saw your mom half dead outside. I see all these people in and out of your house. Then your vanishing act. We're not going anywhere until you tell me everything."

I keep checking out the back window. "Okay, but just drive."

He doesn't move.

"You know I'm not Meg Jones," I begin. Ethan nods. My heart races. I can't believe I'm about to say this out loud. "Well, I'm not Avery Preston, either." Ethan's head drops forward slightly. "My name is Anna Boyd. I'm from Scottsdale, Arizona. Right outside of Phoenix."

I'm getting the *what the hell* look, and he hasn't even heard the worst part yet.

"My family is in the Witness Protection Program. All those suits you saw at my house are part of the U.S. Marshals Office. We're under their protection from some really nasty bad guys. The marshals will be looking for me soon, and I was hoping to get a little farther than two blocks down the road." I put my hand over my mouth. There's no going back now.

Ethan's jaw drops, but at least he starts driving. He glances at me a few times. "Okay, spill it."

"I can't give you any details that will hurt you later. I'm sorry I've gotten you this involved, but trust me, you don't want to know any more than necessary. I need to get out of this town. I need to get to Shreveport." I'm almost sitting backward in the truck, keeping a lookout for any activity behind us.

"Why are you running from the marshals?" Ethan asks.

"I can't tell you that. Even if you stop the truck again." We stare at each other for a few seconds before he turns his attention back to the road.

"Will they be looking for you because they're worried about you and want to make sure you're safe, or really looking for you, using every resource the government has to track you down?"

I bite my bottom lip. "Probably closer to the second one." The suits know I remember. They know I can testify now. They've been waiting me out for months and months. They won't let me just run away.

"Where are you going once I take you to Shreveport?"

"Ethan, please. It's better if you don't know."

He looks at me squarely. "Tell me or we stop right here."

It looks like he means it. "I'm taking a bus to Scottsdale. I'm going home."

The truck swerves. "Are you crazy? Why are you going to the first place they'll look for you?" His voice is incredulous.

"You can let me out here, but I'm not telling you. I've told you too much as it is."

Ethan shakes his head. "So U.S. Marshals are gonna be looking for you. Soon. Maybe even whoever these *bad guys* are, too. And you're gonna get on a bus and head to Scottsdale?"

Okay, the way he says it does shoot a few holes in the competency of my plan. "Yes. I did have a really good plan, but everything got screwed up. I wasn't planning on leaving until Friday. Things have changed, and I have to go tonight."

"Do you have any money?"

There's cash in my bag. Between what I already had and what I stole from Dad, it's about one hundred seventy-five bucks.

"Yes."

Ethan makes a couple of turns as I continue to stare out the back windshield. I get that creepy hair-standing-up-on-the-back-of-my-neck feeling when a black Suburban a few cars back makes every turn with us.

"Uh-oh."

Ethan's head swivels around. "What do you mean *uh-oh*?"

It looks like the same Suburban that was in the parking lot the night the power went out in the laundry room and that was behind us on the way to Ethan's last night. "There's an SUV following us. I think I've seen it before."

"Is it the marshals?" Ethan makes a quick right turn, and a few seconds later, the Suburban does the same.

My palms get sweaty. "Don't know for sure." It's physically hard to get my next sentence out. "Maybe not."

Ethan swears under his breath and makes a quick left turn, the speed of the truck increasing.

I twist in my seat, scanning the area for any other vehicles. Shit! What are we supposed to do now?

"Hold on." Ethan throws an arm across me and makes a very sharp turn.

"Where are we going?" I glance at the speedometer, which is inching up to seventy miles an hour. The Suburban isn't far behind us.

"The farm."

The farm! What are we going to do at the farm? Sic the hog dogs on them? I don't say what I'm thinking; I just hold on and watch for the SUV.

When we get close, Ethan pulls out a square device from under his seat. He clicks it, and I see the slow mechanical gate start opening.

The tires squeal when we make the turn onto the farm road. He clicks it again, just as we pass through the opening. The Suburban slows in front of the gate. It's almost all the way closed now. A few seconds later, the Suburban pulls away. I collapse in the seat.

"What do we do now?"

"We're going out the back side. It takes five or six minutes cutting through the farm, but twenty if you have to go around. And that's only if you know where the other side comes out."

The farm is pitch-black. The crop rows flicker past the window, and I'm mesmerized watching them.

We finally get to the other gate, and Ethan clicks it open. We sit at the road for a few seconds but don't see any lights either direction.

Ethan peels out of the farm. We drive for a few more minutes before pulling into a dark, gravel driveway. It's long, probably half a mile.

"What are you doing now?"

"Saving your ass. You won't make it out of Louisiana if I put you on a bus." He grabs his phone and his coat and hops out of the truck. My body is glued to the seat until he pounds on the hood of the truck to get me moving.

This is more than I bargained for. I can't put him right in the middle of my disaster. "Wait. Ethan, this is too dangerous. Maybe you should take me home."

He stops and turns to me. "If I take you home, will that stop you from trying to get to Arizona?"

I don't answer for a few seconds. "No. I have to go back."

He spins back around and heads toward a house next to the driveway. He's walking fast, and I have to hurry to keep up.

He says over his shoulder, "I don't think that was the marshals.

The gate wouldn't have stopped them. If it is whoever is after you, I don't know why they didn't bust through the gate. Maybe they're waiting us out. Thinking we couldn't get off the farm another way. I'm guessing the marshals don't know you're missing yet. When do you think they'll figure it out?"

I think for a second. "Probably around six in the morning. They're planning to relocate us first thing. I don't think they'll come in my room until then."

This makes Ethan stop cold.

"They're moving you?"

I almost run into his back. He sounds pissed. "That's why I have to go tonight. Tomorrow will be too late."

He looks at me a moment, then turns around and starts walking again. He glances at his watch. "It's about eleven thirty now, so six and a half hours."

We walk up a few steps to the back door. Ethan knocks loudly.

A light pops on just as the door opens. It's Pearl.

"What in the holy hell are you two doing out here?"

"Pearl, we need a car, some money, maybe pillows and blankets, food, and water."

She eyes Ethan carefully, then looks at me. "Are you in some kind of trouble?"

I nod. "Yes, but I didn't do anything bad." I feel guilty, the way she's looking at me. "My family is in some trouble, and I'm trying to get us out of it," I say softly. "I wish I could tell you more, but I can't."

She holds her stare for a few seconds. Probably the longest few seconds of my life. She's either going to help us or try to turn me in.

"Well, come on in and let's get you what you need."

Ethan and I follow her in to the kitchen, where she grabs a small ice chest from the pantry and starts filling it with food. Ethan grabs several bottles of water and a few Cokes. Pearl hands him a paper bag to put them in. They work together in silence, Pearl never asking a single question.

I'm shocked. We could have just robbed a bank, or killed someone, and she's making us lunch to go.

She digs around in her purse. "I guess you only want cash."

"Please," Ethan answers.

She pulls out several one hundred dollar bills and hands them to Ethan. "This is all I have on me here."

"That's enough. We both have some money, too." He shoves the bills into his back pocket.

I look at Pearl. "I'm so sorry to show up here like this. I'll pay you back."

"Just get yourself back here safe." She puts her hand on Ethan's shoulder. "You're a good boy. I trust you, maybe more than I should. Don't make me sorry for it."

He hugs her tightly. "I won't. I'll explain everything when we get back."

Pearl lets him go and turns to me. "Is Mary all right?"

"Yes. She's with my dad."

Pearl looks back at Ethan. "What about your parents?"

"I'll send them a message once we get going."

She hugs him one last time. "You're positive this is something you can handle?"

I look between them. There is so much Ethan doesn't know. I

start to speak, to tell them both I'll do this on my own, but Ethan looks directly at me, and his expression tells me not to say anything.

He whispers to Pearl, "Meg needs me."

"Well, let's get you a car so y'all can get out of here."

We follow Pearl to a barn out back. Ethan helps her open the two huge double doors. There are three different cars and one truck inside.

Ethan walks to a black car in the back. "This one still in Fred's name?"

Pearl's left eyebrow pops up. "Yeah." She walks to a cabinet on the wall to get out the keys, then tosses them to Ethan.

"What kind of car is that?" I ask.

Two sets of eyes flicker to me. "Girl, that's a 1970 Ford Mustang. I shouldn't even let you ride in this car if you don't know what it is."

"Sorry, cars aren't really my thing." I let out a small, nervous laugh.

Pearl comes close and hugs me. Her embrace is so warm and tight, I can hardly make myself let go.

"If I can, I'll call Fred to get a message to you. I'm gonna drive my truck around to the old barn," Ethan says.

Pearl nods. "I'll try real hard not to be scared watching the two of you pull out of here like this."

"Pearl, we'll be fine." I hug her one more time.

We throw our things in the back of the car, including the ice chest and drinks, and get inside.

Pearl steps up to the car, and I roll the window down. She pokes her head in. "I'll tell whoever's asking that I haven't see you."

It's hard to swallow. These two people I didn't even know a month ago are now risking so much for me. "Thanks, Pearl. I'll explain everything as soon as I can."

She ambles back off to the house. Ethan pulls up next to his truck. "Follow me in the car."

He cranks his truck, and we drive into the back pasture. There's an old barn that looks like it will fall down at any moment. He jumps out and opens a side door. Once the truck is inside, he stacks some square hay bales in front of the door. You can't even tell there's an opening now.

I climb over to the passenger side as Ethan opens the door. "We've got one more stop to make before we hit the road."

I wrap my arms around my waist and stare out the front windshield. "Where are we going?"

"Ben's."

Okay, definitely not what I was expecting. Ethan dials his number as we pull into the driveway.

"Hey. Can you come outside a minute?"

Ethan hangs up the phone, and we both hop out of the car. "I don't get why we're here."

Before Ethan can answer, Ben comes out of a side door.

He's in pajama bottoms and a Natchitoches Football T-shirt. He rubs his hands together, blowing out a puff of warm air. "You better have a good reason for dragging me out here."

"I need a favor. Forget all the stupid shit, I really need your help."

Ben gets serious. "What do you need?"

"We have to get out of town for a while. A couple of days. I need everyone to think me and you are headed to the cabin. Drive your truck there and stay until Sunday."

Ben folds his arms across his chest. "What's wrong?"

Ethan shakes his head. "It's not my story to tell. Just do this for me."

Ben waits a few seconds, then says, "When do you need me to leave?"

"Now if you can. Here's my phone. I got a text waiting to be sent to Mom. I need you to send it and one to your mom when you get there."

Ben takes the phone from Ethan. "Anything else?"

"No. That's it."

Ben and Ethan stand there looking at each other. "You're gonna owe me big-time."

Ethan nods. "Yeah."

They shake hands, then Ethan motions for me to get back into the car. I just witnessed hell freezing over.

We stop once right on the outside of town to fill up with gas, grab a map, and use the bathroom.

Ethan spreads the map across the hood and studies it. "Scottsdale is a helluva long way from here."

I stand next to him. "I can still take the bus."

He laughs at me and says, "It's far but it's almost a straight shot. It's all interstate from the minute we leave Louisiana until we get to Arizona. If we don't make too many stops, we can probably make it in a little less than twenty-four hours."

I nod, looking at the path he traces with his finger along the map.

He glances at me. "It's gonna be a hard trip doing it that fast."

The last eight months have been hard, but this trip is the only thing I have any control over. "I'm ready."

Ethan folds the map and pulls me in for a hug. "It's strange to look at you and not think of you as Meg. Or Avery."

I giggle into his chest. "Think about how I feel. Before I open my mouth, I have to think, *Okay who am I and what's my story?*" I giggle again. I'm half delirious.

He shakes his head, like he still hasn't quite absorbed all of this yet.

We get back in the car and hit the interstate. I spend the first hour riding backward, looking for the Suburban. About ninety percent of this trip will be on interstate, and while that's great for making good time, it's awfully boring out the window. Especially in the middle of the night.

We've been in the car about an hour and a half and haven't spoken once since we left the gas station. And neither of us has touched the radio. The silence is thick.

I'm still in awe of Ethan. He jumped into this road trip with me blind and has more sense about it than I do. He's left this awesome fake trail, and I was just going to grab the earliest Greyhound out of Shreveport. And I know what we're up against. My plan sucked. He's right, I'd have never made it out of Louisiana on the bus once the suits started looking for me.

I grab a pillow and lean it against the door to watch him drive. "Who's Fred?"

Ethan frowns and then smiles. "Fred is Pearl's boyfriend she thinks no one knows about."

"Where's the cabin?"

"South Mississippi, near the Gulf. It's a fishing cabin Pearl's husband had before he died. She lets me go there whenever I want."

"What made you pick this car?"

He cocks his head and looks at me. "Blame it on all the movies I watch, but I'm trying to drop us off the face of the earth. The Feds can pull credit cards. Cell phone records. They can track us through OnStar or GPS. They'll probably go to Pearl first, then me. They know what my truck looks like. Even though this car is a little flashy, it's Fred's. Not many people know him and Pearl are an item, so hopefully they won't be looking for his car. And when Ben gets to the cabin and sends that text, that's where it will look like we are." He chuckles after he says this. "They may pick us up on the street cameras if they go back and look at tonight's tape, but there's not much I can do about that. There's hardly anybody else on the road right now to blend in with."

Good Lord. He's thought of everything.

"What does the text to your mom say?"

"If I keep answering these questions, you have to answer some of mine." He smiles and the dimple digs deep in his cheek.

I would have never gotten this far without him. He deserves a few answers.

"Okay, deal."

"The text says, 'Heading to the cabin for a few days. Everything's fine. Don't be pissed. See you soon.'"

"I can't believe you thought of all of that. So, basically your phone will send a text from somewhere in Mississippi, and Ben will be there waiting. You know once they get to him, they'll know what we did."

He laughs. "Yeah, but they'll be over in Mississippi scratching their heads. It'll buy us some time. They can jump on a plane or whatever. We need all the help we can get." We drive a few minutes before he asks, "Why's your family in Witness Protection?"

I stare out the windshield. "It's nothing we did. It's not like I'm part of some crime family. It's just one of those being-in-the-wrong-place-at-the-wrong-time kinda things."

The only protection I can give Ethan is his ignorance. Maybe when this is all over, I can tell him everything.

"How many times have you moved?"

I curl up in the seat. "Natchitoches was our sixth placement since the beginning of June last year."

He lets out a quiet laugh. The kind of laugh that you do not because something is funny, but because it's all too much to take in. "Everything makes sense now. All these nagging little things I had in my head about you. You seemed so normal one minute, and then you'd wig out the next."

I playfully slap his arm. "I think I held it together pretty well."

"What was the original plan? I'm hoping it was a hell of a lot better than the one you concocted tonight."

I let out a huff. "It *was* a good plan. Catherine and I were going dress shopping in Shreveport on Friday. I was going to give her some lame excuse and get on a bus to Phoenix. I was going to take care of what I need to take care of there and then head back to Shreveport on Sunday. I could have been back in class by lunch on Monday."

Ethan laughs. Loud. He looks at me and shakes his head. It's actually a few minutes before he quits laughing. I stare out the side window, trying to ignore him. It was a good plan until Mom fell apart.

"So they were gonna move you in the morning. Would I have ever seen you again?" His voice is serious now.

I look at him. "No. There would've been no sign we were ever there."

He reaches for my hand. We both seem content for the moment to just watch the miles drop away in front of the headlights.

Chapter 25

RULES FOR DISAPPEARING BY WITNESS PROTECTION PRISONER #18A7R04M:

Never tell anyone your secrets. They're called secrets for a reason.

MY eyes feel gritty and I'm having trouble opening them. The light is bright, blinding me when I'm finally able to crack them. Someone is shaking my shoulder.

Finally, the dark fuzzy shape comes into focus. It takes me a few seconds, and then everything comes crashing back. Ethan.

He looks exhausted. I sit up quickly. "How long have I been asleep?" A glance out the window does not help pinpoint our location. We're stopped at a gas station right off the interstate.

"We're on the other side of Fort Worth, about halfway to Abilene. You're gonna have to take a shift because I don't think I can keep my eyes open for another mile."

"Why didn't you wake me up sooner?" I quickly undo my seat belt and hop out of the car. My legs are wobbly, and I really need to pee.

Ethan looks at me from over the roof. "I'll fill the car up. Go get whatever you need inside."

I reach into the car for my bag. I half walk, half run to the store, trying to get my legs to work. Once inside, I quickly spot the restroom.

Cringing, I step inside. It's gross. Somehow, I manage to use the toilet while keeping the plastic bag on my lap. There's no way I'm setting it on the floor in here.

Another balancing act at the little sink. I wash my hands and pull my toothbrush and toothpaste out of my bag. Once my teeth are brushed, I actually feel human again. My eyes are burning and red from sleeping in the contacts. They're coming out. They'll work well in Scottsdale, but I'm done with them until then. I get out the little case to put them away.

Back in the store, I grab a honey bun and fix a cup of coffee, then wait in line at the checkout. Ethan walks inside. When he gets close, his eyes squint as he looks at me closer. Not paying attention, he walks into a display of chips.

He changes course and comes to me in the line. He gets really close. "I knew your eyes were different in that newspaper article, but they are really blue."

I giggle. "Yes. They are."

He whispers in my ear, "Once we get back in the car I'm sleeping for a couple of hours and then we're talking. Really talking about all of this."

I love this car. It's a totally different experience driving an old muscle car than any sports car on the market today. You really feel the engine when you hit the gas, and it makes a pretty cool rumbling noise, too.

Ethan told me before he completely passed out to watch my

speed. The last thing we need is to get pulled over. It's hard, though. I want to gun it and feel this car haul ass, but I restrain myself.

Maybe on the way home.

I glance over at Ethan, like I've done a hundred times since he fell asleep. He's reclined, mouth wide open. He's dead to the world.

He's gonna want answers when he wakes up. I don't blame him, but hate pulling him into this. As much as I want to keep him ignorant of the finer points, I don't think I can talk him into letting me go to Price's alone once we're in Scottsdale. Not that it matters. I don't know if I can do what needs to be done alone. It would be worse to let him walk in there and not know what we're up against.

My mind wanders as I drive. Will I run into Elle or Laura? Probably not. Do I want to see them while I'm there? No, not really. With Brandon dead, a lot of my anger at them is gone. Laura could have been with him, and then she'd be dead too. I like to think my disappearing on Elle and Laura that night may have been the reason Laura and Brandon weren't together at his house. Maybe overhearing what I did saved her life.

I drive for a few hours. There is nothing, and I mean nothing, to look at through this part of Texas.

Ethan starts to wake up as we pass through Midland. He tosses and turns in his seat for a few minutes before he finally gives up. He raises the seat and rubs his eyes.

"Where are we?" His voice is scratchy.

"Just passed Midland. Sign said Odessa is next." I turn to look at him. "Do you need to stop?"

"Yeah, but I can wait until Odessa." He reaches into the backseat and opens the ice chest, pulling out a Coke. He holds it out to me. "You want one?"

I shake my head. "No, I had coffee."

He settles back in his seat and cracks the can. Yawning big, he stretches his legs and arms out.

"You can go back to sleep. I'm fine to drive a while longer."

He arches his back and rubs his face with his free hand. "No, I'm good. How long was I out?"

I glance at my watch. "About three hours. Not long enough."

He takes a deep drink of the Coke. "You didn't sleep much more than that. It's enough for now." Ethan leans back against the seat and turns his head toward mine. "Okay, blue eyes. Spill it."

"Can I tell you everything but the exact details of what put us in the program? I'd rather not name names."

"For now. But you're gonna have to tell me eventually. Whatever you need to do in Scottsdale, I'm going with you."

I nod and take a deep breath. "I lived in Scottsdale my whole life until last June. My dad was a pretty successful CPA there. Not a big firm but a handful of really big clients. We lived in a nice house in a golf course community. Lots of nice things—cars, clothes, you name it." I take another deep breath. I had no idea how hard this would be to say out loud.

"I witnessed something I shouldn't have. Something terrible." I don't want to tell him I didn't remember it until a few days ago. I don't want to tell him I've hated my dad for months for something he didn't do.

Ethan nods, urging me to go on.

It's enough encouragement for me to keep going. "The longest we stayed in a placement was ten weeks. Most we were only there four or five. It was hard, all the moving. Changing names, new schools, new towns. Mom didn't handle it well."

"Is that normal—to move that much?"

I shrug. "I don't think so."

A tear escapes, sliding down my cheek, and I brush it away with the back of my hand.

We pass a sign for a gas station at the next exit.

"Pull over. Let's take a minute to talk," Ethan says.

I take the exit and pull into the gas station, stopping in front of the pump. We turn to face each other in the car.

"Mom was a casual drinker. But she started drinking a lot once we were in the program. It was too hard for her. She was a very social person back home: lots of committees, lots of clubs. The suits took her to a detox facility last night. I don't know where she is right now." I'm crying and I can't stop. I haven't had anybody to talk to about this, and now it's just bursting out of me.

Ethan reaches behind the seat and tears off a paper towel from the roll Pearl gave us, and hands it to me.

I mop up my face while Ethan watches and waits for me to continue. "There's something in Scottsdale that may help us stop running. I'm the only one who knows for sure where it is. I didn't tell Dad I was leaving. With Mom gone, he has to stay with Teeny."

Ethan smiles when I say Teeny's name. "That's the second time you've called her that. What's her real name?"

I let out a short laugh. "It's Elena. Elena Boyd. Teeny has been her nickname forever. It's what we all call her when it's just us. I about died when I said it in front of you the other day."

Ethan shakes his head. "Does she have blue eyes, too?"

"No, just me. But we're both blond. She was hardly speaking by the time we got to Natchitoches. All this moving was getting to her, too."

Ethan looks like he doesn't believe me.

"It's true. She's different around you and Pearl."

"So what are you trying to find in Scottsdale?" he asks.

I lean back against the door and close my eyes. "I'd rather not tell you. You're better off not knowing." Especially when he gets questioned by the suits.

"I'm gonna see it whenever you get it. Open your eyes and look at me."

My eyes open. Ethan holds my hands and pulls me in close. Our faces are inches apart.

He speaks quietly. "I'm in this. It doesn't matter if you tell me what it is or not; I know more than the marshals or anyone else wants me to. I'm not gonna say this doesn't scare me. It scares the shit out of me. But the best thing you can do is prepare me. Let me know what I'm up against. Keeping me in the dark is not going to help."

He's right. I tell him the whole story about Mr. Price and Brandon and the man with the scar named Sanchez. I tell him about losing my memory and the accounting ledger I'm hoping to find in Price's wall.

Ethan is quiet a minute and then pulls me in for a kiss. It takes me by surprise but not for long. I'm kissing him back. His hands are in my hair and the scratch of his whiskers rubs me raw. His hands skim my sides, and I want to crawl across the seat, into his lap.

Several quick raps on the window makes us both jump as if we'd been shot. An old man in overalls is peering into the car.

"Either pump or move this car." He turns and walks off.

Ethan throws on a baseball cap and hops out. God, we're sitting in a parked car at a gas station, making out. I'm almost embarrassed to get out. A few minutes of kissing and all rational thought flies out of my head.

No matter what, Ethan is in this all the way now.

With the tank full, we spare a few minutes in the store, then it's back to the Mustang.

Ethan pauses before putting the car in reverse. "I'm starving. Let's eat real quick before we get back on the road."

My stomach rumbles at the mention of food. We eat in the car, picnic style, with the food from the cooler. Pearl threw in lunch meat, bread, cheese, and mustard. We make some sandwiches and share chips out of the bag.

"If you're gonna give the ledgers to the Feds, why didn't you just tell them where they are and let them come get them?"

I take a drink of my Coke, thinking about the best way to answer this. "I'm not. Sanchez, the man who killed my dad's boss and his son, has sent someone after me. He knows I know where the ledgers are, and he wants them back or he'll kill my family. The suits can't protect us from him. Dad wants to make a deal with him—the ledgers for our safety. But he shot my friend Brandon just for walking into the room. I don't know how smart it is to make a deal with these people."

Ethan has stopped eating, and his mouth is hanging slightly open. "Holy shit." He stuffs the rest of his food into the paper bag we're using for trash. "Holy. Shit."

I feel guilty now. This is so much more than he thought he was getting into.

"You can let me out here. I'll find a way to Scottsdale. I'm so sorry for dragging you into this." I start gathering my things, and Ethan puts a hand on my arm to stop.

"Can you please just give me a minute to let this crazy shit sink in before you decide to run away?"

He leans his head against the back of the seat. "So if you aren't giving the ledgers to the Feds and you aren't sure about giving them to this Sanchez guy, what are you going to do with them?"

I lift my shoulders and say, "I haven't worked that out completely. The original plan did not include being chased by suits and killers! I was going to have some time to figure it out."

Ethan gathers our trash and hops out of the car to throw it away. I pack everything else in the cooler.

Once he's back in the car, he says, "Let's worry about getting the ledgers first, then we'll figure out what to do with them. We need to get back on the road. It's already ten thirty. I'm sure they've been looking for a while now, and we still have a long-ass way to go."

Reality check. As much as I want this to be some great little getaway with my cute boyfriend, it's not. I look at the map. Long-ass way is right.

Ethan thankfully changes the subject once we're back on the road. "Tell me the worst place you lived."

I sip on my water and answer, "Definitely our first move. It was Hillsboro, Ohio. None of us understood what any of this meant. We were jerked out of our home, lost our friends. I was used to

Scottsdale. It was the first two weeks of the summer before my senior year. Always sunny, always something to do. They plopped us down in this ridiculously small town. School was out, so there was no real way to even meet people. They put us in this tiny little house in a semi-bad area. I had no car, nothing. It was horrible."

"How long were you there?"

"Not long. Maybe four weeks."

"What was your name there?"

"Madeline Holmes. Teeny's name was Hayden."

Ethan moves his cap over his head a few times. "Do you get to pick your names or what?"

"The suits give us our last name and we get to pick our first name. Teeny picks people off TV."

Ethan laughs. "What'd you do? Just come up with a name? This is crazy."

I laugh back. "It is crazy. Picking my name was the hardest part for me. Each time we moved somewhere, I thought I better pick a good name because I'll be stuck with it forever. Never thought I'd go through so many in such a short period of time."

This seems to be fascinating to Ethan. "Okay, so why did you have to leave Ohio? Did something happen?" he asks.

I curl up in the passenger seat with the blanket. It's really cold out in this barren part of west Texas. "That placement was only a transitional one. They explained to us about the program and what would be involved. We knew going into Ohio that we wouldn't stay there long. I didn't stress as bad about my name there, but it was still a big deal because it was my first fake name."

"So where after Ohio?"

"Springfield, Missouri. After being in Hillsboro, I was actually excited about this move. Springfield was tons bigger. Our house was decent, and there were kids our age down the street. We moved there in the middle of July."

Ethan had bought a cheap pair of sunglasses at the last stop, so I can't see his eyes, but I can tell he's getting a kick out of this, for some insane reason.

"What was your name there?"

"Isabelle Mancini, and Teeny was Vanessa."

Ethan pulls down the shades and says, "Italian, really?"

I imagine myself back in Springfield, my high hopes there, and how naive I was. "Yes, and I really embraced it. Made sure my first name sounded Italian, too."

"So what caused that move?"

I look down into the folds of my blanket. "That move was my fault." I tell him about going to the party and my drunken escapade on the Internet. And the birth of the go-bag.

"That sucks. How fast after you used the Internet did they come get you?" he asks.

"I'm not sure. I passed out next to the computer. Maybe a couple of hours."

Ethan stares out the windshield, and I know what he's thinking. This kind of response time does not work well for us and our current situation.

"We were only there about four weeks," I add.

We travel the next few miles in silence. Ethan seems lost in his thoughts. I pick at the blanket. Finally, he turns to me again, recovering some of his earlier enthusiasm.

"Where next?"

"Naples, Florida."

"Avery Preston. I was wondering when we were gonna get to her."

I snuggle in the blanket. "I loved Naples. It reminded me the most of Scottsdale. We lived in an apartment three blocks from the beach. We were there the longest, ten weeks maybe. You said you fished Paradise Coast?"

"Yeah. Me, Dad, Ben, and his dad. I was ten." He pushes his hat up on his head.

"Y'all *were* close."

He smirks. "Listen to you. *Y'all.* You're halfway to being a Southern girl."

I pull the blanket up to hide my grin. "What's the other half?"

"You gotta eat a piece of Pearl's Cajun pizza. And love it."

I make a fake gagging motion. "No way in hell. That's just wrong to put all that on a pizza."

"What was Teeny's name in Naples?"

"Sydney." I wonder if they hounded her this morning about where I was, or if she shut down with Mom gone.

"Naples is cool. We stayed there one night."

I nod. "That was the hardest one to leave. I made friends, joined some clubs at school. We were there until the end of October. It was tough when we left."

"What caused that move?"

I shrug. "No idea. They just showed up and we were gone." It seems forever ago that I sat in that apartment and waited for Tyler. Leaving him was nothing compared to what it would be like to leave Ethan.

Ethan takes his sunglasses off and rubs his hands over his eyes. "You know how bizarre this is, don't you? I can't imagine moving like that, changing names."

"You have no idea."

He voice gets soft. "When did your mom's drinking get worse?"

I swallow hard and beg myself not to tear up talking about this again. "When we left Florida. The suits dropped us in Bardstown, Kentucky. Talk about shell shock. It was almost worse than leaving Scottsdale for Ohio. Florida was doable. I could have stayed in Florida." Knowing he is about to ask, I add, "I was Olivia Taylor, and Teeny was Amanda."

"How long were you there?"

I lean against the door and run my hands through my hair. "Almost two months. We left right before Christmas. And I don't know what happened there either."

"Okay, so that's four places. One more before Natchitoches?"

"Yeah. Conway, South Carolina. I was Gabrielle Chandler, and Teeny was Sabrina."

He laughs. "You went for fancy names, didn't you?"

Madeline, Isabelle, Gabrielle, Olivia. "Yeah, I guess I did." I hadn't really thought about them all together like that.

"Meg was a good choice. It fits you. The others are a little too . . . I don't know, too much. So how was South Carolina?"

"Pretty cool—better than Bardstown, really, but my family was going down the drain. We could've been anywhere; it didn't matter. We were there until we came to Natchitoches. It was a scary move. They came in the middle of the night and yanked us out of bed."

Ethan's eyes get big. "You're shitting me."

"No. One minute I'm sound asleep, the next I'm in the van."

"And then you're sitting in the office of my high school. No wonder you didn't want anything to do with anybody. I'm surprised you talked to me at all."

Warmth spreads through my chest. He gets it. He understands. I reach my hand over and hold his.

"That was my plan. No friends. I hate leaving people behind." I rub my thumb over his hand. "It would've devastated me to leave you. To never see you again. And then for you to wonder where I went. I didn't want that."

Ethan glances from me to the road and back. "I don't want that either." He brings my hand to his lips and kisses my knuckles. "Anna," he says quietly. It's the first time he's said my real name. He watches the road a few minutes more, then says, "It's nice to meet you, Anna Boyd."

By midafternoon we're headed down I-10 toward New Mexico, a stretch of interstate that runs close to the Mexican border. I've napped off and on, but now I'm just trying to find something decent on the radio.

"I really miss my iPod right about now," I say, turning the small knob across the FM dial.

Ethan laughs. "Yeah, in these parts it's either gonna be mariachi or country."

I snarl at the radio. At least it's warmer here. I've shed a few layers, and we may actually have to turn the air conditioner on soon.

Ethan points to a sign up ahead. "Let's stop when we get to El Paso. I gotta get out of this car awhile. We'll find somewhere to eat."

I nod. I'm getting cabin fever, too. It's better to have silence than the noise coming across the radio, so I cut it off.

"How pissed do you think your parents are going to be that you did this?" I ask.

"Dad'll be furious. Mom will just be worried, but I'm eighteen. I can legally come and go as I please." His face is smug.

"My dad is probably freaking out. I bet they still tried to move them, but he won't leave while I'm gone."

Ethan takes the off-ramp, and we both look at our roadside restaurant choices. Mexican, hamburgers, or truck stop diner.

I shrug, not really caring which one we go to.

He pulls into the parking lot of Dos Amigos restaurant. It's a seat-yourself kind of place, so we take a booth in the back. This restaurant looks sketchy. It's old and the painted walls were probably once pretty vivid, but now it's just faded red, green, and yellow. The floors are worn, and the vinyl cushions in the booth are cut in places. But the smells coming out of the kitchen are incredible. It's late for the lunch crowd, so there aren't many people inside.

A young Hispanic girl approaches our table carrying water, menus, chips, and salsa. "*Hola.* You want something to drink?" Her accent is thick.

Ethan looks at me before answering. "Two Cokes."

The waitress leaves, and we both look at the TV in the corner of the room. The news is on and we watch it for a few minutes.

"Do you think the Feds will go public with their search for you?" he asks.

I shrug my shoulders. "I would think no because they wouldn't want to show my picture and name. The real one or the fake one."

"That's what I hope, too. It'd suck if we were all over the news like some wanted felons."

"Well, they have to go easy here. We're in the program for protection. It's not like we did something wrong and are giving evidence to get out of trouble." I hate to admit that was what I thought was the deal.

The waitress brings the drinks, and we order. I can't say I'm very adventurous when it comes to food, so I stick with two tacos, rice, and beans. Ethan, on the other hand, goes for some crazy combination platter. We talk awhile about regular things, both of us wanting a break from what we're really on this trip for. But it doesn't last long.

"We need to talk about your plan once we get to Scottsdale," Ethan says, scooping a huge amount of rice into his mouth.

"Price lives in the same neighborhood my friend Elle does. It's a gated neighborhood inside a gated community. It's a big house, but the office is on the bottom floor, right off the main hall."

"Does anyone else live there? A wife, other kids?"

"He was remarried to some young woman, but Brandon was his only son. I'm not sure if she still lives there now that Mr. Price is gone." I push my plate away. Just talking about this has gotten me so nervous that I lose my appetite.

"Okay, we have to plan for extra security getting into the neighborhood. We need to assume that the FBI or marshals are watching Price's house. We have to decide how to get in if no one lives there and it's all locked up, or if the wife is home."

"I'm kinda hoping no one is home," I say.

Ethan looks at me, confused. "You think that'd make it easier?"

I take a sip of my Coke. "She'll recognize me!"

He laughs quietly. "Well, I don't know anything about picking locks or disarming alarm systems. Do you?"

"No."

"Are you going to be okay going back there?"

I swallow hard. "I'm gonna have to be, right?"

Ethan finally says, "Anna, once they figure out we're not in Mississippi, they're gonna guess we're going to Scottsdale. They're probably already there now."

I stare down in my drink and watch the ice swirl as I stir it with my straw. "I know."

I describe the house as best I can and the neighborhood layout. We talk about possible entry points and all the things that could go wrong. I tell him where Elle's house is in relation to Price's. I tell him everything but the exact name of the subdivision.

This is insane. Nuts. I can't believe we are sitting here having this conversation. Ethan's right. It won't take the suits long to figure out we're not in Mississippi. And whoever is working for Sanchez could be right behind us, for all I know. The more we talk about the plan, the more scared I get. It was crazy involving him in this. I should've come up with a different plan.

It may piss him off, but there's no way I'm letting him get anywhere near Price's house now.

Chapter 26

RULES FOR DISAPPEARING BY WITNESS PROTECTION PRISONER #18A7R04M:

Never, under any circumstances, try to reenter your old life in any way. You left for a reason, right?

WE'RE back on the road, making our way through New Mexico. I'm driving, giving Ethan a chance to nap. We've been on the road for over fifteen hours now, and we're both feeling exhausted. According to the map, we're only going to be in New Mexico for a short time, but it feels like forever.

Ethan snores softly in the passenger seat. I run through the layout of The Canyons in my head. My house was in the same golf community as the Prices' but in a different neighborhood. While our house was nice, theirs was over the top, located in the exclusive section called The Reserve. It has its own security guard to get past. That makes two guards I'll have to deal with.

I'm not as worried about the main guard station at the entrance. The Canyons is broken down into several smaller neighborhoods as well as the country club that serves the golf course. There're a million reasons I can come up with to get inside, but I'm more concerned with getting into The Reserve. That guard will be harder to lie to. They have to call in for permission to let you pass if you're not on the list. I used to go to Elle's all the time. They recognized me by sight and never stopped me to ask where I was going. That's how I got to Brandon's the night of the shooting without anyone knowing I was coming.

Ethan rolls around a little, trying to get comfortable.

I hope Teeny's okay. And Mom and Dad. Dad's probably worried sick.

Staring at the road, I think back on all the tiny little clues I missed before. I feel like all the pieces have fallen into place. Everything except what triggered all the moves. What was happening that made us run from placement to placement? I hate that I may never know that.

Ethan throws his arms out and says with a yawn, "Where are we now?"

He's so cute when he first wakes up. "Close to the Arizona border. Once we cross the line, it's about three more hours." The sun is low in the sky and it'll be dark soon.

Ethan groans. "Stop at the next gas station. We'll get some gas and use the bathroom. I gotta stretch my legs."

I spot a sign and get off the interstate. In the store, I buy a couple of candy bars and gum, looking for some sugar to keep me going. Ethan finishes pumping the fuel and gets in the driver's seat. Before long, we're back on the interstate.

I hand him a chocolate bar, which he devours in two bites. "Ya know, we're gonna have to find a room somewhere. It's gonna be late when we get there, and we don't have our plan nailed down yet."

I agree. Plus, I'm still figuring out how I'll leave him behind when the time comes.

"It'll be better to find a motel in Phoenix. Everything close to where Price lives is pretty expensive, and I'm sure they'll require some sort of ID."

Ethan nods. "Yeah, I was thinking we need some run-down place. Somewhere that's not too concerned about who's checking in."

I dig through my plastic bag and pull out an old book. I open it to the back cover and pry off a piece of duct tape.

Ethan watches me. "What's that?"

I finish getting the tape off and show him the ID underneath it. "It's an ID card in one of my fake names. I've never been allowed to have a driver's license, but I did get an ID card in Florida. I knew if we had to move that they would take it from me, so I hid it. They asked me about it, but I told them I lost it. They changed my birthday at every move, so this ID already has me at eighteen."

I pass the ID to Ethan, and he holds it close to look at the picture.

"You look so different now. I can't imagine you with all that blond hair," he says.

"Yeah. They cut and dyed it before this last placement."

He hands me back the ID. "This may come in handy."

We make good time, crossing into Arizona just after dark. We're both quiet, having exhausted all conversations possible. I doze off, and when I wake up, we're on the outskirts of Tucson.

Everything looks familiar now. Dad took us to Tucson a ton, and I easily recognize where I am. "You want me to drive now? I could get to Phoenix blindfolded from here if I had to."

Ethan nods and pulls the car over on the side of the interstate. He heads for the passenger seat just as I start for the driver's side.

get caught in the middle. I have one leg across the gearshift, and it gets tangled up with his. Ethan puts his hand on my waist, and I put my weight on his shoulders to bring my other leg over. We're touching each other all over, and it's really got my blood moving. At one point I'm almost straddling him. When we finally get to our own sides, I'm completely flustered. I pull back out on the road, but it's a few miles before I can look at him again.

We get to Phoenix and immediately try to find a motel. We decide on a Motel 6 that's right off the interstate. I laugh to myself when I see the sign, since this is the same chain I thought we should drop Julie and Trey off at when they wouldn't stop making out in the backseat of Ethan's truck.

Luckily, Ethan gets a room without my having to produce the ID. I don't think they would be checking for Avery Preston, but you never know. Ethan pops the key card in the slot in the hall, the door opens, and we both look toward the one double bed. I don't know if I'm excited or horrified.

Ethan sheds his shoes and crawls into bed. He has nothing with him, and I feel another wave of guilt for getting him into this situation. I head to the bathroom with my bag. My fatigue is instantly replaced with nerves. Do I put pj's on? Do I stay fully dressed?

After I brush my teeth, I decide to stay in my clothes, and flip off the switch in the bathroom. The room is dark. I slowly make my way to the bed, then stub my toe on something hard and let out a grunt.

"You okay?"

"Yeah." I can make out Ethan's shape on the side closest to the door.

I crawl into bed and lie flat on my back, hands by my sides. I'm never gonna fall asleep. Ethan rolls toward me, and I press every piece of me into the mattress. His hand reaches out and glides over my waist. He hooks me, pulling me closer to him. My back ends up against his chest, his arm anchoring me to him.

"Is this okay?" he asks quietly in my ear.

"Yeah, it's nice." It's way more than nice, but I'm trying to be cool about it. I don't know how cool I can be, though, with my body so stiff.

I think he's already asleep until he asks, "What were you buying a dress for in Shreveport?"

My eyes get huge, and I'm glad he can't see my face. "Um, Catherine was getting one for the dance at school."

Ethan pulls me in tighter and nuzzles my neck. "What about you? Were you gonna get one for the dance, too?"

I let out a giggle. "I don't know. I could be Peggy Sue Wannamaker from Pittsburgh by then."

He lets out a growl. "No Peggy Sue Wannamaker." His voice gets low. "We're gonna fix this. So I'm officially asking you: Anna Boyd, will you please go buy a cute dress so we can go to the dance?"

I turn over and face him. My hands find his face. His feet tangle with mine. "Yes. Ethan Landry, I would love to go to the dance with you."

He pulls me in for a kiss, and all thoughts of sleep run right out of my head.

My eyes sting when I try to open them. It's still dark, but I see the faint glow of early morning sun through the divide in the curtain. I move my hand slowly, not wanting to wake Ethan, and check my watch. Five a.m. This is the time to make my move. I will slide out of the bed, leave him a note, and grab the keys. By the time he wakes up, I'll be gone and he'll be out of danger.

My back is to him, so I don't know if he's awake or not. Listening to his breathing, it sounds deep and heavy, so I slowly inch my way to the edge of the bed. Once I get there, I roll to my stomach and drop my arm and leg over the side. Then the rest of my body follows. It feels like forever, but finally I'm on the floor on all fours. I'm dying to take a peek, but I don't risk it. I crawl around the bed to the small desk against the other wall. I can't even think about the nastiness on the floor right now.

I get to the desk and pull down the small pad and pen, and scribble a quick note. I fish the keys out of the pocket of Ethan's jacket, then jam my feet into my shoes. My hand goes to the knob.

"There's no reason to do the crawl of shame this morning. I thought we kept it fairly clean last night." I hear the laughter in his voice and drop my hand.

I stand up and look back to the bed. Ethan is propped up on pillows with his hands behind his head, watching my every move.

He pats the bed beside him. "It's early, and you're not leaving without me. So come back to bed, and let's figure out what we're gonna do."

I huff back to the bed, both annoyed and relieved that my plan failed. Ethan pulls me to him, and I snuggle in close.

"What does the note say?" he whispers.

"Don't worry. I'll be right back."

He squeezes my side. "You were really going to leave without me?"

I rise up on my elbows. "I'm not completely helpless, ya know. I have managed to take care of things up until this point." Granted, Ethan got us farther, faster, than I ever would have on my own, but damn, I'm not some damsel in distress.

He runs his hand through my hair. "I know. I'm sorry. I just don't want to miss out on the breaking and entering."

"You've gone insane." I lie back down, my head on his chest.

"I've been thinking about what to do with the ledgers once we get them," he says.

I prop myself up on my hands and look at him. "What?"

"Let's talk this out. So, your dad's boss is dead, and now the asshole with the scar thinks he'll never find the ledgers. He was going to kill you until you told him you knew where they were. He left you alive, knowing the cops were coming, so he didn't really care that you could ID him. Right?"

"Yeah, I guess," I answer. For some reason, I don't like where this is going.

"So I figure, he's confident he could get to you before any trial or testimony, or you'd be dead. But he can't get the ledgers without you. Your dad wants to make some sort of deal with him, but I don't know what you could do that doesn't get you killed in the end."

I take a deep breath and say, "I know. I thought maybe we could make copies and put them somewhere safe, or something like that. Tell him if something happens, they goes straight to the suits—ya know, like people do in the movies."

Ethan nods. "Yeah, we could do that. It'd have to be a great spot, where he can't find it."

I put my head back on his chest, and he twirls his fingers

through my hair. "I hate to let him get away with killing Brandon and Mr. Price. I don't care about the drug stuff or the money laundering, but he shouldn't be able to walk away from that," I say.

Ethan drops his hand from my head. "I just got a crazy wicked idea."

I look up at him. "Oh, God, the way you say that makes me nervous."

"Okay, hear me out. What if we release it to the world?"

"What?"

"We make a video. You tell the whole story about the murders and what you've been through. Then we scan the pages of the ledgers and attach them to the video. Then we could upload it onto Facebook or YouTube or something like that. You can also say if you or any member of your family dies—he did it!"

I sit up in the bed. "That's insane! What would stop him from killing me after that?"

"He's going to have bigger problems than you. All his shit is public knowledge. The cops can arrest him. And then he's got that cartel in Mexico to worry about. What good would killing you do? And the Feds won't need you anymore."

"He'd kill me just because I pissed him off!"

Ethan sits up and pulls me in close. "Anna, there's a good chance he's going to try to kill you anyway. He's found out where you've been even though you are being protected by the government. You think he can't find which safety deposit box you're going to use to hide your copies of the ledgers?"

I pull away from him and roll over, turning my back to him.

He leans in over my shoulder and says, "Just think about it.

That's all I'm asking. Tell me more about the house."

I flip back around. "It's a tough house to get into. We shouldn't have a problem with the main gate; it's the one for his neighborhood that's gonna be tricky."

I describe the layout to him, and we both toss around suggestions, none really feeling right.

"Didn't you say your friend Elle lives behind that gate, too?"

"I can't call her."

Ethan waits a few minutes and then says, "You don't really have to involve her too much. But if we can hide in the back of her car, we're in. We could get into the entire community that way. I have a bad feeling the marshals are gonna be waiting for us there. They know how much you want to go home. And now it makes sense why you don't want them to find you either."

He's right. It would be easy on a normal day to get past the front gate. I could say we're applying for a job at the clubhouse. *Go on back.* Or I could say we're with a pool cleaning service. *Go on back.* It's a joke, really. But The Reserve is different. Nothing but houses. And anyone not on the list has to be okayed by phone before you get through. I'm sure I'm still on the list as Anna Boyd, but that won't work. Everyone looking for me is waiting for something as stupid as that. *If Anna Boyd comes through, detain her immediately!*

"I'm still sort of mad at Elle." It's embarrassing saying it out loud, but true. Most of my anger toward her and Laura *is* gone, but I really didn't ever want to see either one of them again.

Ethan lies down beside me and asks what happened. I cover my face with a pillow and tell him.

"Brandon, this is the guy who died?"

I let out a muffled yes.

"Do they know you heard them?"

I pull the pillow down and look at him. "No, but that's not the point."

Ethan flips me around until I'm on top of him. "If we have to use some two-faced bitch to help get you out of trouble, then that's what we'll do."

I lean down and kiss him. He rolls me over, fitting us together like a glove.

"My mind is so foggy right now. What day is it?"

"Friday. Why?"

I glance at my watch. Five thirty. "You're right. It's stupid not to use Elle to get us in there. I don't want to call her, in case they've tapped her phone, but I know where she'll be in an hour and a half." I'd bet my life she and Laura will be at our favorite coffee shop having our traditional Friday morning cup of latte.

"How much time before we have to leave?" Ethan says between tiny kisses.

I can't concentrate on anything while he does that. "Um . . . maybe thirty minutes . . . or forty-five . . . I think."

He looks at me with that bad-boy smirk. "Perfect, 'cause I was just getting comfortable."

Chapter 27

RULES FOR DISAPPEARING BY WITNESS PROTECTION PRISONER #18A7R04M:

Know when to call in reinforcements.

WE pull up to Sola Coffee Bar in the middle of Old Town in Scottsdale. We're a few minutes early, mainly so we can make sure Elle's not being followed. We're being overly paranoid at this point, but we haven't been caught by the suits or Sanchez's men yet, and I'd like to keep it that way.

Like clockwork, Elle and Laura pull into the lot. I'm a mixed bag of emotions when I see them—the humiliation and anger floods back, but I'm also a bit relieved to see that my spot in the backseat hasn't been filled. I'm nervous now that they're so close. They both get out of Elle's car, and I watch them walk toward the coffee shop. They haven't changed; both still have long blond hair and tanned skin. They look gorgeous. Laura looks a little too thin, though, and it's the first time I think about how she might have felt about Brandon and what it was like for her once he died. Were they getting serious? Did she really like him? Or even love him?

"This was a ritual for us on Friday mornings. It's out of the way from our houses to school, but this is the coolest coffee shop in town. So worth the effort."

Ethan grabs my hand. "Are you ready for this?"

"I haven't even told you thanks once. But thanks for everything."

He pulls me back in and kisses me hard and quick, then we both get out of the car. I have the contacts back in, although I don't think anyone is going to recognize me with the short, dark hair.

Hand in hand, we walk into the coffee shop. I spot Elle and Laura at our usual table in the back, but I quickly look away. This reveal is going to have to be done with the utmost care. We walk toward them, Ethan blocking most of me from their view.

They both glance at us and then again at Ethan with some interest, and I'm ridiculously pleased about this. He's hot. And he's mine. We take a table next to them, and I sit in the chair that puts my back to their table.

Ethan leans in close. "Okay, sit tight."

Our plan is that he will sit down at their table and quietly tell them I'm right next to them. Hopefully they won't make a huge scene. He's not at their table thirty seconds before I hear them squeal and race to my table.

They do a double take, then throw their arms around me.

Ethan comes quickly back to our table, trying to quiet them down.

"Please, y'all, sit down. We don't need all this attention."

Laura and Elle sit on either side of me, taking my hands. Ethan takes the seat across the table. It's weird that they're this happy to see me, and all I want to do is scream, *Why were you making fun of me?*

"Oh my God, Anna. Where in the hell have you been? You just friggin' disappeared one day," Elle says as she squeezes all the blood out of my hand.

"And what did you do to your hair? It's so short. And black." Laura puts her free hand in my hair. "And your eyes! Are those colored contacts?"

Ethan shushes everyone. "Please, let's whisper and calm down."

Both Elle and Laura look at him.

"And who are you?" Elle can sound super bitchy when she wants to.

"This is Ethan and he's my boyfriend." I hate the blush that's creeping up my neck when I say it. "If you'll calm down, I'll explain."

They turn back to me.

"I need you both right now. I can't get into details, but please trust me when I say you cannot tell a single person you saw me here. No one. Not your parents. Nobody." There's no way they won't tell, but hopefully they'll keep quiet long enough for us to stash copies of the ledgers first. Or get them on YouTube. Or whatever we decide.

"What's going on, Anna?"

"The only thing I can tell you is my family is fine." Little white lie. "We won't be moving back to Scottsdale any time soon. I can't be seen here, and you can't tell anyone anything about me. I'm asking you both as my best friends in the whole wide world to please do this for me." Let's see how much this means to them.

They look back and forth between me and Ethan.

"Anna, what do you need?" Laura asks.

"Ethan and I need you to get us into The Reserve. I want you to drop us off in front of that small overgrown section, around the corner from the gatehouse."

They wait for me to say something else. When I don't, Laura says, "Then what?"

I paste a smile on my face. It feels fake and probably looks worse. "That's it. We'll take it from there."

Elle shakes her head. "I don't know what's going on, but I don't like it. If you go in, you have to come out. Won't you need help with that too?"

I'm not telling her the rest of the plan no matter how sweetly she acts. If the ledgers aren't there, I want them to be able to say they dropped us off and never saw us again.

"Anna could get hurt if you don't do things the way she wants." We all look at Ethan. "She'll get there whether you help or not. Trust me. If you do what she's asking, we've got the best chance of making all this work."

Silence around the table. No one speaks for a few minutes. Finally Elle grabs her purse.

"Okay, Anna. But promise me you'll tell me what this is all about soon."

"Of course."

We head outside. Elle and Laura walk on each side of me, and Ethan trails behind. I look so out of place with them now. My poor body has gotten pale living in areas that are too cold to sunbathe in during winter months.

They're both talking fast, catching me up on everything I've missed since I've been gone. I glance back at Ethan and give him a wink. He makes the "talking too much" gesture with his hand and smiles.

I listen with half an ear, not really interested in what they're saying but extremely happy to be moving in the right direction.

But there is one part of this that hurts. The carefree, normal part. The part of me that was lost when we first moved and that I'll never get back.

We get to Elle's car, and Ethan catches up. "Anna, ride with them and I'll follow behind y'all," he says, and jogs to the Mustang. We'd already decided to get our car closer to The Canyons for our getaway, and I don't trust Elle and Laura to ride without me. No telling who they'll call.

I jump into Elle's backseat and the memories overtake me. This could have been any Friday morning from my life here in Scottsdale.

Once we're in the car, Elle says, "Anna, you may already know this, but Brandon died." Laura turns her head to the side, brushing her hand across her cheek. Is she crying? I might not be able to handle that.

"Um, yeah, I heard," I say. I should have been prepared to have this conversation with them, but I'm not.

"It was that same night you disappeared," Laura says, then turns in the front seat to face me. Her eyes look glossy, like the tears are just waiting to fall. "We've been worried about you. What happened to you that night? You never showed at Elle's, and we spent hours trying to find you. Even went to some sophomore's lame party after we saw a picture on Instagram of you making out with some guy. Does your disappearing have anything to do with what happened to Brandon?"

Oh, God. I don't know what to say. "It's complicated. Sorry I've made you worry. And I'm sorry I can't tell you where I've been." This was a bad idea. We shouldn't have contacted them.

Elle looks at Laura and says, "Some things happen for a reason even if we don't get it." She peeks at me in the mirror. "We're just glad you're okay."

Judging from the looks between them, I know I was right. Searching for me that night was probably the only thing that kept Laura from being with Brandon. But then again, if she had hooked up with him—maybe he wouldn't have walked into that room. I lean back in my seat and try not to think about the what-ifs. That will make me crazy.

"What was that crazy post on Facebook about?" Laura asks. "Really, Anna, you can tell us anything. You know that."

"I know. I really wish I could, but please don't ask me."

We ride a couple of blocks in silence until Elle changes the subject. "Okay, that guy you're with seems crazy overprotective and all, but damn that accent is cute. I could just sit and listen to him talk all slow and smooth. He's from the South, right?"

Elle is being sneaky, trying to get me to give something away. "I love his accent too, but that's all you'll get out of me," I say.

The conversation moves to school, our friends, and Elle's many boyfriends this year.

She shrugs. "I'm not getting serious with anybody when I'm leaving for college soon. What's the point?"

Laura shakes her head. "That doesn't mean you have to hook up with everybody."

Elle laughs. "No, that's your job, right?"

They laugh and I let out a weak chuckle, reminding myself they don't know I heard them that night.

"Have you decided where you're going to college?" I ask them both.

Elle nods her head toward Laura. "Miss Smarty Pants over there is going to Brown. Can you believe it?" She looks to Laura. "You know it snows there. A lot."

Laura just laughs. "I know, you tell me every chance you get."

"What about you? Where are you going?" I ask Elle.

"L.A., baby. UCLA, to be exact."

That will put her close to her dad, which is probably the real reason she's headed that direction. She didn't handle her parents' divorce well.

"What about you, Anna? Where are you going?" Laura asks.

Can't tell them I'll be lucky to finish high school at this point. "Undecided."

They both plead their cases for me to join them in their little corners of the country. I tell them I'll think about it. If our plan tanks, I may be enrolled in the Universidad de Mexico, for all I know.

I check behind us several times, just to make sure Ethan is back there. We get close to The Canyons, and Elle pulls into the parking lot of a gas station. She drives to the back and Ethan pulls in next to her.

Elle drives an SUV, so no trunk. We all get out and stare at her car, thinking about the best way to handle this.

Ethan runs his hands through his hair and talks about our options. "We don't know if they're looking for us. If they are, your name"—he points to Elle—"will definitely trigger a closer look."

Elle crosses her arms over her chest. "And who are 'they,' exactly?"

Ethan shakes his head and ignores her question. He walks to the back of her car and looks in the cargo area, then turns to me. "Anna, we can lie down back here, and they can cover us up with these bags and jackets."

Laura looks concerned. "Is this really necessary? This seems so . . . bad." She turns to me. "Are things really this serious?"

I step closer to her. "He's being overly cautious. We're really not sure of anything. We just don't want to take any chances."

"Are 'they' good guys or bad guys?" Elle doesn't want to let it go.

Ethan turns and stares at her. "Both." They're having some sort of pissing contest.

Elle raises the back door and picks up everything inside. I crawl in and lie down on my side, scooting as far back as I can. Ethan crawls in and faces me. Elle and Laura cover us with the bags and jackets. Ethan's face is a few inches from mine.

"You okay riding like this?"

"Yeah. It's not far from here."

He leans forward and kisses me softly. "Are you okay?"

"Yes." And I am.

"Good. I guess this will all be over soon, one way or another."

"Are you sorry you came with me?" I ask.

"No. Not yet, anyway."

I laugh quietly. It's the exact same question he asked me while we were hog hunting, and he returned my same answer.

Elle and Laura get in the car, and we're on our way. It's quiet.

We drive a mile or so before Elle says, "We're coming close to the first guard's station. Seems like there's an extra guy out here today. Usually it's just Miguel."

"How's he dressed?" I call out.

"He's in a Scottsdale PD uniform," she answers.

So maybe the suits are using local guys out here.

Silence for a moment.

"They're making me stop."

Not good. The sticker on Elle's front windshield should allow us to drive past the guard without stopping.

When the car stops, I hear the mechanical rumblings of the window being lowered.

"Sorry to stop you, Miss Perkins, but boss said to stop everyone today." I recognize Miguel's voice.

Elle, speaking louder than normal, says, "That's fine. Why's he looking in my windows?"

Ethan and I freeze.

"Sorry, miss. Don't know why."

We seem to pass the inspection, because the car starts moving again.

"Oh my God, I almost peed on myself. Who is looking for you two?" Elle's voice is about two octaves higher than normal.

Ethan and I don't answer. He finds my hands underneath all the stuff and holds them tight. I'm scared. Really scared this is not going to work.

Elle slows down, and I guess we're at the next guard station. She shouldn't have to stop here either, but she does. She says quietly, "Two more here. Regular guard and another police officer."

I take a deep breath and try to be as still as possible.

The window rolls down again.

This time Elle speaks first. "Frank. What's up?"

"Miss Perkins, sorry for the inconvenience, but we're being a little more thorough this morning. Head office said they've had some reports of suspicious activity."

So that's how the suits are playing it.

"No problem." Elle tries to sound bored, but I can hear the worry in her voice.

"I thought you'd be at school this morning," Frank says.

Uh-oh. No way would the security guard that works in her neighborhood normally ask her this question.

"Well, Frank, I thought since I live here that I could drive straight to my house without being stopped, so I guess we're both confused this morning."

And that's what happens when you question Elle. She doesn't take shit from anybody. I hope this doesn't blow up in our faces.

Frank stutters out an apology, but it's cut off when Elle rolls the window up.

"That son of a bitch is gonna ask me where I'm going? I don't think so." Elle pulls away. "I'm not stopping at the overgrown section. The police officer stepped out in the street and is watching the car. I'm going to my house and pulling into the garage."

Ethan makes a foul expression, and I hear him curse under his breath. This plan is tanking fast.

Chapter 28

RULES FOR DISAPPEARING BY WITNESS PROTECTION PRISONER #18A7R04M:

Always have a backup plan. Enough said.

WE don't move until the garage door closes behind Elle's car. Ethan and I untangle ourselves once the back door opens.

I sit in the cargo area and drop my head in my hands. Why did we ever think we could pull something like this off? The two of us against the FBI, U.S. Marshals Office, local PD, and hit men?

Elle heads to the house. "Come inside. It's not too late to make a new plan."

Laura follows her in, leaving Ethan and me alone in the garage.

"We can still make this work," he says. I don't know if he's trying to convince me or himself.

I shake my head. "No. It's over. We'll never pull this off. The local cops are all over this place. You'll be sucked into this too." I look up at him. "I'll get Elle to take us to the car. We'll head back to Louisiana."

Ethan pulls me in close. "We didn't come all this way to bail now. Plus, if I take you home, you're gone. I have to save you from being Penny Sue Wannamaker from Pittsburgh."

I giggle. "It's Peggy Sue."

"Whatever. We're not done yet."

I pull away from him and pace around the garage. "I'm scared. I'm scared of getting caught by the suits. I'm scared of getting killed by Sanchez or whoever is out there hunting us. I'm scared of what could happen to you and Elle and Laura." I stop in front of him. "I don't know what to do."

Ethan stands up and pulls me into his arms. "Let's go inside and figure it out. The ledgers are so close. We can get them and then all of this will be over."

He leads me to the door and into the house. Elle and Laura are sitting at the breakfast table waiting for us.

"Sit. Talk. Whatever friggin' mess you're in, we can help." Elle pats the chair next to her.

Ethan and I take seats at the table. I give them the short and sweet version. I was at the Price house the night Brandon died. I saw something I shouldn't have. My family is in Witness Protection. There's something in that house that may get us out. I don't mention the ledgers or what I may or may not do with them, since I really don't know what that is yet.

Both of them have dropped jaws and big eyes.

Laura stutters out, "Did you . . . see him . . . when he . . . died?"

I take a deep breath and answer, "Yes."

A tear rolls down her cheek. Almost a year later, Laura is still grieving for Brandon, and I feel so bad for her.

"Can you help me get into that house?" I ask.

It takes a few more seconds, then they're both talking at once. I hold up a hand and they both get quiet.

“Is the house empty or does the wife still live there?” Ethan asks.

“She’s still there. I heard Mom talking about her the other day; she’s about to lose everything. We heard Mr. Price was crooked and someone he did business with killed him. All the money was seized, and rumor is she’s about to lose that house.” Elle turns to me with sad eyes. “The truth is, Anna, most people think your dad was in it with him, and he ran before he could get caught. That that’s why you left.”

My poor dad. Everyone, including me, assumed the worst of him. “Well, that’s not true,” I say firmly.

“We know. I told Elle there was no way your dad did anything wrong.”

Great. Laura had more confidence in him than I did.

Elle continues her story. “The wife still acts like Mrs. Rich Bitch, though. Eats lunch at the club, plays tennis every day. Total denial of what’s about to happen. Or that’s what Mom and her friend Susan were saying. The house was broken into twice and totally trashed. Cops were all over the place for a while. It’s died down since then.”

Great. Just great.

“She plays tennis every day? Would she be playing now?” Ethan asks.

Elle glances at the clock on the oven. “Yeah, I’m sure.”

“So no one’s there?” I ask.

“Just the maid.”

“That’s perfect.” Ethan’s rubbing his hands together like some evil movie villain who’s just thought of the perfect plan to rule the world.

"There's still someone there," I say.

"I know," Ethan says. "Here's what I'm thinking. . . ."

I walk next to Elle along the sidewalk. The plan sucks. I hate the plan. Ethan thinks it's great in its simplicity, but I think he's completely lost his mind at this point. Who volunteers to get in the middle of something as crazy as this? I look at Elle and think of Laura and Ethan in the car around the corner. Make that three insane people.

Elle and I walk up to the Price house. Yes. Walk up to the front door. In broad daylight. And ring the doorbell.

I said the plan sucks.

A few minutes later a woman answers the door. It's Carla, the housekeeper the Prices have had forever. It will be a miracle if she doesn't recognize me.

"Good morning, Carla. Sophie, my little toy poodle, ran away, and I thought I saw her take off into your backyard. Would you mind if we went back there and looked for her?"

Yes. This is also in our plan. We're looking for Elle's little dog. Carla looks in my direction, and I hold my breath. She doesn't spare me a second glance.

"That's fine, come on in." She holds the front door open and we step inside. The second I pass through the door, I'm nauseous. The sights and sounds from that night come flooding back. I'm afraid I'm gonna be sick. We follow Carla through the house, and I can see the office up ahead. It's completely bare. I concentrate on taking deep breaths in and out until we get close to the doorway.

"Sorry, this is kind of weird, but we've been walking around looking for Sophie forever and I really have to pee. Do you mind if I use yours?" I cross my legs together and hop from foot to foot. I'm probably overdoing it, but I'm so nervous. I really do need to go to the bathroom now.

Carla pauses a second and then points down the hall. "Second door on your left."

Oh my God, it worked.

Elle starts moving forward again, leading Carla to the backyard. I walk right past the bathroom and enter the office, then stop and stare at the spot where Brandon hit the floor, dead. There's no sign that anything horrible happened in this room, but I'm finding it hard to breathe. I catch sight of Ethan in my peripheral vision and run to pop open one of the windows. He's waiting on the other side and climbs in.

"Let's make it quick."

I stare at the back wall. It's huge and made of different-sized stones. I feel around, trying to bring back that exact memory. It was right behind the desk, but the desk is gone now.

"Tell me what we're looking for," Ethan whispers.

"I don't know. I saw him put something in a hole in the wall and then lift a stone and shove it back into place." I'm getting hysterical. I'm terrified Carla will come looking for me any minute.

I run my fingers along the mortar of several stones. Nothing. I go over the area again, and this time my nail gets caught on a small jagged piece.

"Ethan, look at this."

There is a tiny crack in the mortar that runs around an entire stone. Ethan pulls a small pocketknife and flips out a blade.

"You had to be a Boy Scout when you were little."

He smiles as he digs the blade between the stone and mortar. "How'd you guess?"

He works the blade, and slowly the stone starts to move. It's loud and slow going. The grating sound echoes through the empty room. We both start pulling, and inch by inch, it's out. Ethan puts the stone on the floor, and I look at it closely. The stone has a mortared edge around it. Without knowing what to look for, you'd have never noticed it could come out of the wall.

"Anna, I think this is what you came for." Ethan pulls out several slim ledgers. Neatly written on the front of each one are sets of dates. "Looks like Mr. Price was keeping these books for a while."

I grab one of the volumes and flip it open. I don't really understand what I'm looking at, but I'm bursting inside. This has to be it!

And then another thought—this is too easy.

I hear footsteps coming down the hallway, and chills race down my spine. Ethan hands me the books and then gets the stone back into place. It grinds the entire way in. It doesn't look perfect, but it'll do. I hand the books back to him, and he stuffs them into a bag just as Agent Thomas walks in the room.

My heart sinks.

Ethan and I exchange worried looks, and I glance at the window. Maybe Ethan can get away, make a run for it. I don't know how we got busted, but there's no way to keep the ledgers from the suits now. We're totally screwed.

Agent Thomas makes his way toward Ethan with his hand extended.

"No."

Agent Thomas turns to me, his eyebrows arched. "What do you mean, no?"

"I mean no. They weren't there. I thought they were but they're not."

Ethan looks nervous and asks, "Anna, who is this?"

"One of the suits," I answer.

"I see we're back to your real name. Seems like you two have gotten pretty well acquainted on your way out here." He takes a step closer to me. "It's over. The man who killed Mr. Price and his son is dead."

"Mr. Sanchez?"

Agent Thomas looks surprised. "You must have spoken to your father, too. Yes, another unit raided his house this morning. We were closing in on him with other evidence that we uncovered, and he put up a fight."

My stomach roils when I hear this. If we could have lasted another few days, this trip wouldn't have been necessary at all.

"The good news is you're out—your testimony is no longer needed," Agent Thomas says. He holds his hand out to Ethan again. "The books, please."

"We didn't find anything, really. And even if Sanchez is dead—what about the other people looking for us? You know, like the hit man or whoever is chasing after us," I ask.

Agent Thomas puts his hands behind his back and cocks his head slightly. "We are aware that Sanchez had associates trying to learn your location, but now Sanchez is dead and there is nothing you can offer the government. Your only testimony was to connect

Sanchez to the murders of Mr. Price and his son, Brandon." He holds his hand out again and says, "I'm not stupid, Anna. Please hand me the bag."

Ethan looks at me, and I shrug, then nod toward Agent Thomas. I never thought he'd really let us leave here with the ledgers, but it was worth a shot. Maybe this nightmare is finally over.

"How did you find us?" I hate how pitiful my voice sounds.

He smirks. "Coming home is all you've talked about. A small contingent of us flew out here last night. I asked the guard to call me if Miss Perkins did anything unusual this morning. She should be at school right now. My partner is questioning her and the housekeeper in the other room."

"So what happens now?" Ethan asks.

"Agent Williams is at the main guardhouse. He's not going to be happy you got past him. I'll give him a call, and he'll make arrangements to get you both back to Louisiana."

Back to Louisiana. A smile breaks out across my face, and I feel like I can breathe easy for the first time in months.

"Is Elle in trouble?" I ask.

Agent Thomas ignores me and looks in the bag, fingering through the books. "We searched this place top to bottom." He looks at me. "Where were they?"

I nod my head toward the wall. "One of those stones slides out."

Agent Thomas lets out a sharp laugh and drops the ledgers back in the bag. "You both stay put here while I call Agent Williams."

Agent Thomas leaves the room, and I sink to the floor. Ethan drops down beside me, pulling me in close.

“At least it’s over,” Ethan says.

“Yes! It’s over.” I smile again and pull his face to mine for a kiss.

I snuggle in close while Ethan runs a hand up and down my back. Then his hand stills. “Anna, something’s not right. How’d he know what we were here for? You said the Feds didn’t know you knew where the ledgers were. And we didn’t mention it to him, but he knew we had them.”

“Uh . . . Oh, God, I don’t know.”

“And that agent has been gone for a long time, and I don’t hear anyone else. Do you?”

Silence.

“No.”

We both jump up and race out of the room. I follow Ethan to the back of the house, and we see two people lying on the grass.

“Elle!” I scream, and run through the back doors. Elle and Carla are bound and gagged on the ground.

Chapter 29

RULES FOR DISAPPEARING
BY WITNESS PROTECTION PRISONER #18A7R04M:

Don't ever think it's over. Even when you're sure it's over, it's not over.

WE race outside and Ethan drops down next to Carla while I go directly to Elle. For a split second I think they're both dead. Until Elle moans when I pull the gag out of her mouth.

"Elle! Elle! Wake up!" I try to rip the plastic tie that's binding her hands, but it's too tough.

I glance at Ethan, and he's got his pocketknife out and frees Carla's hands, then turns to Elle. A quick swipe and her hands fall to her sides.

"Do you think that agent did this or the men working for Sanchez?" Ethan asks.

I don't know what to say. Or think.

He hands me the small blade and says, "I'm going to look around. Maybe that agent got attacked, too." But I'm thinking that something with Agent Thomas is really wrong. Ethan's right: how did he know what we were here for?

He leaves before I can beg him to stay. The sun is beating down and it's hot, but I can't stop shivering. What in the hell just happened?

Elle starts moving around, and I help her to a sitting position.

"Elle, are you okay? What happened?" I push her hair out of her face and feel a huge knot right behind her ear.

She moans and grabs her head. "I don't know. We walked outside. Carla was right next to me, and then all of a sudden she was falling. I reached for her, and that is the last thing I remember."

Carla whimpers but doesn't wake up.

I scan the lawn, praying that whoever did this is long gone. I almost hope Ethan finds Agent Thomas around the corner so he's not what I think he is.

Ethan comes back, drops down beside me, and says, "Nothing. No sign of that agent or anyone else. Didn't he say his partner was talking to Elle and Carla?"

I nod and ask, "What about Laura? Is she okay?" Laura was waiting for us in Elle's car around the corner, ready to help us make our getaway.

"She's fine. Never saw a thing. I sent her to the gatehouse and told her to wait there with the guard and call the cops."

I hand Ethan his knife back, and he stands over us, keeping guard until I hear sirens. I can't help but think of Agent Thomas and wonder who he really is.

The place is swarming with cops and suits. Agent Williams paces around the room in front of us. He *was* in the main guardhouse, so it didn't take him long to get here. He's a big man with shocking white hair that is surprisingly long in the back. I remember Dad saying Agent Williams was on his side about not forcing the return of my memory, and I wonder if he regrets that now.

Elle and Carla are being looked over by paramedics while Laura is outside freaking out. They won't let her in, but I can hear her calling our names from the front yard.

Ethan and I sit with our backs against the wall in Price's office. I explain as best I can how everything went down, starting with our cross-country trip and ending with Agent Thomas. Of course I don't mention that I wasn't planning on handing the ledgers over to the suits.

It's so quiet when I finish, I don't think anyone even breathes. Agent Williams finally explodes. "Who is this Agent Thomas?" He barks orders to the suits behind him. "Find out if this place has security cameras and look for a picture. Get the tech guys in here." He whirls around. "Did he touch anything in here?"

My eyes close as I bring back the image of him entering the room. "No. We gave him the bag with the ledgers. He said he was calling you, and then he left."

"He got into this house some way. Get someone over here to dust every doorknob." Agent Williams screams at everyone in the room, "How did this happen?"

"I put the tracker in the bag." Ethan's voice is firm but quiet.

Silence.

"What tracker?" Agent Williams bears down on Ethan.

"A GPS tracker we use with our dogs. Anna had one, so I threw it in the bag with the ledgers. I figured it couldn't hurt."

The room erupts in chaos. Ethan asks to borrow a smartphone and pulls up the Web site that shows where the ledgers are. Agent Williams starts barking orders, handing the phone over to a suit before he runs from the room.

Agent Williams turns to me. "I don't even want to get into why you came out here on your own, but why would you give the ledgers to someone you didn't know?" His voice is raised, and his face is red and splotchy.

"What do you mean? I did know him. And he told me Sanchez was killed last night—that you wouldn't need me to testify anymore," I say quietly.

Silence.

"Sanchez is alive and well—I saw surveillance tape of him this morning. How did you know this man?" His voice is controlled but angry.

What the hell. Sanchez is alive?

I flash my eyes around the room, stopping at Ethan. He's back next to me and holds my hand. "He found me one day in a coffee shop in Natchitoches. I skipped class. When the school couldn't get Mom, they called you guys. He came and tracked me down."

Agent Williams lets out a deep breath and closes his eyes. "The U.S. Marshals Service is not listed as a contact at a protected person's school." He opens his eyes. "Did you see him any other time?"

I swallow hard. This is really scaring me. "Yes, he came to the laundry room where we live. Said he needed to talk to me about Mom. That he had just been talking to Dad, but Dad wasn't being helpful."

A vein ticks on the side of Agent Williams's face. "A U.S. Marshal will never approach a minor outside of the presence of her parents unless it is an extreme emergency. Like this. Is that it?"

I shake my head. "No, he gave me his business card. I called him because I wanted to know what would happen if I left the program.

He came and checked on me at Pearl's once, too."

Agent Williams holds out his hand. "Do you still have the card?"

I pull the card from my back pocket. I hate to admit that he would have been the one I called if Ethan and I got into trouble.

"What made you call him and not some other agent? You have a hotline number if there's a problem."

I shrug, feeling helpless. "I don't know. He seemed nice. He's the only one of you who ever really talked to me." I feel so stupid.

Agent Williams holds the card by the edges and inspects it closely, turning it over several times. "This is a fairly good copy. Don't know that I would recognize it as a fake." He drops it into a plastic bag that is offered by one of the other suits.

The tech team arrives, and the suits direct them around the house.

Ethan and I are ushered to the den, and we sit on the edge of the couch. Carla and Elle are gone. I'm assuming they left with the paramedics. I don't hear Laura screaming anymore either. Mrs. Price came home at some point, pointing her finger and threatening lawsuits, but they moved her out pretty quick.

Agent Williams crouches down in front of us. "I'm going to bring a few people in. In case they can't get him, we're going to need you to remember as much as you can about the conversations you've had with this man. There will also be a sketch artist. Work with him and let's see if we can get some sort of idea of what he looks like. The housekeeper and your friend never saw him, but luckily, you both did."

Yeah, real lucky.

Agent Williams stands to leave, and I crumble into Ethan's arms. All the adrenaline is gone. I'm left with the sinking feeling of being right back where I started. If the ledgers are gone and they know my memory has returned, I'm back on the chopping block. I'm worried the suits will still want me to testify against Sanchez, but I'm more worried Sanchez still wants me dead.

We're drained. Ethan and I have been questioned all afternoon. I repeated my conversations with Thomas over and over to make sure I remembered every detail. The artist was here and created a pretty accurate drawing of what he looks like. Ethan and I couldn't agree on a few things, like the exact shape of his eyes, but all in all it's good. The techs collected a ton of prints.

Ethan and I lean back into the couch. My head is on his shoulder as we watch all the activity around us.

Ethan turns his head toward my ear. "We could make a run for it."

I smile. "If I thought we could get away with it, I'd be the first one out the door."

He plays with my fingers. "So, what does this mean?"

I shrug. "I guess I'm back in the program. I don't know. With the ledgers gone, I'm all they've got."

"You could refuse. If Thomas worked for Sanchez or the drug cartel, he could have killed us both this morning. Why didn't he? Two quick shots and we'd be gone."

I get goose bumps when he says this. It's a thought I've had crawling around in the back of my mind, but I was too scared to let it come to the surface. Ethan's right. We should be dead right now.

In fact, Thomas has had a handful of times to kill me.

I curl up and bury my head in the cushions. I can't take any more of this. Nothing is what I thought it was, and I feel like I am going crazy. Ethan keeps a hand on my back but doesn't say anything else. I turn my head and watch the room. It's still full of people writing reports and talking on phones; it reminds me of that first morning at my house when we entered the program. My world is falling apart and it's business as usual. Agent Williams is in the corner, his phone to his ear. He's listening to the conversation but watching me, and his expression is not good.

He hangs up his phone without saying a word. He shouts, "Everyone's got what they need in here. Let's take what we have and start looking for this guy."

The suits pack everything up and scatter one by one, leaving Ethan and me alone with Agent Williams.

He sits down in a chair, looking at us both. His hair is sticking up in the back, and his eyes are tired. "I just got a call from one of our agents following the tracker. They traced the signal to Eduardo Sanchez's home. Sanchez is dead. The tracker was stuck in his pocket, and his body was still warm. We've had agents on him ever since the shooting, but no one saw anything this morning. In fact, they didn't realize there was a problem with Sanchez until the other agents showed up looking for the tracker."

"Was it Thomas?" I ask.

Agent Williams looks deflated. "No one knows. No one saw anything."

"How did he die?" Ethan asks. I don't know if I want to hear the answer.

"His neck was cut from one side to the other."

I bury myself in Ethan's side while he stares at the floor.

"So what does this mean?" I ask.

"Well, that's the kicker. For you, it's actually good news. There's no one to testify against. And no reason anyone should come looking for you. If Thomas wanted you dead, that's all we would've found when we got here."

I should be relieved. But I'm sick inside. And confused. For whatever reason, Agent Thomas let us live, and I'll probably never know why.

Chapter 30

THREE WEEKS LATER

THE doorbell rings, and I struggle to get the door open without messing up my nails. Catherine, Julie, and I got mani-pedis for the Mardi Gras Ball tonight. The polish I picked was called "Cajun Shrimp." I thought that was appropriate since my family has decided to make Louisiana home.

"I have a delivery for Anna Boyd."

I can't help but squeal at the huge daisy arrangement filling the doorway. My boyfriend rocks!

The last three weeks have been crazy. It was three days before the suits let us leave Arizona. Dad flew out and was so pissed at what Ethan and I did that he lectured us off and on for two days. And when he wasn't scolding me, he was hugging me and telling me over and over how sorry he was that this happened to us. In the end, they flew us back to Louisiana while a couple of agents drove Fred's Mustang home.

I carry the flowers back to my room. Dad stayed with the factory but moved to the accounting department, so we were out of the tiny cottage and into a house not far from Ethan's.

Teeny pokes her head in a few minutes later and says, "Don't forget Ethan said I could take a ride in the limo before you go to the dance."

"We won't forget," I answer.

Teeny is better, but she still freaks if we don't get home when we say we will. And I don't think she'll ever get over her fear of men in suits.

She stayed with Pearl when Dad was with us, and she didn't speak to me or Dad for three days after we got back. She was mad we left her behind.

But she forgave Ethan immediately. Figures.

It's chaos when Ethan and the rest of the group finally show up at the house. We're riding with Will, Catherine, Julie, and Trey. Dad drags us all in front of the fireplace for pictures. He takes shots of us as a group and then of each couple. It's pretty embarrassing.

I hug him on my way out, and he whispers, "I'll e-mail these to Mom. She'd love seeing you all dressed up like this."

Mom is in a treatment facility in Baton Rouge. Dad's the only one who's seen her and has been trying to talk me into visiting her soon. Not sure I'm ready for that yet.

We take Teeny for a ride through the neighborhood; she presses every button and climbs all over us.

The school dances are different here. In Arizona, the school would have rented a ballroom from one of the best hotels. We would have had a three-course meal first, then danced to a well-known band. Not in Natchitoches, though. The ball is in the gym, and decorating means throwing tons of green, yellow, and purple streamers on anything that stays still long enough. There are not one, not two, but three balloon arches. It's pretty cheesy but I love it.

Ethan and I head straight for the dance floor, where a slow song is playing. He pulls me close, and we sway in rhythm to the music, my face buried in his neck and his arms tight around my waist. It's hard to believe I'm here. With him. In a cute dress Catherine and I went shopping for last week.

It's moments like this when Thomas creeps into my mind. When I realize how lucky I am to be here. There's not a day goes by that I don't try to figure out why he didn't kill us. And I still have the nightmare at least once a week.

I raise my head slightly and look over Ethan's shoulder to see Ben and Emma dancing nearby. "I'm still not sure it's a good idea for us all to go to the cabin together," I whisper in Ethan's ear.

"It'll be fine. Will and Catherine will be there too. I owe Ben a weekend at the cabin, and he's holding me to it." The suits tracked Ben down about an hour from the fishing cabin and held him the rest of the weekend, not believing he didn't know where we were. "And just think—a road trip with no drug smugglers, hit men, or government agents. It'll be great."

Ben and Ethan have made some headway in repairing their friendship. Emma and I have formed an unspoken truce. We'll probably never be friends, but at least she's not hostile anymore. I can't tell if she's scared of me or impressed by me.

Ethan and I are sort of like rock stars at school now. No one knows the whole story, but people have heard just enough to make us seem really cool and mysterious. I'm back to my original name, hair, and eye color, and it seems to freak people out.

"When do you have to be home?" Ethan asks. Dad's loosened

up a lot and even helps Ben's dad with his books. There's a small chance now that his family might not lose his farm.

"Not for a while. I told him we'd be late." Ethan and I have been inseparable since we got back. I don't think he'll ever know what it meant to me that he was there when I needed him, but I'm trying every day to show him.

Catherine waves to us from across the room. "I think everyone's ready to head to Will's," Ethan says.

Time for the after-party.

I step away, and he pulls me back quickly, kissing me on the small daisy tattoo that's showing on my bare shoulder, before letting me go again.

I giggle and walk toward the closet where they're keeping our coats.

The party at Will's starts as a small group of us hanging out around his pool, but it isn't long before his house is packed.

I'm curled up next to Ethan on one of the loungers, sipping a beer. It's chilly out, but that doesn't stop Will from taking some stupid bet to jump into the pool and stay there for at least two minutes. He will apparently do anything for ten bucks.

"Will's such a dumb-ass," Ethan says.

"Yes. He is. Look at Catherine, she's pissed."

"She's pissed because she just wanted it to be a few couples here tonight." I turn toward Ethan, moving in closer, and just before he can kiss me, the chair we're in gets bumped and I almost fall off.

Ethan sits up and looks around, but whoever knocked into us has moved on. "Damn, I'm with Catherine. There are way too many people here." He looks at my beer and says, "I'll grab us a couple more, then we'll get the limo driver to take us for a ride. Get away from the crowd for a little while."

"Sounds like a good plan."

Just as Ethan turns to leave, I tug on his pants and say, "I forgot to thank you for the flowers. They are beautiful."

He stops and looks at me funny. "Flowers? What flowers?"

I sit up and stare at him. A creepy feeling washes over me, and I ask, "You didn't send me a bouquet of daisies today?"

He looks really confused. "No."

I let out a nervous laugh. "It must have been Dad. He knows how much I love them, too."

Ethan waits a few long seconds before he nods slowly and walks away. I don't think he believes Dad sent the flowers. I don't think Dad sent them either, but who else would do that?

With him gone, I get cold. My coat is hanging off the back of the lounger, so I pull it over me and use it like a blanket. But there's something inside—it feels square and hard. I dig around in the coat and realize it's in the pocket, so I pull it out. It's my journal, with a single daisy stuck between the pages. A sinking feeling comes over me, and I search for Ethan, but he's across the patio, talking to Trey.

I shove the journal back in the pocket and jump up from the chair. Oh, God . . . Oh, God . . . Oh, God. I race to the bathroom, but Ethan stops me before I make it there.

"What's wrong?"

"Nothing. I've got to go to the restroom. I'll be right back." And I pull away from him.

Once I'm alone, I lock the door and slide down the wall to the floor, opening the journal to where the daisy is.

And there, scribbled on the page, is a note for me.

> *Dear Anna,*
>
> *I'm sure you have questions, and someday maybe I'll answer them for you. I thought it was important for you to have this back. I hope the nightmares that haunted you are gone. Maybe one day we'll meet again.*
>
> *T.*
>
> *P.S. Tell your friend the tracker was a clever move.*

Oh, shit. *Maybe one day we'll meet again.* What in the hell does that mean? I rip the page out and tear it into pieces. Then do the same with the flower. How did this get in my coat pocket?

Then I remember someone just knocked into our chair, right where my coat was draped over the back. I scramble from the floor and race back out to the pool, ignoring Ethan calling my name.

I search the crowd, looking for Thomas, but he's not here.

Ethan comes up behind me and says, "Anna, you look scared. What's wrong?"

I turn and bury my head in his chest, squeezing him tight. "Nothing. It's nothing."

He leans his head close to my ear and says, "I'm here if you need me."

I move my hands to his face and bring his lips to mine, kissing him softly. "I know. And that's the only thing that makes everything okay."

He hugs me tight while I look behind him, scanning faces like I did a few seconds ago. And like I will do for the rest of my life.

Acknowledgments

THERE were *so* many people who made this first book possible, so if you will indulge me . . .

A HUMONGOUS thank you to:

My agent, Sarah Davies, for pulling me out of the slush pile and making my dreams come true. I'm so thrilled to have found a home at Greenhouse Literary.

Elizabeth Schonhorst, for the invaluable help on the early version of this manuscript.

My amazing editor, Emily Meehan, for loving this story and making it better. From our first conversation, I knew Anna and Ethan would be in good hands. And to Laura Schreiber, for your tireless work and making this entire process delightful. Thank you both for being so good to me.

Elizabeth Holcomb and Monica Mayper for their careful copyediting, along with the entire team at Disney-Hyperion, especially everyone in marketing and publicity, and all those behind the scenes who helped get this book into the hands of readers. Your support is so appreciated.

The design team, especially Marci Senders and Theresa Evangelista, for the awesome cover. I adore it.

Moriah McStay Lee, the Grammar Queen and my first critique partner, for always being honest even when I didn't want to hear it. So happy I sat down next to you at the lunch table at that SCBWI conference, and so glad you were as clueless as I was.

Elle Cosimano and Megan Miranda, critique partners and agency sisters, for answering panicked e-mails with mind-blowing insight, for dragging me through that haunted jail, and for being incredible friends. This last year would not have been the same without you.

The wonderful online community of readers and writers. I would have never gotten past the query letter without you.

The Lucky 13s, for your full support and safe haven.

Kari Olson and Katharine Brauer, for donating critiques for charity and giving such wonderful advice. You are both quite incredible.

My mom, Sally Ditta, for introducing me to the wonderful world of books when I was a little girl, especially the Nancy Drew series, and for telling me I could do anything I put my mind to. I love you very much. And to my step-dad, Joey Ditta, for always making me feel at home and for being such a good friend.

My dad, Tony Bruscato, for showing me the world and talking about the law and your cases and all of the other things I once thought boring. Some of that stuff actually sank in.

Uncle Charles and Aunt Bitsy, for always being there for me and making sure I had what I needed when I needed it. Especially the 1987 Nissan Pulsar. I loved that car.

My in-laws, Richard and Lennis Elston, and my husband's entire family, for welcoming me into your family with open arms and never letting go. And special thanks to Lennis, for your invaluable accounting knowledge and for not freaking out when I asked how to launder money.

Bubba Salley, hog hunter extraordinaire, for answering my endless questions about hogs, hog dogs, and other really random things.

My friends who listened endlessly about my road to publication and who were the most gracious first readers a girl could have: Christy Poole, Elizabeth Pippin, Jennifer Bond, Kylie Reeves, Missy Huckabay, Lisa Stewart, and Christa Drake, the original "Sissy."

My young friends who inspire me: Danlee, Carlie, Allie, Avery, Skylar, and Adeline. And to my New York traveling buddies: Mignon, Alexis, Julianna, and Rebecca, thank you for letting me crash your thirteenth birthday trip as the favorite aunt. And to my siblings, Jordan, Sidney, and Molly. I couldn't write these acknowledgments and NOT mention ALL of you. Thank you for being so excited about this book.

My family and friends from whom I borrowed names for the characters in this book. And if you got stuck with the bad guy or mean girl, please don't take it personally.

And saving the best for last: Thank you to the most important people in my life—my husband, Dean, and our sons, Miller, Ross, and Archer Elston, for understanding when I was a bit crazy on a deadline and being okay with grilled cheese sandwiches for dinner when my head was lost in a Word document. Thank you for the overwhelming support. I could not have done this without you, nor would I have wanted to. And, boys, even if it was just for a minute, thanks for thinking I was cool.

Turn the page for a sneak peek at the follow-up to

THE RULES FOR DISAPPEARING.

Chapter 1

"CAN you teach me how to shoot a gun?"

I've been putting off asking Ethan this question for a week. It's now or never. We're in his truck, headed to the farm, and there is a practice range there that Ethan and his dad use to sight in their guns before hunting season. If he agrees, I won't have time to back out before the turnoff.

Surprise flashes across his face. "Are you sure?"

"I'm ready," I answer, hoping it's the truth.

I can tell he doesn't believe me, and I don't blame him.

"I'm not sure I'm ready," he says in a teasing voice.

It wasn't that long ago that I blacked out when I saw him shoot a hog that was attacking his dog. That shot brought back memories so horrible that I had repressed them for months. But I remembered everything now, and I was determined not to cower behind a couch the next time I came face-to-face with a killer. Not if there was anything I could do about it.

"What brought this on?" he asks.

I shrug, not meeting his eyes. "I don't like being scared of anything." And that much is true. I'm terrified of guns, but I'm more scared of returning to the life I led just a few short weeks ago. "I'm ready and we're here. Perfect timing."

My family has only been out of the Witness Protection Program a month and I'll do anything to avoid going back. Our short time in the program nearly destroyed my family.

He reaches for something near my feet and I automatically snatch my purse from the truck floor. The last thing I want is for him to see what I'm hiding inside. He grabs the remote control that works the gate to the farm, which must have fallen out of its usual spot in the cup holder, and gives me a strange look.

Probably because I'm acting like he's a mugger.

"You're jumpy. You hiding another boyfriend in that bag?"

I return his smile with a weak one of my own. Have I been glancing over my shoulder way more than what's normal? Yes. Have I nearly jumped right out of my skin at every little noise? Yes. Do I want to tell him why? No.

Ethan turns serious. "Anna, you've been different ever since the Mardi Gras dance. You know you can tell me if something's wrong, don't you?"

"No! I mean yes, I know. Nothing is wrong. It's all good. Sorry for being weird."

I hate thinking about the Mardi Gras dance.

Hate it.

It was supposed to be the perfect night. I was back to using my real name—no more fake identities—and I had convinced myself it was all over. I no longer dreaded the suits showing up and pulling me away from everyone I'd grown to love, like they'd done so many times before. I no longer worried every time I said good-bye to Ethan that it might be the last time I saw him.

And it *was* perfect—at first. I felt like the belle of the ball dancing in Ethan's arms, and the night was getting even better when the party moved to Will's house.

But that's when everything fell apart. That's when the man I thought of as Agent Thomas re-entered my life.

"I've just been a little stressed lately," I add nervously. And that's the truth.

"And you think now is a good time to shoot a gun?"

"Yes, I do." I drop my purse back down on the floorboard.

"Okay, then. If you really think you're ready, we can try," Ethan says.

I may be good at hiding things from my dad and my little sister, Teeny, but I can't hide anything from Ethan. He knows something isn't right. Gripping my bag, feeling for the hard corners of the journal tucked inside, I think about how much to tell him.

I'm not mentioning the bizarre return of my missing journal . . . or the single daisy that was left in the pages. I'm not telling him about the note that Thomas, fake agent and would-be assassin, left in the pocket of my coat—the note that I tore to pieces, then taped back together hours later. I've re-read that note a hundred times looking for some clue or hidden meaning but there's . . . nothing. It still freaks me out that Thomas managed to get within a few feet of me and I never knew it. I'm not telling him there may still be someone out there watching me.

Ethan clicks the button on the remote and the electric gate

starts to open. "How long have you been thinking about this?"

"For a while."

Ethan glances from me to the farm road, back and forth, like he's trying to solve a puzzle. Given that the majority of the time we've known each other I was lying to him about who I was, I don't blame him for being skeptical.

"I'm not buying that. I'll teach you, but you have to tell me what brought this on. Are you sure nothing's happened?"

I give him a big smile and scoot across the front bench of the truck to get closer to him. I can't tell him. He'll make me tell Dad and Dad will call the suits and I don't ever want to see them again. I fought too hard to get this wonderfully normal life and I'm not ready to give it up.

"Everything's fine. Stop overthinking this. I know I freaked last time but I'm prepared now. I want to learn. I don't want to be scared."

I hope I didn't oversell it.

He moves a hand from the steering wheel to mine, squeezing it tightly. "Just as long as you're sure. I don't know if I can handle it if you pass out. That damn near killed me seeing you on the ground like that."

And I don't know if I'll ever get tired of hearing him talk in that slow, smooth Louisiana drawl or seeing that dimple dig deep into his cheek. This moment, in the truck with him, reinforces why I will not go back to the way things were. I want this life. I deserve this life. But I need to learn how to protect myself. I don't ever want to be a victim again.

"Does your dad know you want to do this?"

"No. But it's not like I'm hiding it from him. He wouldn't understand and I don't want to try to explain it. He won't get it."

The first twenty-four hours after Thomas returned my journal and left the creepy note, I was terrified. I stuck to Dad and Teeny like glue, not willing to let them out of my sight. And Ethan, he knew something was wrong, but I dodged his questions like the seasoned evader I am. There were a million times in that first day that I teetered on the brink of telling Dad everything, but I couldn't say the words that would surely bring the suits back into our lives. And what would they do, anyway? All they know about Thomas is that he's some sort of assassin, or killer for hire, or something horrible like that. But that's it. They would have no idea how to catch him—so they'd probably just toss us back into the program.

After that first day, when nothing else happened, I decided that maybe Thomas did mean exactly what he said in the note: He just wanted me to have my journal back. I know enough about Thomas to know that if he wanted me dead, I would be dead.

Ethan pulls through the front gate of the farm and I rub my sweaty hands down the front of my jeans.

I can do this.

I have to do this.

There are several tractors working in the distance and I spot Ethan's dad's truck parked at the barn. I was hoping we would be alone—I don't need any witnesses if I am, in fact, *not* ready to do this.

Ethan turns off the truck and pulls me in closer, kissing me gently on the lips.

"We'll start slow. You can hold the gun, load it, get a feel for it.

If that seems all right, then maybe we'll try to fire a few rounds. If you start feeling bad, tell me and we'll stop. Don't push yourself on this. You're safe with me. You just have to put all of the other bad stuff out of your mind."

I drag him toward me, away from the steering wheel, and crawl in his lap, kissing him deeply. He knows and understands me like no one else ever has and that is a serious turn-on.

It's not long before we're totally making out in the front of his truck.

We hear a four-wheeler approach and I jump off Ethan's lap and move back to my side of the truck just before his dad stops on Ethan's side. I'm sure the slightly fogged windows give a little clue as to what was happening inside.

Ethan chuckles as he rolls down his window. "Hey, Dad."

He nods, sneaking a peek at us when he says, "Hey, son. Anna." He looks as embarrassed as I feel.

"Hi, Mr. Landry." My face is on fire.

"Dad, I'm going to teach Anna how to shoot this morning."

Mr. Landry jerks his head to me quickly. He also witnessed my meltdown the last time I was around a gun. "Are you sure?"

I nod and Ethan says, "We're going to ease into it. No rush."

No rush. I hope he's right and I won't need this skill anytime soon.

Chapter 2

RULES FOR DISAPPEARING
BY WITNESS PROTECTION PRISONER #18A7R04M:

~~Live on the fringe of society. . . .~~

NEW RULE BY ANNA BOYD:

Screw that.

I try not to hyperventilate. Ethan's got everything lined up: the gun, the bullets, safety glasses, and even a pair of earmuffs to deaden the sound.

We're on the back part of the farm where they do target practice. There's a wooden structure that's used as a gun rest at different heights so you can either stand or sit while shooting. In front of us are targets at varying distances.

"First thing I want you to understand is this is a completely safe situation. We're far enough away that there is no chance you will hit anyone or anything other than the target or the hay bale behind the targets. It's just me and you, Anna. No one else."

I nod and stare at the gun. As much as I try to keep the memories away, my mind instantly fills with the images of dead bodies and pools of blood.

Taking a step back, Ethan sees I'm having trouble and wraps his arms around me. "Anna, we don't have to do this today. Or ever. It's okay."

I shake my head and answer, "No, I don't want to be scared anymore." He thinks I'm talking just about the gun, but it's so much more than that.

"Do you want to talk about it?"

Ethan knows all about my family's time in the Witness Protection Program but he's only heard the cold, hard facts that Agent Williams laid out. I witnessed two murders—not only was my dad's boss killed in front of me, but so was his son, Brandon, the boy I'd had a crush on for years.

It was so traumatizing I blocked that night out completely, and had no memory of it for months. But that memory returned right here on this very farm when I rode along on a hog hunt with Ethan. His dog, Bandit, was hurt and he was forced to shoot the feral hog attacking him. The sight of the gun, the crack of the blast, and the smell of the smoke flooded me with memories of that night.

Until that night on the farm, I thought the reason we were in the program was because my dad had done something horrible.

But it was me all along. I was the one the suits were protecting. I was the reason we were forced to leave our home in Scottsdale, our friends, everything we'd ever known.

I was the reason my mom turned to drinking. She couldn't handle staying in the program indefinitely while everyone waited for my missing memories to return, the suits showing up in the middle of the night because our location had been compromised. I was the reason she nearly drank herself to death and is now recovering in a treatment facility in Baton Rouge.

I drop down on the small stool next to the gun rest and bury my head in my hands. Ethan crouches down beside me, running his hand over my head in slow, calming strokes.

"Talk to me," he whispers.

"I can still see Brandon on the floor in that room. When I shut my eyes, he's there. One leg was at an odd angle and his shoe was untied. And the blood. It was everywhere. The room smelled like gun smoke and blood. . . . His body was just so . . . still."

Ethan pulls me in closer.

"And then the man who shot them, Sanchez, found me behind the couch where I was hiding and I knew I was next. He put that gun in my face and it was like everything was moving in slow motion. I thought I was dead."

A broken sob escapes my mouth and Ethan brings my face to his.

"But you survived because you are strong and smart. Don't forget that part. You are strong and smart."

"The only reason he didn't kill me was because of those ledgers. What if I hadn't seen Brandon's dad put them in that wall safe? What if Sanchez hadn't wanted them back badly enough and he shot me on the spot? If the cops hadn't shown up when they did, I would have told him the location and then he would have killed me."

Those ledgers are what kept my family and me alive for months. The suits wanted me to get my memory back so I could testify against Sanchez. But the drug cartel that Sanchez worked for had heard from him that I knew the ledgers' location. Ledgers that showed all of the ways Brandon's dad, who was the head of the accounting firm where my dad worked, had laundered their drug money. It would have completely shut down their operation.

And that's how "Agent Thomas" came into my life. He wanted the ledgers and knew I could get them for him. He drew me in, making me trust him. I thought he was the only suit who really wanted to help me.

"You're safe now. Sanchez is dead, remember? He can't hurt you."

He's dead because Thomas slit his throat from one ear to the other. Once the cartel got the ledgers back, they cut Sanchez loose. Apparently there are no second chances in the drug cartel business.

Except for Ethan and me. Thomas could have killed us in Scottsdale, but he didn't and no one knows why.

"Anna, please tell me why you want to do this."

"I want to be able to protect myself." And this is the truth, even if it's not the whole truth.

I stand up and give myself a good shake. "Please help me, Ethan."

His expression is guarded but I know him well enough to see that he is struggling with this. He wants to help me, but he doesn't think this is a good idea. At all.

"First, pick up the gun. It's not loaded. Feel it in your hand. See how you do with that."

I run a finger over the handle. It's cold even though it's been sitting in the sun, and shivers race up my arm.

Taking a deep breath, I wrap my hand around it, lifting it from the gun rest. It's heavier than I thought it would be. My fingers fit perfectly in the grooves on the handle.

"This is a Glock. It's small and there's hardly any recoil so I thought it would be an easy gun to start with. Let's practice holding it the right way and aiming before putting any bullets in."

Ethan moves behind me. His hands move on top of mine and he brings them up, pointing the gun at the targets in front of us. He repositions my hands until the right one is holding the gun, my pointer finger on the trigger.

"You fire a gun with the same hand you write with so for you that's your right hand. Your left hand will help support the gun like this," he says, and positions my left hand around the underside of the gun.

Ethan's body surrounds me completely. His arms line up with mine, his chest and legs mold against me. As nauseating as it feels to have this gun in my hand, I can't help but feel safe. It is a strange sensation.

"How do you feel?" Ethan asks.

"Scared but not scared. I know nothing bad will happen while you're here with me."

"Do you want me to step away? Let you hold it on your own?"

I'm terrified for him to let go of me. I'm not sure my body will support itself once his moves. But then I think of the journal—and Thomas. He took it from me—I assume for the secrets he thought may be written in it—and then inexplicably gave it back. What reason would he have to bother me once he had the ledgers? I have no idea, and that scares me more than this gun.

"Yes. Let me try it on my own." My voice sounds shaky, but I can't help it.

Ethan peels his body away from mine and it's agonizing, like slowly pulling off a Band-Aid.

I stand on my own, still aiming the gun at the target, and try to control my trembling limbs. I concentrate on that pit of fear in my belly. It churns and spins and makes me dizzy so I push it down. It will not control me. I will not live in fear. I will not lose this new life I have.

"Show me how to put the bullets in."